WHERE THE POPPIES DANCE

ANNEMARIE BREAR

Historical Saga Author
AnneMarie
BREAR

Image cover: Arcangel.com

A SISTER'S SACRIFICE

Book 1

Yorkshire, England, 1914

Olivia Brodie is a devoted parlourmaid serving the Broadbent family at Hawthorn Manor and spending precious time with her father and brothers at the family forge. But everything changes the day Spencer Middleton, the Broadbents' charming and enigmatic grandson, arrives. Sparks fly between Olivia and the army officer. Their connection is undeniable—but so too are the rigid boundaries of class and propriety. When Spencer departs, promising to return, Olivia dares to dream of a future that defies society's expectations.

However, tragedy strikes Olivia's family, devastating her. Compounding her grief is the news that the manor is sold, leaving her homeless and jobless. With her younger brother Lachie to care for, she is forced to seek work in the nearby bleak industrial town, and Olivia finds herself far from the countryside she loves—and from the man who captured her heart.

Desperate to keep Lachie out of the perilous coal mines, Olivia finds hope when she secures a position as housekeeper to Stephen Sheridan, a gifted but reclusive pianist haunted by his past. As danger follows her through the dark alleys of the town and Sheridan's secrets begin to surface, Olivia must decide who she can trust.

Torn between the memory of first love and the comfort of newfound companionship, Olivia faces an impossible choice. Can she build a new future from the ashes of her old life—or will love find its way back to her against all odds?

Set against a backdrop of social upheaval and changing fortunes, this is a poignant tale of love, loss, and the resilience of a young woman determined to forge her own destiny.

The story continues in *Where the Poppies Dance...*

To all those heroic men who served
To all those who fell and never got back up
To all those who were wounded
To all those who came home changed
To all the women who served as nurses and ambulance drivers
who were told not to go to the front lines but did anyway
To all the women who took over men's jobs
To all the families who kept hope alive at home
They lived through a changing world
A brave generation who deserve nothing but respect
And should never be forgotten for the sacrifices made
They died for us
Lest We Forget

WHERE THE POPPIES DANCE

CHAPTER 1

Wakefield, Yorkshire, England
May 1915

THE GOLDEN SPONGE cake Olivia Brodie brought out of the oven filled the kitchen with a delicious aroma. It was her youngest brother Lachie's sixteenth birthday, and she wanted to make him a treat, and he loved a bit of cake, did Lachie. She'd have liked to put on a good spread for his special day, but since the war had started the year before, certain foods had become expensive, and the government urged everyone to buy only what they needed to limit waste.

She untied her apron and placed it on the hook on the back door and gave the kitchen a final check. She'd spent all day tidying and scrubbing the rooms of their terraced home at number seven Woodcock's Square, needing to keep busy on her days off work so she wouldn't worry about Spencer, the man she loved.

War news dominated the newspapers, and each day she

scoured the casualty lists looking for the name of Captain Spencer Middleton, who was currently serving somewhere in the trenches on the Western Front in northern France.

His last letter had arrived three days ago, a short note telling her he was well, and he would write a longer letter in the next day or two once they had settled into a new area.

She'd placed that note into the bundle of letters Spencer had written to her since they'd reunited last August. Another bundle of letters was upstairs beside her bed. She re-read them constantly.

They'd found each other again after being parted when his battalion was sent to Ireland, and she'd lost her job working at his grandparents' manor. Spencer hadn't known where she'd gone after her father died and his blacksmith forge was given up. He had no way of knowing she and Lachie had left the countryside and ventured into Wakefield to look for work.

By chance, Spencer's friend Mr Parkinson, Parky, had seen her at the theatre where she'd been listening to her new employer's concert.

Fate had brought her and Spencer back together after months of him searching for her, but their meeting had been short-lived, and Spencer had soon been deployed to Belgium to face the advancing German army.

Everyone said the war would be over by that Christmas of nineteen fourteen. It hadn't. Now, nine months later, the battles were continuing, and the lists of the dead and wounded were always growing.

Olivia shivered and put the kettle on the gas hob to boil. Lachie would be home any minute from his job at the iron foundry, and they'd have some tea. She wanted to give him her present before they went to the cinema to watch Charlie Chaplin's latest movie film.

The back door opened, and her neighbour, Tess Hobson, came in. 'Is the birthday boy not home yet?'

'No, not yet. Tea?'

'Aye, that'll be grand, lass.' Tess sat at the table, wearing a large white apron over her brown dress. Grey liberally streaked through Tess's dark hair now. 'Are you icing that cake?' She nodded at the cooling cake on the sideboard.

'I don't have any icing sugar.'

'No, I don't have any either. I doubt the neighbours would have any. How spoilt we were before the war to have as much sugar as we could buy?' Tess tutted. 'Now we skimp and scrape for a few ounces. Damn those Germans stopping the food ships from reaching our ports.'

'Did you get any letters today?' Olivia asked. Receiving letters from those serving was the main topic of any conversation that anyone spoke of if they had someone in the army or navy. Tess and her husband Larry had two older boys, Lance and Simon, serving; Lance in the army and Simon in the navy. Their three younger boys, Jonnie, Jules and Colin, worked alongside their father down the coal mine, where Lachie had worked until his accident last year.

'No, nowt today.' Tess sighed. 'My Lance is dreadful for writing at the best of times, he's worse since the war started. You?'

Olivia poured the boiling water into the teapot and let the tea leaves steep for a while. 'No. I'm expecting a letter from Spencer any day now. He mentioned being sent to another area. He'll write once he's settled.' A swell of love filled her chest for the handsome man who had stolen her heart last spring.

'Is it a quieter spot than where he was? Ypres, wasn't it? Such strange names we are learning.'

'I hope he's away from the fighting, but I doubt it. You know they can never give out their exact location, and Spencer is normally in the thick of it.' She shivered slightly and poured out two cups of tea.

Spencer had been in the main thrust of the fighting since he landed in Belgium at the beginning of the war. The German advance had caught them all by surprise and swept the British and allied soldiers back in a hasty retreat in those first awful months of the war. Place and battle names like Mons, Aisne, Flanders, Ourcq, Marne and so many more became of interest. Olivia borrowed an atlas from the library to find where they were on the maps so she could follow the progress the newspapers reported.

'Your captain writes as regularly as clockwork.' Tess began to spread strawberry jam on one half of the cake while Olivia started to cook the sausages and fried onions and potatoes for her and Lachie's evening meal.

Olivia relied on Spencer to be honest in his letters. She wanted to understand what he was going through, and she read those types of details to Tess and Lachie, leaving his words of love to read only for herself.

Spencer wrote of his war, telling her of the fatigue, of the mental struggle of seeing his men die in front of him, but he also spoke of the bravery and sometimes of the light-hearted situations that happened amidst the carnage. Most of all, he told how much he loved her and couldn't wait to see her again. In return, she told him of her uneventful life at home, where she counted down the days until they could be together again.

Olivia glanced at the clock on the mantlepiece and turned the sausages. 'Lachie is late. It's ten to seven now. He should have been home twenty minutes ago.'

When Lachie was injured in the mine accident last year, she made him promise never to go down the pit again. It took nearly two months for him to recover from his injuries, but he'd kept his promise and instead found a job at the iron foundry on Vicarage Street in town. Being the son of a blacksmith had given him a background of working with iron, which helped secure the job.

Tess sipped her tea. 'Perhaps he's working overtime? So many businesses are so busy since the war began. The new munitions factory is taking on more women, did you hear? They can't keep up with demand for shells and the like. Some people will be making some money out of this war, and that's for certain,' Tess said knowingly.

'He has worked overtime in the past.' Olivia flipped the fried onions and potato slices. 'He knew we had plans.'

Tess sandwiched the cake together. 'Oh, I got word that Keane's Butcher's in Warrengate has some rabbits coming in tomorrow morning. I'll grab us one each. It's on the quiet.' Tess tapped her nose to indicate it was a secret. 'We can't let anyone know about it. I can't be dealing with the neighbours whining they don't have one. I can't supply the whole square.'

'Thank you. I'll make a stew with it once I'm back from work.' She sat down opposite Tess, looking at the clock again. 'We planned to go to the cinema. He needs to hurry up, or we'll be late for the eight o'clock showing. He's got to have a wash and eat before we leave.'

'Well, he's not with my Colin, as he's on nights and has already left for the pit. Have you got a little bit of icing sugar? Just a tiny bit to dust the top of the cake?'

Olivia rose and went to the larder and brought out a tin. She opened the lid and peered in. 'About a teaspoon's worth.'

'That'll do, it's better than nowt. Pass me the sieve.'

She did as asked and while up turned the sausages and lowered the heat to not burn them. 'Lachie has made a few friends at the foundry. They're a bit rough, if you know what I mean. One has been in prison.'

'You can't control who he works with, lass,' Tess said calmly, dusting the cake. 'You just have to hope his upbringing will make him sensible enough to decide who he calls friends.'

'Yes, but Lachie isn't always sensible, is he?' Olivia sighed and made a pot of gravy with beef gravy powder.

'He's a lad. Lads take a while to grow up. I should know,

having five of them, but Lachie is a good lad, and you know it. So, stop worrying.'

She drank some of her tea. 'I try not to, but after my brother Stu leaving us and Father dying, Lachie is all I have left of my family. The foundry can be a dangerous place to work.'

'Safer than the pit. At least at the foundry the roof isn't going to cave in on him like his last accident. Lass, he's just running late, he's not been injured.'

Olivia nodded, knowing she was being overprotective.

'I like that outfit.' Tess nodded to the deep-blue skirt and matching jacket with the white frilled blouse that Olivia wore beneath her white apron. 'Blue is your colour, it brings out your lovely eyes, not that they need it.'

'Thank you. I bought it from the little shop near the market at the end of Brook Street. Mathers, I'm certain it's called.'

'Is it newly opened?'

'Last week, I think.'

'Aye, I've not been inside it yet,' Tess said as the front door opened. 'Oh, here he is. Happy birthday, lad.' Tess beamed at him as Lachie came through from the front room into the kitchen.

His clothes and face were dirty from working in the iron foundry, nevertheless, he wore a huge grin. He'd grown tall recently, easily surpassing Olivia's height of five foot seven by several inches. He shaved now, and his shoulders had widened from working the heavy machinery at the foundry. He reminded her so much of their late father with his blond hair and blue eyes, which she herself had also inherited from him.

'Thank you, Mrs Hobson.' Lachie bowed formally and then impulsively kissed the older woman's plump cheek with a grin.

'Get away with you, lad.' Tess laughed, pushing him away.

'Did you get me a present, Tess?' he teased.

'Did I heck get you a present, lad! But you can have some advice for free. Don't make a habit of coming home late.' Tess nodded wisely.

Olivia attended to the food. 'Happy birthday.' She poured him a cup of tea. 'Did you have a good day?'

'Aye, it was fine.'

'Go and have a wash so we can eat. The cake has no icing, I'm afraid.'

'I don't mind.' He stood in the middle of the small kitchen, still smiling, fidgeting, his laughing blue eyes, so like Olivia's, kept darting from her to Tess and back again.

'What's wrong with you?' Olivia chuckled. 'Did you lose a penny and find a shilling or something?'

'A shilling, yes. The King's shilling,' he announced proudly.

A chill went over her. To take the King's shilling was a saying when men enlisted and were paid to join the army. She instantly dismissed his words. He was too young, only sixteen.

'What do you mean, lad?' Tess glowered. 'Tell us you've not done owt stupid.'

'It's not stupid to fight for one's country, is it?'

Olivia felt the blood drain from her face. 'You can't enlist. You're not old enough. Nineteen is the enlistment age.'

'I lied about my age, told the recruitment officer I was nineteen today,' he boasted.

Anger grew in her chest. 'Then you can march straight back down to that office and tell them the truth, and if you don't, then I will!' She glared at him.

'Aye, lad, go and tell them you were mucking about,' Tess prompted. 'You're just a lad.'

Lachie tensed. 'Lad, am I? I work twelve-hour shifts, using machinery that would crush bones. I'm taller than most of the men in the foundry. I bring home a wage. I'm not a child. If I can survive being buried down a pit, then I've got what it takes to fight for my country.'

Olivia thought she'd go mad with rage. 'You're not going, and that's an end to it.' She grabbed her hat, food forgotten. 'I'll go to that recruiting office myself and demand they release you.'

Lachie folded his arms defensively. 'If you do that, I'll just go to another office, and the next time I won't tell you. I'll just go.'

'Just go? Without a word? Like Stu did?' Olivia slumped against the counter. 'You're happy to leave me?'

'Liv—'

'You know how worried I am about Spencer. Do you want to put me through that worry over you as well?'

'I have to do my bit, Liv.' Lachie softened his stance. 'Those damn posters of Kitchener pointing his finger are everywhere. It feels like he's always pointing at me.'

'That's the point of them, to trick young men into signing up,' Tess muttered. 'The country went hysterical at the beginning of the war, hundreds of thousands of men enlisted, all thinking it were a great laugh, something exciting to do to get away from their jobs in mills and factories and pits, but you're not stupid, Lachie. You've read the newspapers, lad, seen the reports coming through now. The casualty lists: the dead, the wounded, the missing.'

Olivia took a step closer to him, her anger gone, to be replaced with dread. 'I've read you parts of Spencer's letters. He writes so much about the life of a soldier in this war. You know the truth of it out there. It's no picnic.'

Lachie pulled out a chair and sat down heavily. 'Our foreman, Mr O'Toole, announced this morning that his second son, Herbert, had been killed in action somewhere in Flanders. Mr O'Toole broke down and couldn't finish speaking. He's lost two sons now. At Christmas he lost his oldest son in action, remember? We all sent up a cheer for Mr O'Toole, for his sons, and then a group of us decided to enlist after our shift to honour Mr O'Toole's sons, to do our bit. We can't let the Germans win, Liv.'

'When you're old enough, if the war is still continuing, then you can do your bit,' she suggested. 'But not at sixteen.' She reached for his hand and gripped it tightly. 'Lachie. I'm begging you not to do this.'

'I'm sorry, Liv, but I'm going.' He stood up and walked out into the small backyard to wash.

Tess shook her head. 'If you stop him this time, he'll only do it again. He's as stubborn as you.' She stood as well and patted Olivia's shoulder. 'The best we can hope for is that those in charge see through his lie and send him home, other than that, they give him a role far to the rear of the front lines in a supply company or something like that.'

'You know, Lachie. He'll not be content with that.'

'He might be once he's over there, lass, and see it all for how it really is.' Tess smiled sadly. 'Don't let the time you have with him now be full of arguments.' She let herself out.

Alone in the kitchen, Olivia plated up the food and put it on the table, her appetite gone, her mind and heart at odds.

Lachie came in from outside and quietly closed the back door. He'd washed with the bucket of water and soap she'd left out for him and changed from his work clothes into his second-best suit. He sat down and began eating. 'Are we going to the cinema then?'

The last thing she wanted to do was sit and watch a film when dealing with the news that her brother would soon be fighting.

'Liv, I'll be gone to a training camp soon. We need to make the most of the time I have at home.'

She folded a tea towel and placed it over the edge of the sink. 'Did you think of me in any of this?'

'You should be proud of me! I'm defending this country like so many other men.'

'Men who were of age!' she argued. 'You're leaving me alone to worry about you and Spencer.'

'You're not alone. You've got Tess next door, Sadie on the other side, and all the other neighbours.'

'It's not the same. You're my family, all I have.' She didn't have to mention their other brother, Stu, who'd left the family last year and gone off travelling without telling anyone where he was going. They'd not heard from him since.

He gripped his knife and fork. 'I want to do this. I left the pit because you asked me to, but this time I'll not listen to your pleas and make my own decisions.'

'Why can't you join the volunteer unit in town instead and defend here at home?' She spoke of the citizen's militia groups that were springing up all over the country to defend the population in case of invasion. It was mainly made up of older men and retired ex-soldiers who were too old to fight.

He snorted. 'I'd be a laughing stock. The volunteer units are a joke, parading around with wooden rifles. No one takes them seriously.'

'They are in the service of the crown. Doing their bit.'

'They wear armbands with GR on them for Georgius Rex. Folk call them God's Rejects, a load of old men pretending to be soldiers. No, thank you. I'll fight with the real army.'

All argument left her. His determination was clear on his face, in his tone. She'd not win the quarrel. He was becoming a man before her eyes, but that didn't lessen the terrifying fact that he was going to war. 'When do you leave?'

'They'll notify me in a couple of weeks where I'll be sent for training.' He couldn't keep the excitement out of his voice.

'And training at the camp is for a few months?' she asked hopefully. By then, the war might be over.

'Yes, a good three months here in England the officer told us at the recruiting office, and then more training once we get to wherever they post us.'

She took a deep breath. With luck, Lachie wouldn't be anywhere near a battlefield until the end of the year. The war could be over by then. She wished she could talk to Spencer about it. She'd write to him later tonight.

'Try not to be upset, Liv,' Lachie said gently.

'I'll try.' She nodded. For him, she'll put on a brave face, but it will be difficult. 'Let's go to the cinema. If we hurry, we'll make it before the start of the movie.' She untied her apron and grabbed her purse from the table, forcing a smile. They had to grab every moment of happiness.

CHAPTER 2

Flanders
Late June, 1915.

ON A WINDLESS, hot summer's day, Captain Spencer Middleton walked beside his company of men as they trudged along the dirt road. Refugees spilling out of towns further north in Belgium hindered their way. Many times, the men had to part to allow horses and loaded carts to pass. Young children and old people sat high on the wagons atop of furniture and belongings, while dejected and fearful their family members plodded behind, fleeing from all they'd known.

Spencer hated seeing such wretchedness. The peaceful countryside of Flanders no longer resembled lush farmland and woods filled with birdsong. Instead, it had been replaced with an artillery-despoiled wasteland of shell holes, destroyed buildings, dead animals, broken trees, and miles of trenches dug into a rolling flat landscape.

Worse than any of that was coming across hastily erected graves of soldiers who had fallen in the greatest sacrifice. Army burying parties were often seen and never spoken of by soldiers marching past. His men, hardened soldiers, would take off their caps in respect as they passed the ugly mounds of dirt and rudimentary wooden crosses made up of bits of broken duckboards that lined the bottom of the trenches. Sometimes, the grave mounds held no cross at all, and that saddened Spencer more than he liked to admit.

Spencer checked his map and used his compass. They were close to the next line of trenches, which crept along the edge of a devastated area that had once been a small forest. His orders were to hold a section of the trench of roughly two hundred yards, reinforcing the Allied front line, which stretched over four hundred miles from the North Sea in Belgium to the Swiss border in the south. The unit that held this stretch before had been withdrawn under heavy shelling, and this was a hole in the line that needed plugging.

'Sir?' Lieutenant Dawes came alongside him. 'My map says this area to the right is where we should be.'

'So does mine.' Spencer folded his map and compass away. 'But we are not staying near this road. We're to head into those shattered trees and build a new trench to join up with the French on our eastern flank.'

'But I thought we were to defend the road from attack?' Dawes questioned, something he often did.

Spencer looked at the younger man, a replacement for a lieutenant killed last month in battle, a day before they were pulled out of the line for a rest period. Spencer had welcomed three new lieutenants into his company in ten months. He hoped Dawes wouldn't get himself killed as the other two did. However, Dawes was impatient and acted as though he knew everything, and that rubbed Spencer up the wrong way. 'Lieutenant, if we are in the woods, we have some cover. We can set watches on the road but be protected in a trench. We are not going to be sitting beside a road in easy view of any passing

German bi-planes, sniper attacks or raiding parties. Understood?'

'Yes, sir, but—'

'There are no buts, Lieutenant.'

'How long are we told to hold this section, sir?' Dawes asked. He had an intensity about him that Spencer wasn't sure if he liked or not. The man was straight out of military college and seemed intent on being a textbook officer. Only, after the baptism of fire Spencer and his men received on landing in Belgium and facing the might of the German army, Spencer knew textbooks didn't always have a ring of truth or reality about them.

'We'll hold this section until we receive orders to the contrary, Lieutenant.' Spencer studied the lay of the land. Using binoculars, he could see to his right in the distance movement of other units, likely the French in hastily erected trenches.

Spencer signalled to Dawes to use his binoculars. 'Take your platoon into this wood on the right. See it? You are to walk until you find the nearest allied unit and identify yourselves to that unit's officer and tell them of our location and gather any intelligence.'

'Sir, perhaps a sergeant could attempt this task?' Dawes argued. 'I can be of better use overseeing the men dig in correctly.'

'I have sergeants to do that, Dawes.'

'But—'

'Are you defying an order, Lieutenant?'

'No, sir, merely discussing better options.'

Spencer clenched his jaw. Why did this fellow always argue his orders? 'It's not up for discussion. Be as quick as you can. Keep low.' Spencer saluted him and then turned to find the private who was his runner.

Spencer quickly wrote in his notepad their location and intentions to hold the line. He requested from his superiors back at headquarters, a mile and a half away, armoury supplies and food.

After speaking to his two other lieutenants, Spencer instructed for the men to start digging. He wanted the ditch along the wood to become a deep trench. As the men began digging, Spencer ordered for sentries to be posted at intervals for two hundred yards.

'I want parapets every twenty yards. A decent fire-step the whole way along.' He spoke of the ledge the men would stand on to fire over the top of the trench wall. 'Dugouts need to be reinforced with any wood you can find,' he said, walking between the men. 'I don't want men buried alive while they sleep. There are enough broken branches lying about to use as supports.'

He stopped beside a private. 'Put that cigarette out, Private. Your head is still showing above ground. Smoke when you don't risk a bullet hitting you between your eyes!'

For hours, Spencer dictated his instructions, helped by his junior officers, making the men see his vision of a neat, high-mounded and orderly trench. The trench zig-zagged, hindering the enemy's advantage of shooting straight if they got into it.

Small dugouts were built into the side walls for the men to take shelter, sleep, or rest when not on lookout duty.

'Sir.' Dawes reported back as the setting sun cast a golden glow over the landscape. The sky was a mixture of orange and pink hues, contrasting against the ugliness of the ruined land below.

'You were gone a long time, Dawes,' he reprimanded, supervising the location of a latrine pit some distance behind the trench.

'The French unit was leaving when we got there, being replaced by a new Canadian unit, so I thought to speak to the French as well as the Canadians.' He handed over his extensive notes. 'The French have had periodic bouts of fighting for weeks. They say it's been quiet for two days, which is making them uneasy.' Dawes pointed to a ridge in the distance. 'The Germans have dug in along that slight ridge below the horizon. Apparently, night raiding parties occur often, every couple of days. Sometimes not long after dark and sometimes just before dawn. We're advised to double the sentries at night.'

Spencer used his binoculars to study the ridge, seeing the smudged markings of the German front line. He wondered if a German officer was doing exactly as he was right now and gazing upon the Allied line, knowing that there were men waiting to kill him.

He lowered the binoculars. 'Very good, Lieutenant. Get your men sorted. Dig in. Eat. Rest. We'll have a meeting for all officers and NCOs at twenty-one hundred hours. Tell the others, please.'

'Sir.' Dawes saluted and walked away.

Spencer had only walked ten feet before Private Bishop, his batman, came up to him. 'Yes, Bishop?'

'I've made you a dugout, sir. Your kit is in there, ready for you. I've made you a cup of tea, and there's some bread and cheese.' Bishop, a boy of only eighteen, smiled proudly.

'Bread and cheese?' Spencer enquired, falling into step with him back towards the trench.

'I managed to find some before we left the village.' He grinned. 'The farmer's daughter was most obliging.'

Chuckling, Spencer didn't fully believe him. Private Bishop was known to be a bit of a larrikin. Spencer had taken him on when his former batman left the army after getting married and moving to America before the war started. Bishop was a cheeky fellow from the back streets of London who had the talk and the ways of acquiring anything Spencer needed, whether it was sanctioned by the army or not. Always ready for a laugh, Bishop hadn't let Spencer down in any of his duties. His role was to care for Spencer, and he did it uniquely and enough by the book not to get into trouble, *just*.

The dugout was a large square in the side of the trench wall with enough room for Spencer to sit and have his kit spread out beside him. Bishop had lined and supported it with broken branches gathered from the shelled woodland. He'd tacked a waterproof sheet over the front of it so that when Spencer slept, he had some form of privacy, but also, he could write by lamp-light without giving away his position to the enemy.

'We'll build a better one once the timber and sandbags are sent up from HQ, sir.'

'You've done well, Bishop. Thank you.' Spencer rubbed his forehead and checked his notes. He had so much to do.

Bishop handed him an enamel mug of black tea made on a Tommy cooker and a slice of bread with a chunk of cheese on it.

Suddenly hungry, Spencer sat in the dugout and ate and drank while reading his orders from his commanding officer. They were to hold their line until they were relieved. When that would be, Spencer had no clue, and he suspected neither did his commanding officer.

The surrounding noise of men settling in ebbed and flowed as sergeants gave orders to the men to dig deeper, reinforce a wall and all the other tasks employed in trench life.

In the distance, the low boom of artillery fire hummed like an annoying whine of a wasp, and he hoped that none of it would come their way until the men were sorted and had more cover built up.

His lieutenants were also busy taking some of the strain from him as carts rolled up the dirt track from headquarters filled with ammunition, and supplies, including rolls of barbed wire, which one of their tasks was to roll out in front of the trench tonight once it was fully dark.

Finishing the last mouthful of bread, he checked his watch and signalled to Dawes nearby it was time for 'stand-to', at which point orders were given down the line for all the men to stand on the fire step armed and ready for attack.

After the initial rustling of the men getting into position, a tense quiet enveloped the area. Stand-to was ordered twice a day, dawn and dusk, and the men would stand ready for an hour and a half, prepared to meet the enemy should it come.

Spencer and his officers walked behind the men, checking their stance, giving them a note of advice or simply a nod of acknowledgment. At one point, Spencer used his binoculars to check the fields stretching out over No-Man's-Land. He strained his eyes and concentrated on any slight movement in the grass across the mile or so to the enemy's trenches. Nothing seemed out of the ordinary. So far, so good.

Much later, close to midnight and after the officers' meeting, Spencer sat in his dugout. On his lap balanced a small portable secretary, something of an extravagance considering the environment, but a useful writing board his grandparents had bought him in Paris and sent to him a month ago for his birthday. The walnut wooden secretary was of a slim design, with a carved indent at the top to hold a pen and inkwell to stop them from moving. The lid lifted, revealing a place underneath to keep paper and envelopes. Although not army issued, Spencer used it constantly. Bishop knew to guard it with his life.

By lamplight, huddled behind the waterproof sheet, Spencer began a letter to Olivia.

My dearest darling,

You would laugh if you saw me at this particular moment. I'm crouched in a hole much like a fox in a den! I hope I can be as wily as a fox should the enemy come knocking.

We left our billet at the village three days ago (when I sent my last letter to you). My men enjoyed the rest, but it was over before we realised, and for the last two days, we've been in the reserve line waiting for orders to go to the front line.

We arrived at our new location this afternoon and are living at the edge of a shattered woodland. The area would have been peaceful farmland not so long ago.

You asked in your last letter what you could send me. If possible, any food in tins would be most welcome. Bishop, as I reported in my last letter, is clever at purloining bits and pieces, but tasty food is scarce, and army food is not the best, as I've commented before. Bishop kindly asks for blackberry jam, his favourite—the cheek of the man. Ha!

Seriously, anything you can spare is welcome. My grandparents and sister Anthea have sent out parcels, but Grandpapa has been unwell, and I do not want to burden them with requests. My father and Parky have also been excellent in sending me goods, but mail is not always reliable when we are moving about so much.

I've written to my brother, Ralph, and given him your address. He wishes to write to you, as does Mildred. I hope that pleases you? They think kindly of you, always have done since the days at Hawthorn Manor.

When I ponder that summer, when we met, and the short time we shared, I am always frustrated at not doing and saying more when I had the opportunity. I know we've written about this subject before, many times, since I was sent out here to fight, but I still feel robbed of the time we could have had if only war had not been declared, and if I was not a soldier.

I will make it up to you, Liv, I promise.

Spencer paused and took a deep breath. He was desperate to see Olivia, to hold her and kiss her. Their exchange of letters was the only link they could have, but he wanted so much more. If he survived the war, he would never leave her again.

Have you seen Parky recently? He wrote and told me he would visit you soon when he is next in the north, but he has become very involved with the War Office and spends most of his time in Whitehall with the

Quartermaster's Branch, who are responsible for supplying the army with everything we need. Of course, Parky would be enjoying that, being in the thick of things but in no fear of getting shot at! By the way, he has a gift for you from me. In my heart, I am there with you when you open it.

I will sign off on this letter, and it will go with the morning's post.

I miss you, my darling.

With all my love and devotion,

Spencer. XX

He sealed the envelope and added it to the pile of post in the canvas mail bag. Rummaging in his kit bag, he pulled out the pile of Olivia's letters. He'd kept every one and in quiet times, right before sleep, he'd read one or two and even though he knew them off by heart, he liked to read them for it brought her closer to him. For a short time, the war could recede from his mind, and he'd ignore the danger, the dirt, the noises of men, the bland food, the lice and the rats and all the discomforts and he'd be with Olivia. He'd hear her voice, see her smile, touch her pale blonde hair, drown in the depths of her blue eyes. Just for a little while.

CHAPTER 3

July 1915

Using her key, Olivia opened the back door of the elegant terrace house of number eighteen Belgrave Mount, a mere ten-minute walk from where she lived on Woodcock's Square, and not far from where she used to work as a housekeeper for a pianist, Mr Stephen Sheridan, an Austrian, who had fled to America after the war was declared because of his father's political views.

She wasn't a housekeeper for Mr George and Mrs Ida Rochdale, but more of a part-time daily. Spencer had asked her not to work in the munitions factories that had sprung up since the war started, stating it was too dangerous, and he generously sent her money each month, which paid for the rent, but since losing her position with Mr Sheridan, she needed to do something. It wasn't in her nature to sit about the house all day and do nothing.

Working for the Rochdales gave her some money and independence. She earned enough to buy personal items for her and Lachie and Lachie's wage covered the food, gas and coal. With careful management they were coping.

At times, she felt guilty for only working four days, but the arrangement suited the Rochdales, who left every Friday morning to take the train to spend three days with Mrs Rochdale's sister, Mrs Dewhurst and her husband in Manchester. Therefore, neither Olivia nor Mrs Wilmott, the cook, were needed full-time.

Mrs Dewhurst was an invalid and Mrs Rochdale helped to look after her younger sister each week for the Dewhursts didn't have the money to employ a nurse. Olivia admired Mrs Rochdale for the diligent care of her sister, especially at her own advanced age.

Working only four days, gave Olivia time to write long letters to Spencer, to clean and do her shopping and to knit the numerous pairs of socks and scarves that she donated to the many charities who sent care boxes to the troops. Working less also pleased Spencer who didn't want her employed at all. It was easy for Spencer to wish that she didn't work, he came from a class where the women stayed at home, their only requirement was to marry well, supervise the staff and run efficient homes and provide heirs. She wasn't from that world and as much as Spencer said she needed to get used to the idea of doing no manual labour when they married, at the moment they weren't married, and she needed to earn.

'Morning, Olivia,' said Mrs Wilmott as she cracked eggs into a bowl.

'Good morning, Mrs Wilmott. How are you this morning?' Olivia hung her hat and bag on a hook in the scullery and joined the cook in the kitchen.

'Well as can be.' Mrs Wilmott exhaled heavily. The older woman was rarely happy and seemed to suffer through life though, as yet, Olivia had failed to understand just why the cook was so miserable all the time. Mrs Wilmott had a good job and lived with her widowed sister in town. Although called Mrs, she'd never married and admitted she never wanted to be.

'I'll go through and get a start on the dining room.' Olivia donned a large, bibbed grey apron, wrapping the ties twice around her narrow waist.

'I heard thumping above, so Mr Rochdale is awake. I left a jug of hot water on the landing table for his morning shave.' Mrs Wilmott frowned. 'I'll have a pot of tea ready for us before they come down.'

'Right, I'll crack on then.' Olivia took a box of cleaning items with her into the hallway and turned into the dining room.

Being summer, the fires in each of the rooms weren't lit, giving her less to do. She opened the heavy curtains, swept the carpet rug and then dusted the furniture before polishing the table and setting it for breakfast for two.

The Rochdales hadn't been blessed with children. The old couple lamented often about it just being the two of them. Although not extremely wealthy, the couple lived well, employed two servants and possessed a lovely house filled with solid furniture. Mr Rochdale retired some years ago as a senior engineer and Mrs Rochdale once mentioned to Olivia she'd inherited the house many years ago from her father, who had been a doctor.

Number eighteen wasn't on the grand scale of where Olivia had worked for years at Spencer's grandparents' home of Hawthorn Manor, but this house had a charm of its own, with two front rooms and a dining room at the back and three bedrooms upstairs. Each room was filled with ornaments, paintings, glossy-leafed plants on pedestals, and the Rochdales, despite being in their seventies were happily married and still laughed together, creating a warm and contented atmosphere. Again, it was opposite to her last employment at Mr Sheridan's house which had been a quiet, intense house full of secrets.

Once the dining room was prepared for the day, Olivia went

into the front hallway and swept and mopped the tiles before taking the rug out the back and banging it free from dust. She collected the newspaper from the front doorstep and brought it inside for Mr Rochdale to read when he was at breakfast.

Back in the kitchen, she quickly drank a cup of tea with Mrs Wilmott and ate a slice of toast and jam.

'Have you heard from your fella?' Mrs Wilmott asked.

She smiled, love filling her heart. 'Yes, a letter arrived yesterday. Thanking me for the tins of jam and peaches I sent previously.'

'That was weeks ago you sent them.'

'True, but Spencer has been moved again. Still in Flanders but elsewhere now.'

'I thought the men aren't allowed to tell us back home where they are?'

'They aren't, and Spencer doesn't give me precise details. Simply a F stands for Flanders, that kind of thing. All I know is that they've been involved in small battles before being withdrawn to the reserve lines and so on.'

'Sounds tedious.' Mrs Wilmott flipped the bacon frying in the pan. 'I'm so glad I don't have any family involved in any of this war nonsense. Men are so stupid to start wars.'

Olivia nodded in agreement and took her cup and plate to the sink in the scullery to wash later. She heard movement on the staircase and swapped her large apron for a smaller frilled white one to serve the Rochdales their breakfast.

She carried in a tray of fresh tea, hot toast, a dish of butter and two small crystal bowls, one of strawberry jam and the other of orange marmalade. 'Good morning, Mr Rochdale.'

'Good morning, Olivia.' Mr Rochdale greeted her with a warm smile, sitting at the head of the table and opening the newspaper. He wore a plain grey suit, and his sparse white hair was neatly oiled and combed.

'Your bacon and eggs are nearly ready.'

'Thank you. My wife will be along presently.'

When Olivia returned to the dining room with another tray full of crispy bacon, scrambled eggs, sausages and kidneys, Mrs Rochdale was seated next to her husband.

'Oh, Olivia, good morning.' Mrs Rochdale was dressed in a lavender skirt and bodice, her grey-white hair pinned up in a sleek chignon that she did herself. 'Have you heard when your brother is going to training camp?'

Olivia's stomach churned. 'He leaves this evening, Mrs Rochdale.'

'Wasn't he meant to go last week?'

'Yes, but his leaving was delayed by over a week. They are sending him to a new training camp that's been built on the other side of Pontefract. While he's been waiting, the army have arranged smaller training groups in town that he's attended each day. Strangely, he's enjoying it. He comes home each day telling me about doing drills, route marches and learning about handling a weapon.' She was amazed at how quickly Lachie had become a soldier.

'He'll get a taste of the true army discipline when he gets to the training camp,' Mr Rochdale murmured, adding food to his plate. 'It's not all fun and games like what they've been doing in town. I've seen them marching, holding wooden rifles wearing their own clothes. The army will make a man out of him for certain.'

'How you will miss him,' Mrs Rochdale said carefully, knowing how upset the whole thing made Olivia.

'I'm hoping that the war will be declared over while Lachie is at the camp, and he never leaves England.'

'Some believe the war will continue for another year at least.' Mr Rochdale stabbed his fork at a piece of egg. 'A damn waste of fine men, that's all that's happening, I can tell you.'

'George,' his wife reprimanded with a frown before giving

Olivia a reassuring smile. 'Let us hope it's all over quickly and before your brother is in uniform.'

For the rest of the day, Olivia cleaned, tidied and sorted the house as Mrs Rochdale requested before going out to visit a friend and attending a flower show. Cleaning usually gave Olivia a sense of wellbeing, of contentment. Seeing a room polished and shining after she'd finished it was a great satisfaction. However, Lachie's departure played on her mind, and nothing could stop her worrying.

Mrs Rochdale let her go home early to say goodbye to Lachie, and since it was Thursday, Olivia wouldn't be back until Monday morning.

'Now, keep your chin up,' Mrs Rochdale said to Olivia. She'd come into the kitchen as Olivia was putting on her hat and grabbing her bag. 'Your brother is doing a fine thing. You'll miss him but remember that he is someone to be proud of and that you are not alone in sending a loved one away. Women are doing it all up and down the country.'

Olivia nodded, though she wanted to argue that not all women were sending off a sixteen-year-old who should be at home safe.

Most evenings on the walk home, Olivia stopped at the butchers or grocers to buy a bit of food, something to cook for Lachie when he got home from work, but not today. His train was leaving at four and he finished his last day at work at three. He wanted to have a bath and pack.

Olivia hurried home, eager to spend as much time with him as possible.

Inside number seven, she found Tess in the kitchen, making a beef sandwich. Out the back, Tess's son, Colin was pouring water over Lachie's head as he sat in the bath.

'I didn't know what time you'd be home,' Tess said. 'I thought to make him a quick bite to eat.' Tess put the sandwich on a plate. 'The tea is mashed. He's outside in the bath chatting away to Colin as though it's a bloody seaside holiday he's going on.'

Seeing the emotion in Tess, Olivia went straight to her, and they hugged.

'He's like another son to me. With two of my boys already fighting and now Lachie…' Tess wiped her eyes. 'I could slap him stupid for enlisting and giving us both this extra worry.'

'You can, after I've done it. At every opportunity I've asked him to change his mind. He won't. I have to accept it.'

'Stubborn little bugger.' Tess sniffed.

Olivia smiled sadly. 'Lachie will be fine. I have to believe that, Tess, or I'll go mad. It's bad enough I have Spencer over there. Now, with the two of them fighting…' She took a deep breath and pasted on a smile she didn't feel. 'We have to be strong and be here ready and waiting for when they come home.'

'I've told my three other boys that I refuse to allow them to join up. Thankfully, they have no inclination at this point to do it and are in a special occupation which is rammed home to them before the start of every shift by their underground over-men. Even the pit manager repeatedly tells them all how important it is that they continue to work on digging out coal.'

'No matter what job Lachie had, even if he was still at the pit, I don't doubt he would still have enlisted. There is something in the Brodie blood that makes us want to be adventurous, spontaneous. My grandfather started it by leaving Scotland and coming to England. Stu needed to go and see the world, and at times I too want to see what else is beyond Wakefield.'

'Aye, if you'd accepted Mr Sheridan's proposal, you'd be in America by now.'

She thought fleetingly of Stephen Sheridan. She hadn't loved him, for her heart was taken by Spencer, but she'd been close to going with Stephen to a new life in America if Lachie hadn't had his accident at the pit. She hoped wherever Stephen was, he was safe and happy.

The walk to the train station passed in a blink and Olivia waited on the crowded platform as Lachie greeted some fellows from the town training groups that were joining him on the same journey.

Finally, he came back to her, grinning with excitement. 'I'm in good company, Liv. There are few fellows from the foundry that I know and some from the training I've been doing at the barracks in town.'

'Good. You won't be lonely then.' She did her best to keep a positive tone. 'Are sure you've got everything you need?'

'Yes, as I've said for the last eight times you've asked.'

The train hissed and the station master blew his whistle. Suddenly everyone waiting were shaking hands or giving cheeks a kiss as mothers and fathers waved to sons boarding the train, girls gave sweethearts a final embrace and wives held babies up to fathers for a final kiss.

Olivia grabbed Lachie in a tight hold. 'Behave. Listen and do as you're told.'

'Yes, Liv. I'll be fine.'

'Write as much as you can and tell me everything you're doing.'

He kissed her cheek. 'I'll see you in a few months. I'm allowed home for a few days before I'm sent overseas, apparently.'

She refused to cry as he climbed aboard. He was only going to a training camp, he was in no danger for now. So, she smiled and waved, her chest tight but wouldn't let him see. She watched the train until it was gone from sight.

'He'll be back before you know it, lass,' an older man said, walking past her.

She turned for home, not eager to start living by herself. She'd never lived alone before. At twelve years old, she'd gone from a warm happy family to live and work at Hawthorn Manor who employed a large group of indoor staff. After leaving the manor when it was sold, she'd left the countryside with Lachie when their father died and moved into the square where they'd been accepted and welcomed instantly.

When she turned into the square, many of the neighbours were sitting out in the evening sunshine, some of the men were drinking ale and the women enjoying cups of tea.

'He got off all right then?' Sadie asked from number five.

'Yes, fine.'

'Come and sit with us for a bit, lass.' Tess waved to the empty chair beside her.

Ezra, a single man who worked at the coal mine with Tess's husband, Larry, and their sons, gave her a pat on the shoulder as she passed him. A kind man who would help anyone, Ezra didn't need to say anything to show his support.

Sitting between Tess and Sadie, Olivia accepted a cup of tea from Mrs Muldoon from number ten. 'Thank you.'

She didn't want to enter an empty house just yet, that would come soon enough. It would take some getting used to being in the house on her own with no one to talk to, no one to care and cook for, but that was something she'd face later. For now, the sun was warm on her back, and she was surrounded by her friends.

'You know what you need?' Sadie said to her.

'No, what?'

'A cat to keep you company.'

'I'm not fond of cats.' Olivia sipped her tea.

'A bird then.'

'Yes, one of those parrots that talks to you.'

Olivia chuckled. 'That would be different.'

'She can have my kid anytime she wants noise and disruption.' Winnie offered, from number one, juggling two-year-old Martha on her knee.

Mrs Betts, a widow from number nine, shook her head. 'No, all Olivia needs is for her captain and her brother to come home, as do all the families around the world fighting in this hideous war.'

It warmed Olivia's heart that the whole square knew of Spencer even though the neighbours had never met him. But Tess had soon spread the word when Olivia and Spencer reunited and told everyone they were to marry the minute the war was over. Which meant Spencer was an honorary member of Woodcock's Square despite him never having stepped foot on the square's cobbles.

When she and Lachie first moved here, she was upset to be living in such poor surroundings. Woodcock's Square was nothing like living in the country at her family's neat cottage or in the splendour of the manor. It had taken some time to become used to living so closely with strangers in the small poky terraced housing where you heard your neighbours day and night and where everyone knew each other's business and where barely anyone knew how to knock on a front door but just opened it and came inside.

Yet, gradually, Olivia had come to warm to these people as their generosity and kindness became apparent. Her neighbours had very little money or possessions, but they were happy to share whatever they had with her and Lachie, and she was soon accepted as one of their own.

One day, when she married Spencer, God willing, she would leave this square, but she'd miss those she called friends, especially Tess, who was like a mother to her.

Suddenly a sleek silver motor car pulled to a stop at the edge of the square on Norton Street. All the neighbours stared and the men home from work gave low whistles and murmurs of admiration.

'That's a Rolls-Royce Silver Ghost,' Ezra said in awe.

'That would cost a bob or two,' commented Mr Muldoon.

Olivia paid attention. Spencer's best friend Mr Parkinson was the only man she knew who owned a car, but this wasn't the car she'd seen him drive.

Even the children playing hopscotch and marbles grew quiet as a chauffeur climbed out and opened the back door for his passenger. A tall gentleman stepped out of the car wearing a fine suit the colour of charcoal.

'He must be lost or something,' Sadie said knowingly.

For some reason, Olivia put down her cup and stood. The gentleman placed his trilby on his head and the action reminded her of Spencer. Her stomach flipped.

Ezra strode down to the road to the gentleman and held out his hand. 'Good evening, sir. May I be of help?'

The gentleman shook his hand with a smile. 'Ah, good evening. Yes, I hope so. I am looking for Woodcock's Square? My driver asked someone out on the other street, and they pointed to here, but this street says Norton?'

'Aye, it does. But this square behind us is Woodcock which you can only access from Norton Road.' Ezra swept his arm behind him to show the L-shaped terraced houses and the back of the shops and the pub fronting Stanley Road.

'I am wishing to visit Miss Olivia Brodie. Does she live here?'

Ezra stiffened. 'May I ask who you are, sir?'

'Mr Stanford Middleton.'

Olivia left the group and walked closer to the two men and could clearly recognise an older version of Spencer. 'Mr Middleton. I'm Olivia Brodie.'

Stanford Middleton took off his hat and smiled with a kindness in his eyes so like his son's. 'Of course, you are. Spencer described you perfectly. May I kiss my future daughter-in-law?'

She nodded with a smile and went to him to receive his kiss on the cheek. 'I'm pleased to meet you, Mr Middleton.'

'Call me, Stanford, my dear. We are to be related after all.'

Abruptly, Olivia wondered why he was here, and a shiver of

apprehension chilled her. 'Have you heard from Spencer? Is he well?'

'Yes, yes, oh my dear, do not be alarmed!' He quickly took her hand. 'No, nothing has happened to him. I come with good news.'

She sagged with relief.

Tess had come beside her, obviously thinking the same. 'Everything all right, lass?'

'Yes. This is Spencer's father, Mr Stanford Middleton.'

Tess shook the man's hand. 'Perhaps you should take him inside, lass?'

Olivia led the way through the neighbours and into her front room where Mr Middleton frowned as he looked around the cramped living conditions.

Tess came with her. 'I'll put the kettle on.'

Olivia waved Mr Middleton to the armchair by the unlit fire, and she sat on the little sofa while Tess went into the kitchen.

'I have received word from Parky,' Mr Middleton began, then paused. 'You do know of Parky?'

'Yes, Spencer's friend, Mr Parkinson. I've met him several times.'

'Good, well, Parky was meant to come and see you, but he has been sent to Italy on some secret army mission, apparently, so he told me when I saw him in London two days ago. Parky is fluent in Italian and French, you see. How he has managed to become so engaged in army business is beyond me, but he was always a clever fellow and has many friends in high places.'

'Spencer joked that Mr Parkinson would help win the war without ever coming close to an enemy's bullet.'

Mr Middleton laughed. 'My son is so right on that score. Anyway, Spencer had entrusted him with a task of his own, to come and see you.'

'Spencer did mention it in a letter.'

'That task has now fallen to me.' From his suit jacket pocket, he pulled out a small box and an envelope. 'This is from Spencer.' He gave both of them to her.

Surprised, Olivia took the box and envelope. She opened the box first, expecting a little trinket inside, instead she stared at a beautiful sapphire nestled in a gold band. 'Oh, that's so beautiful.'

'It was my wife's, Spencer's mother's ring.' Mr Middleton gazed at the ring.

Olivia opened the envelope and took out the piece of paper.

My darling,

Forgive me for instructing others to do what I so wished to do myself.

Months ago, I asked my father for one of my mother's rings to give to you as an engagement ring. You know how much I wish to marry you the first moment I'm able to do so.

My father allowed me to pick my mother's sapphire ring, which was his mother's ring as well. I hope you will adore it as much as my mother and grandmother did.

I'd give anything to slip this ring on your finger but know that I do it in my heart. So, as you can guess, I am formally asking you to marry me.

Wear the ring knowing it is given with all my love and devotion.

Your ever-loving (fiancé,)

Spencer.

Olivia folded the note and gazed at the ring in the box.

'Will you wear it, my dear?' Mr Middleton asked.

She glanced up at him, noticing Tess stood in the doorway carrying a tea tray. 'Yes, I'll wear it with pride, Mr Middleton. I love your son very much and will marry him the instant I'm able to.'

He nodded happily. 'Good. Excellent! That is all I needed to hear.'

'And you accept us being together? Accept me?' Olivia had her doubts that Spencer's family would welcome her with open arms. The class divide could be a hurdle too high to jump.

'I do. We all do. I have only heard lovely things about you from Spencer and Parky, and also my in-laws, Mr and Mrs Broadbent. You and Spencer have become a topic of conversation within the family.'

Olivia stilled. 'I've been talked about?'

He saw the look of disappointment on her face. 'My dear, it is to be expected. Spencer has never been keen on any young woman enough to offer marriage. The army was his life. Until you.'

'Does your family deem I'm not good enough for Spencer? After all, I was your in-laws' maid. That would have shocked them.'

'An undeniable truth, indeed, it was a shock.' He smiled kindly. 'But not an insurmountable problem. Spencer has been very open and honest with us all. He loves you and wants to marry you. I wrote to my mother-in-law Seraphina in Paris when Spencer first mentioned you to me. She was surprised by the development, but Spencer had warned her and his grandfather, Anthony, of his plans as well. Seraphina gave Spencer her approval, which can sometimes be difficult to obtain. We know Spencer would have continued with your relationship with or without the family's approval, that is the kind of man he is. He is like me, and when we love, we love deeply. However, his grandmother's endorsement made him exceedingly happy. You must not worry. If my son is happy, that is all that is important to me.'

'Despite the class difference?' Could she believe him?

'Spencer told me that you are a decent, well brought up young woman, with intelligence and kindness. Is he wrong?'

'No.'

'And you love my son? The man, not the soldier or his position in life?'

'I love your son, Mr Middleton. I would love him even if he suddenly became poor and was without a home or family connections. He makes my heart spin like a windmill in a gale. He is everything and all I would ever want.'

Mr Middleton reached for her hand and held it. 'Then what more could any father ask for in a daughter-in-law?'

'I will do my best to make Spencer happy for the rest of my life,' Olivia said solemnly. 'I understand it won't be easy. We are from different worlds, but I'm willing to try to make it work for us.'

'Those worlds are colliding closer and closer, my dear. This war is bringing changes to all classes and only a fool would remain blind to it. Just love my son, and the rest will fall into place.'

Behind him, Tess beamed and brought forth the tea tray. 'This tea is getting cold, though we should have more than tea for this occasion,' she said. 'An engagement!'

'I have champagne in my motor car,' he announced.

'Lord, you should have said!' Tess nudged him. 'Go and get it, man. We've got to celebrate!'

Chastened by a woman of a class much lower than him, Stanford Middleton laughed and went outside.

'Let me look at it then.' Tess took the box and inspected the ring. 'It's beautiful, lass. I'm right pleased for you.'

'Thank you.' Olivia felt happy, naturally, but she wished more than anything that Spencer was here.

'Put it on!'

'Should I? Without Spencer?'

'Yes. Goodness knows when you'll see him again. Wear it. Enjoy it.'

Olivia slipped the ring onto her finger and held out her hand to admire it. 'It's more than I ever could have imagined.'

'Aye, it's a sparkler that's for sure. Don't be losing it down the sink drain.' Tess laughed. 'He's a looker is that Mr Middleton, isn't he? If your Spencer is anything like him, you've struck it lucky, girl, and no mistake.'

Olivia chuckled. 'I know I did.'

'Come on, let us go out into the square and celebrate with everyone else.'

'Really?' Olivia held back not sure if Mr Middleton would want to be surrounded by the working class of the square.

'They are your people, lass.' Tess read her mind. 'Mr Middleton might be soon your father-in-law, God willing, but for now, we are your family, and we want to share this happy news with you.'

Nodding, Olivia fetched glasses from a cupboard and joined her outside where Tess announced the news and everyone cheered and clapped. Mr Middleton was accepted into the fold as though he was a fellow neighbour instead of a wealthy gentleman, but he didn't seem to mind and happily poured mouthfuls of champagne into a mixture of glasses and teacups held out to him. Even his chauffeur was invited to join them as more cheers were raised for the newly engaged couple.

'I hope Spencer can sense all this,' Olivia murmured to Mr Middleton as he came to stand beside her.

'I hope so, too, Olivia.' He clinked his glass against hers. 'I was thinking I would like to write to you, if that is agreeable with you?'

'I'd like that as well.'

'Good. We need to get to know each other, don't we? Once the war is over, and Spencer resigns from the army, I expect you and he will come to York and live with me, or perhaps in my townhouse in London? I'd like him to become involved in my businesses.'

His comment surprised her. Spencer had mentioned to her in a letter that after the war he wanted to resign his commission.

'Oh, I'm not sure where we'll live. It seems impossible to plan a future with the way things are right now.'

'That is understandable. I shall mention it to Spencer in my next letter. He has been a career soldier since leaving school. I suspect he, and you, have many decisions to make.'

'Yes, but not until after the war.' She smiled at Sadie and her husband Gerry who raised their glasses towards her.

Mr Middleton studied the last drops of champagne in his glass. 'As I said, I am hoping Spencer will join me in my businesses. I need to leave them to someone. Ralph is committed to the church and Anthea is well cared for by her husband in Paris. Spencer is the only one who might take on all that I have built. Your late father had his own business, did he not? Spencer told me you have brothers? Did your father want them to follow in his stead?'

'My father was a blacksmith. Hardly a businessman such as yourself.'

'He still ran a business, no matter how small.'

'Well, my brother Stu left us. He had no intention of following our father into the business. Stu fought with our father the day he left, and father died of a heart seizure afterwards. We had to give up the forge, so my youngest brother Lachie didn't get the chance to take over from our father.'

'Fathers and sons. I was not best pleased when Ralph informed me he was joining the church not long after Spencer left for South Africa, but what could I say? I wanted both my boys to be involved with my businesses. I built it all for my family, but young men have to find their own way.'

'So, it seems. My brother Lachie would have followed Father's lead if Father hadn't died so suddenly while Lachie was still a boy. We had no choice but to leave our cottage and come to Wakefield to find work.'

'And Spencer could not find you to make other arrangements.'

'No. We didn't communicate very well with each other before he left for Ireland.'

'Spencer told me he made mistakes and didn't recognise the depth of his feelings until it was too late, and you were gone.'

'Neither of us did. Everything happened so fast. Unlike now, where we take the time to write to each other and reveal everything in our hearts. Not a week goes by when I don't receive a letter from him, and I send him the same.'

'He adores you very much. I know my son and I know when he feels something keenly.'

'Be assured that I love him just as much, Mr Middleton. He means everything to me.'

Mr Middleton sighed heavily, a sadness creeping into his eyes. 'We just need this damn war to be over.'

'I couldn't agree with you more.' She sipped her champagne with a heavy heart.

'Enough talking, you two.' Tess declared. 'Ezra, play us a tune on your mouth organ. This is a party!'

Mr Middleton's expression grew a little concerned. 'Should I leave?'

'Heavens no!' Tess took his hand. 'We'll have a little dance.' She turned to Mr Muldoon. 'Head over to the pub and get some more drinks in.'

'Old Spinney won't let me bring them out here,' Mr Muldoon spoke of the pub landlord.

'Tell Old Spinney if he ever wants to see my Larry and my lads in his bar again, then he'll send out some drinks. Invite him to come out and have a drink with us.'

The square soon filled with a jaunty tune played by Ezra and Sadie's husband, Gerry, who accompanied him by playing the spoons. Children ran about as lanterns were lit to replace the dwindling light.

The inhabitants of the square didn't have much, but they

knew how to enjoy themselves with very little, and even when times were bleak.

CHAPTER 4

Northern France,
October, 1915.

In an abandoned farmhouse on a cold windy evening with a hint of rain in the air, Spencer sat at a makeshift table conducting a meeting with his officers and NCOs. The rest of the men were resting, spread across the farm in the barn, stables and outbuildings.

'Right, gentlemen.' Spencer glanced at the officers sitting or standing around the table in the dark kitchen that was lit but only one candle stub. 'Our orders have been sent to me and are as follows. At zero hours, a reconnaissance party will leave this farm and investigate the village two miles to the north of this position. They will return at three hundred hours and report on their findings. I have been informed that the village has been abandoned. The enemy held it for several months, but their troops have been withdrawn.'

'How do we know the Germans are gone for certain?' Lieutenant Dawes butted in.

Spencer gave him a cool look. 'We don't, Lieutenant. That's why we are going to send a party to gather intelligence. If they deem the village safe and abandoned by the enemy, then at four hundred hours we shall march on the village and take it under our control. We will hold it until we are relieved by another company. Any questions?'

'This could well be a trap that we are walking blindly into,' Dawes muttered.

'A trap?' Spencer tightened the grip on his pen in annoyance. 'The reconnaissance party will ascertain whether the village is clear of Germans or not.'

'And what if they are seen? The party could all be killed and we'll not know about it,' Dawes argued. 'The Germans will then know we are likely to be holed up here at this farmhouse. One call to their artillery and we'll be shelled like sitting ducks.'

'Our orders are to take the village, Lieutenant, but before we do so, I am sending a party out. I can do no more. We take our chances.'

'Then we should march there, in force, before dawn and spring a surprise attack, sir.'

There were general mumblings around the room for and against the plan.

A growing anger simmered in Spencer's chest. 'We are not walking blindly into a village without first getting clear intelligence about it, our *own* intelligence.'

'This farm is in the middle of miles of open fields. It's a possible target by itself, and if there are Germans in the village, they might know of our position already and attack us first either tonight or tomorrow. We should be ready to defend this farm first.'

Spencer strove for patience. 'We only arrived at this farm two hours ago, Lieutenant. If there are Germans in the village, and for them to know we are here, then they would have to have roaming reconnaissance parties, and one of those parties would have to be close to this farm in the last hour of daylight to see us just as we arrived. Many factors would need to be aligned for that to happen, wouldn't you agree?'

'It could've happened.'

'The intelligence I've been given is that the Germans have left the village,' Spencer said in a tone that held an edge to it.

'We don't know if it was a bluff by the Germans.'

'In this instance, I don't expect it to be a bluff.' Spencer gathered his paperwork, eager to be finished.

'We don't know the intelligence of the enemy, sir,' Dawes said stubbornly.

'No, we don't but we should always assume they are cleverer than we are. To reason the enemy as stupid is a weakness on our part.'

'I don't consider the Germans are stupid at all. They have shown intellect when at times we have not, sir. A German unit might be hiding in the village or marching towards this farm as we speak. We should stay here and defend this farm.'

Spencer leaned towards him, anger sharping his tone. 'Are you arguing about your orders, Lieutenant?'

'I'm arguing about the futility of them, yes.'

'You are disobeying these orders?' Spencer challenged.

A gasp echoed around the room.

'You're putting words into my mouth!'

'Putting words into your mouth, *sir!*' Spencer reminded him of who was exactly in charge.

'Forgive me, *sir.*' Dawes barely kept the sarcasm out of his tone.

'You will lead the reconnaissance party, Lieutenant Dawes.' Spencer decided as punishment for the man's confrontation. 'I have every confidence you will find out whether the enemy is in the village or not. I shall select the men to accompany you.'

Dawes's chin jutted out furiously. 'Surely on such a mission I should pick my own men, sir?'

Before another word was spoken, the back door opened and in walked a familiar face, Alfred Dunbar, Spencer's friend and fellow battalion captain. All the men stood and saluted.

Alfred saluted them and grinned at Spencer. 'What's all this then?'

'What are you doing here?' Spencer shook his hand, grateful to see his friend.

'Oh, I heard you were in need of a superior company to help you out,' Alfred joked.

'And they couldn't find any, so they sent you and your men?' Spencer chuckled.

'Steady on,' Alfred warned with a grin, glancing about the table. 'Something is afoot. You'd best tell me all about it.'

Sometime later, Spencer walked around the farm's buildings alongside Alfred. A weak moonlight lit their way. The wind had dropped slightly, but the night had grown colder. Most of the men were indoors in the outbuildings, except for the sentries on duty.

'That Lieutenant Dawes is an intense type of fellow, isn't he?' Alfred said, stopping beside a barn wall to light a cigarette.

'He's a pain in my arse, that's what he is. Ever since he joined us, he's been challenging my every decision.'

'A bit like you used to do to our officers when you first arrived in South Africa.'

'Our officers were fools. I am not.'

Alfred laughed. 'I'll give you that.'

'Dawes could be a fine damn soldier if he just dropped the textbook rules and used his initiative.'

'Butting heads with him won't help that, you know. He's the type that you need to get on side.'

'I've tried. The kid is twenty-one and straight out of military school. He thinks he knows everything.'

'Didn't we all at twenty-one?'

'It seems so long ago, doesn't it?' Spencer sighed and took a drag from Alfred's cigarette. He didn't smoke but at times, like this one, he felt the need to. 'Ten years ago. I was in a war then and I'm in another one now.'

'When did you start smoking?' Alfred asked in surprise.

'I don't, not really. This war is driving me to it.'

Alfred fished in his jacket and pulled out a silver flask. 'I forgot to congratulate you. An engaged man. I wish you all the best, Spence.' He passed the flask to him to take a sip. 'Shame it isn't champagne.'

Spencer smiled. 'My father took champagne to Olivia, along with the ring. She wrote to me telling me about the little party they had in the square. I should have been there.'

'Anyone might have thought it was your father proposing to Olivia,' Alfred joked, sipping rum from the flask.

'My father wrote to me telling me how delightful Olivia is, and he's pleased I've chosen so well, despite her working-class origins.'

'A barbed compliment that only parents can make so well.'

'So true.' Spencer shrugged. 'I care not a jot what anyone else thinks. Olivia is beautiful and clever and kind and she's mine.'

'When's the big day? Once this conflict is over?'

'No, before then. On my first leave if we ever get any,' he said flippantly. 'It's been over a year since we crossed the Channel.'

'You don't have to remind me, my good friend.' Alfred took another swig and then held it up to Spencer. 'To you and Olivia, may you be blessed with a—'

'Don't say it!' Spencer cut him off. 'Don't say anything but congratulations, nothing else about long lives or a blessed future, not here, not now.' He shivered, any talk of a long and happy future was bound to bring bad luck and a bullet through his head.

'Congratulations, old pal,' Alfred said soberly. 'And to everything left unsaid.' He clapped Spencer on the back in a mark of solidarity and hope.

Spencer touched his jacket pocket where Olivia's latest letter sat close to his heart. She'd written only two days ago, telling him that Lachie was doing well at a training camp near Pontefract and that she and Tess were making her wedding dress and that his father had opened a bank account for her and put money in it and would continue to do so, which she found very generous, but she would still work for the Rochdales because leaving them would be wrong. She also needed to keep busy while she waited for him to return to her.

Distant shelling drifted on the breeze and with it the smell of gunpowder. On the dark horizon spurts of light lit up as bombs exploded.

He glanced up into the night's sky, finding the moon peeking out between whipped clouds and hoped and prayed that he would indeed return to her.

* * *

December 1915

'It's cold enough to freeze the balls off a brass monkey out there!' Larry said, coming into the kitchen from outside and pulling up his suspender straps to his trousers.

'Larry Hobson! Language!' Tess barked at him, pushing dirty clothes into the steaming water in the copper boiler.

'Sorry, luv. Sorry, Liv.' Larry put down the folded newspaper that he'd been reading in the lav and sat at the table with the women.

'So, you'll come to us for Christmas dinner?' Tess asked Olivia.

'Of course, and thank you. I couldn't bear to sit by the fire alone all day.' She was dreading Christmas Day in two days' time. It would be her first without any member of her family present.

'I'd have not let you anyway,' Tess said in a no-nonsense tone, adding more hot water into the boiler from the kettle. 'Did Lachie write and let you know when he might be finished with his training?'

'His letter arrived just this morning, that's why I've come over to tell you that he said they will be finished by the first week in January. He's hoping to get a couple of days at home before he leaves for deployment.'

'Does he know where they'll send him?' Tess hung clothes over the clothes hoist suspended from the ceiling.

Larry tapped the newspaper. 'I doubt it'll be Gallipoli. They've withdrawn the Australians and New Zealanders from there. I doubt it'll be long before the British leave the place as well. That campaign has been a disaster. Back door to Europe they said, more like the back door to hell.'

Tess looked at her husband in surprise. 'The navy as well? Our Simon's ship is in that area, isn't it?'

'Aye, it was, but he could be anywhere by now,' Larry told her sadly. 'I meant our army. If they are brought home, they'll only be sent elsewhere. Just like young Lachie will be.'

Olivia stood and helped Tess, hating the thought of Lachie being sent anywhere. She looked lovingly at her engagement ring. She'd not heard from Spencer in over a week, which was so unlike him, and she was beginning to worry even more than usual.

Tess bustled about the kitchen, her own worry for her boys clearly showing on her face. 'Well, Christmas will come despite the war and so we need to be prepared. I'll go shopping in the morning and see what food I can buy that'll keep. I've paid for a bit of roast beef at Keane's, the butchers, that's been put aside for me to collect late tomorrow. Keane will be closing early on Christmas Eve.' Tess consulted her shopping list.

'There's a good chance me and the boys might be working Christmas Day, luv,' Larry ventured with a sad expression.

Tess rounded on him. 'Working! On Christmas Day! Why have you only told me this now?'

'It's not set yet. But with some of the men enlisting, we're getting low on manpower. Double shifts are occurring more and more. We can't get the coal out fast enough to meet demand.'

'Listen to me, Larry Hobson. You and my boys will be at this table on Christmas Day, or I'll march down to that pit top and have a word with your manager.'

'Now, Tess, lass, you know production is up because of the war. This is us miners doing our bit, even if that means missing a bit of Christmas. It's the least we can do, isn't it?' he soothed.

Tess grew red in the face. 'The least we can do!' She fumed. 'I've already got two sons in the war. I'm doing my bit knitting scarves and sending care boxes to soldiers. You and the boys are working all hours. This family is giving *enough*.' She stormed outside.

Larry rose to go to her, but Olivia put up her hand to stop him. 'I'll go.'

She found Tess crying in the alley that runs behind the terraces' backyards and put her arm around her shoulders but remained silent. She'd never seen Tess cry.

'I'm an awful woman, aren't I?' Tess mumbled. 'I'm moaning about Christmas and wanting my family at the table when so many mothers will never have their sons or husbands at their table again.'

'You aren't awful at all.' Olivia rested her head against Tess's shoulder. 'You're allowed to be upset.'

'I suppose if Larry and the boys are working, you and me can finish your dress. There's not much left to do.' Tess wiped her eyes with her apron.

'That sounds like a good plan.'

The back gate opened, and Larry stuck his head out, looking worried. 'Liv, there's an army officer out the front of your door. He looks official.'

Olivia felt the blood drain from her face.

'Now then.' Tess took control and grabbed Olivia's arm. 'It could just be someone checking on Lachie's age or something. Bad news usually comes in an envelope first. So, don't panic yet that it's about your Spencer.'

Her feet were stuck to the ground. She couldn't face whoever was out the front. Whoever it was wouldn't be bringing good news.

'Come on, lass.' Tess gently guided her through her own back gate and into her house.

It was Tess who opened the front door and stood stiffly demanding the officer's business. Olivia waited in the kitchen, summoning courage to face the news.

'Good afternoon, madam. I'm Spencer Middleton. I'm looking for Olivia Brodie.'

'Spencer!' Tess exclaimed but was abruptly pushed aside as Olivia flung herself into Spencer's arms.

'Oh, my darling.' Spencer held her tightly, squashing her into him.

Olivia thought her heart would burst with happiness. She held onto him, frightened to let go in case it was all a dream.

Eventually, Spencer loosened his hold and smiled down into her face. 'Good afternoon, Miss Brodie.' He grinned, kissing her.

She melted into his arms, not caring that she was kissing him on the front doorstep for the whole square to witness.

'Come inside, you two.' Tess beckoned them in.

Reluctantly, Olivia dropped her arms, but she took his hand and brought him inside and closed the door to introduce him to Tess properly. 'This is Mrs Tess Hobson.'

'It's a pleasure to finally meet you, Mrs Hobson. Olivia mentions you in every letter, so I feel as though I know you quite well already.'

'I hope she only writes the good parts, Captain,' Tess joked.

She shook his hand with both of hers. 'My, it's a happy day now you've arrived, Captain, and that's for sure.'

'How long can you stay?' Olivia asked, bracing for him to say only an hour or so.

'I've five days with you, my darling. I've lost a day in travelling here and I'll lose one travelling back.'

'Five days!' She hugged him again.

'Now.' He gently cupped both her cheeks. 'What do you think about getting married tomorrow?'

Olivia stared. 'Tomorrow? How can we possibly do it tomorrow? It's Christmas Eve!'

'Ah, you see things have been happening.' He winked cheekily.

'What do you mean?'

'For the last month, my father has been pulling a lot of strings and has managed to obtain a special license from the War Office for us to be married. My commanding officer has also agreed, and since my battalion was due some leave, my commanding officer said now would be the perfect time for us to do it as who knows when I will have leave again. Is that suitable to you?'

'Er... yes, but we need to speak to the vicar.' Her mind was in a flurry.

'My brother Ralph will arrive tomorrow and marry us. He knows the vicar of St Andrew's Church, which I understand is where you have gone to services before?'

'Yes, it is.'

'Ralph has been in constant contact with the vicar to arrange everything once Father told Ralph of the license.'

'Goodness. It's difficult to take all this in. You're here and we're getting married tomorrow?' She wanted to laugh at the madness of it all. She glanced at Tess who frowned.

'We need to finish your dress!' Tess ran out of the house and through her own front door.

Spencer pulled Olivia closer. 'What do you say? Shall we get married then?'

Olivia grinned. 'Well, I had nothing planned to do tomorrow, anyway…'

He laughed a delightful sound and crushed her into him to kiss her deeply. It was some time before they broke apart.

'I couldn't write and tell you about all this because it's all happened within days of us being pulled out of the trenches and sent to the coast to board a ship. I sent a telegram to my father, and he sprung into action sorting everything out for tomorrow. I hope you don't mind?'

'How could I mind about any of that? Your father is so generous and considerate to organise it all. I'd marry you in the middle of the square if that's all we could have. All I care about is that you're here now.' She kissed him again. 'I can't get over it. You're in my arms. I've missed you so much.'

'I've missed you. The whole time I'm away, all I think about is you.' He returned her kiss tenderly. 'You mean everything to me, you know that, don't you? I know I say it in my letters, but I mean it.'

Knocking on the front door drew them apart. Olivia opened it to find Mr Parkinson standing there holding a box of chocolates and a bottle of champagne, both of which he thrust into Olivia's hands. 'Mr Parkinson!' She was shocked to see him.

'Parky?' Spencer's eyes widened. 'I thought you were in Italy.'

'I was and then summoned by your father to return home. Apparently, I have special duties as your best man to perform?' He raised his eyebrows and bowed like a knight.

Spencer embraced him. 'It's good to see you, old friend.'

'Less of the old, my good fellow.' Parky slapped him on the back and then turned to Olivia. 'Now, Miss Brodie. Shall we open that champagne?'

'Absolutely.' Olivia busied herself in the kitchen finding glasses and ashamed she didn't have flutes, but ultimately what did it matter? Spencer was here and tomorrow they would be married. She could hardly believe any of it was happening. Her head was spinning with the notion of not only being a bride in the morning but a wife to Spencer, something she'd only ever dreamed of being.

She smiled to herself on hearing Spencer and Parky laughing in the front room. She wished Lachie was here, but at least he was safe for now at the training camp.

Impulsively, she went next door and asked Tess and Larry to join them, which they did. The little party soon drank all the champagne, prompting Larry to go and buy bottles of ale for the men, while Tess and Olivia put together plates of sandwiches and cut up slices of fruit cake.

Olivia sat next to Spencer on the sofa, unable to keep her gaze from his. She wanted to constantly touch him to make sure he was real. 'I'm still so surprised you're here.'

'There's nowhere I'd rather be. It's been too long, my girl.' He held her hand as Parky dominated the conversation with his witty stories about Italy.

As the afternoon turned into evening, Parky stood and drank the last of his ale. 'Well, Miss Brodie. You must forgive me as I need to whisk your intended away for the night, but I shall have him at the church bright and early in the morning.'

Everyone stood up and said their farewells.

Tess gathered the plates and empty bottles. 'Come around after you've said goodbye, lass, and we'll work on the dress. We should have it finished by tonight. I'll call in and ask Sadie to give us a hand.'

When Olivia was alone in the front room with Spencer, she walked into his arms and held him tight. 'I don't want you to go.'

He lifted her chin with a finger, his green-hazel eyes filled with love. 'Just imagine, tomorrow, we'll be married, and for the next three days after that I'm here with you.'

'I still can't believe any of this.'

'Believe in this...' He kissed her reverently. It was a kiss full of promise and hope and building passion.

She stood on the doorstep and watched him join Parky in the square and they walked along to Norton Road where Parky's motor car was left. Spencer gave her a wave and climbed into the motor car.

'Good God, you could have warned me how handsome the captain is!' Tess said coming out of her house carrying the wedding dress. 'He's a right head-turner, isn't he?'

Olivia laughed. 'I did tell you.'

'You two make an extremely handsome couple.' Tess spoke as though it was a unique phenomenon. 'I can see now why Mr Sheridan or Ezra never stood a chance with stealing your heart. The captain owns it wholly.'

'Yes, he does.'

'Right then, lass, let's get started.' Tess laid the dress over the sofa. 'Sadie is coming over to help, and I thought you could have a bath and wash your hair while we finish the dress?'

'What would I do without you?' Olivia kissed the older woman's cheek.

'Stop all this messing about, lass. We've got work to do!' Tess's smile showed her pleasure of the bond between them.

CHAPTER 5

With her stomach churning with excitement, Olivia stood in front of the mirror and stared at herself. The white satin dress was overlaid with a fine-lace pattern and studded with white sequins in select places within the pattern. Her gossamer lace veil covered her pale blonde hair and was held in place with a mother of-peal comb, a gift from Tess. Sadie had artfully arranged her long hair up with pins and dotted several small artificial white roses around the combs.

'You look incredible, lass.' Tess came into the bedroom, dressed in her Sunday best outfit of pale green.

'All thanks to you.'

'Nay, I just wrapped the parcel. Your parents gave you the goods.' Tess winked. 'Are you ready? Mr Parkinson said the ceremony was to start at ten o'clock. It's half nine now. Larry has gone out to find us a hansom cab, the rest of the neighbours are walking. It's a clear morning, though a bit cold. You'll have to wear your best coat over your dress.'

'No, I'll wear the silver cape you got me last year to wear to the theatre.'

'Oh, yes. How could I forget that?' Retrieving the cape from the wardrobe, Tess helped to drape it over her shoulders as voices drifted up the stairs. 'That'll be Larry back. Have you got your flowers?'

Olivia collected the bunch of cream silk material flowers, all Tess could manage to get from various neighbours at such short notice. Being December, fresh flowers grown in hothouses were expensive, she was happy with her material ones.

Downstairs, Olivia expected to see Larry in the front room, but instead she was surprised to see Mr Middleton.

'Good gracious Lord,' Mr Middleton gasped seeing her enter the room. 'You are magnificent, Olivia.'

Embarrassed at the fuss, she blushed. 'Thank you, Mr Middleton.'

'Stanford,' he corrected.

'Stanford.'

'I have brought my car to take you to the church.'

'That is so kind of you. Thank you.'

'I bought you another gift as well.' He walked to the front door.

'Really, you shouldn't have. You've been too generous as it is.'

With a flourish he opened the door and presented a young man in uniform.

'Lachie!' Forgetting any decorum, Olivia rushed to hug her brother. 'This is so wonderful.' Crying, she turned and hugged Stanford. 'Thank you. Thank you!'

'My pleasure, my dear.'

Tess embraced Lachie, tears in her eyes. 'It's good to see you, lad.'

'And you, Mrs H.'

Tess sniffed. 'Right, let's be going. We can't be standing about here all morning.'

Olivia stared at her brother as they climbed into Stanford's motor car. Lachie had grown inches and filled out. He looked older and so handsome in his uniform. A man. He could easily pass for eighteen or more. No one would question him now. Olivia held his hand on the short drive to St Andrew's Church. 'I'm so happy you're here.'

'Mr Middleton arranged it.' Lachie grinned mischievously. 'I have to be back at camp by six o'clock tonight, not a minute later.'

'I shall drive him back in plenty of time, or my chauffeur will, do not worry,' Stanford assured her.

'I can't thank you enough,' she said to Stanford.

'I assumed you would want your brother to walk you down the aisle.'

She reached for Stanford's hand. 'I was going to ask you if you'd like to do that.'

'And I would have been honoured, but it is your brother's place.'

All too soon they were at the church. The low sun shone from a light blue sky. The air inside the church was crisp but not unbearably cold when she removed her cape and handed it to Tess. The neighbours who could make it were standing blocking her view of Spencer.

The organ began to play, and Olivia's stomach tied itself into more knots as she linked her arm with Lachie's.

'I'm glad you're marrying Captain Middleton, Liv. You've never looked so happy.'

'This is the happiest day of my life. I'm marrying the man I love, and you are here to share it with me. I only wish the whole family was here.'

Lachie's eyes dulled for a moment. 'Father should be doing this, not me. If Stu hadn't argued with him and caused the heart attack, then Father would still be alive now.'

'We can't spend our lives wondering what if? It would send us mad. But we have this moment. Let's enjoy it.'

'This is the last time it'll be just the two of us.' He coughed to cover his emotion.

Her heart swelled with love for him. Their lives had changed yet again. Only this time it was for the better. 'Spencer is a good man, Lachie. I'm lucky to have him. He's part of our family now and we should be thankful.'

'Let's make it official then.' He patted her hand, and they set off.

The ceremony passed by in a moment. Spencer, standing tall and splendid in his officer's uniform, never took his gaze from hers as they made their vows in front of his brother Ralph, before God and their guests.

Olivia's hand shook slightly as Spencer slid the gold wedding band onto her finger to join the sapphire ring. She wished her parents were here, even Stu, to witness her happiness, to share in the best day of her life.

'It is with great pleasure that I pronounce you as husband and wife,' Ralph declared.

Parky whooped and clapped heartedly making everyone laugh.

Spencer could hardly kiss her he was smiling so much. She giggled at him as their lips touched.

'My wife at last,' he whispered.

She was Mrs Olivia Middleton. Was she dreaming? Was it possible to be this joyful?

Outside of the church, Stanford held up his hands. 'At this short notice I was not able to secure a venue to hold the wedding breakfast, I do apologise.'

'Never mind that, Mr Middleton,' Larry announced. 'Me and the neighbours have put our heads together and this morning we hired the back room of the Butcher's Arms on Stanley Road, and they said they'd put on a simple spread for us, some sandwiches and pork pies whatever they can cobble together. The Butcher's Arms often do wedding breakfasts or christenings and funerals and such like. It's our gift to the happy couple. Everyone is invited.'

'That's very kind, Larry.' Olivia was overwhelmed.

'You must let me contribute, Mr Hobson,' Stanford said.

'I'll never say no to someone giving me money, Mr Middleton,' jested Larry.

At the Butcher's Arms, Olivia took off her cape and stood by the roaring fire with Spencer to receive everyone's good wishes. She was deeply moved when Ralph and his wife Mildred came over.

'Welcome to the family, sister,' Ralph said with meaning. 'I'm delighted to see how happy you've made my brother.'

'Thank you, Mr Middleton.'

'I insist you call me Ralph.' He was not as handsome as his brother, but his words were kind, and his eyes showed sincerity.

'You look fabulous, Olivia,' Mildred said in her quiet and unassuming way. 'I hope you do remember me?'

'Of course I do, Mrs Middleton. You were very kind to me when I worked at Hawthorn Manor.'

Mildred relaxed slightly. She was a small, plump woman with a gentle way about her. 'I wasn't going to come, but Ralph insisted. I didn't want to embarrass you by turning up at your wedding uninvited.'

'I'm pleased you came. We would have been disappointed if you hadn't made it.'

'I'm terribly fond of Spencer, though we've hardly spent any decent time together as he has always been away with the army since I married Ralph, but he writes such lovely letters to Ralph and me. It is a shame Anthea and his grandparents couldn't make it, but with such short notice and the distance from Paris, there would not have been enough time to arrange everything.'

'At least Spencer has some family here.' Olivia glanced around at the room and the working-class people who filled it. 'This is a much simpler wedding than you would be used to I imagine?'

'Not at all. As a vicar's wife I have attended many such weddings. I confess I usually enjoy them more than the ones full of pomp and ceremony. Ralph may have been born into a wealthy society, but I was not. My father was a reverend attached to a country manor. You must never think of me as someone above you simply because you have served me at Hawthorn Manor. Like you, I married up.' She had a tinkling laugh.

'That is good of you to say, Mrs Middleton, but a vicar's daughter is more esteemed than a blacksmith's, or a housemaid.'

'Never think low of yourself, Olivia, especially not now. You're a Middleton now and that name demands respect in many circles, more than you know. Our father-in-law is an important man in London. He has the ears of a good number of influential people, including the royal family.'

'Goodness, I never knew. Spencer didn't tell me.'

'Apparently, we are not meant to know everything, even Spencer would not know it all. I only am aware of some of it because I overheard Seraphina talking about it one Christmas when she had too many sherries and Stanford had disappointed her in some way.'

Olivia thought of her former mistress. 'I remember the mistress would get melancholy at Christmas over her daughter's death.'

'Indeed, and Seraphina blames Stanford.'

'Why? Spencer's mother died in childbirth.'

'A child she shouldn't have conceived as far as Seraphina is concerned. Spencer and Ralph's births were an ordeal for her daughter. The doctors advised caution on having any more...' Mildred suddenly shook her head. 'Gracious me, why I am telling you all this on your wedding day?' She laughed self-consciously. 'Forgive me. My tongue has run away with itself. I was simply trying to put you at ease.'

Olivia smiled, liking her new sister-in-law. 'Thank you, Mrs Middleton.'

'Come, we are sisters now. It's Mildred.' She squeezed Olivia's hand. 'We shall write to each other often, yes?'

'I'd like that.'

'So should I. Being a vicar's wife can be lonely. Ralph is out caring for his parishioners at all times day and night. I often keep busy with doing good works within the village but it's such a small village I'm not as busy as I'd like to be, and I have only an older brother who lives in Halifax. We do not visit each other hardly at all, and my father is dead. So, writing to you will give me something else to do.' She paused. 'May we come and visit you, or you could come to us?'

'That would be lovely,' Olivia hesitated. 'But I still work.'

'Oh, yes, of course.' Mildred smiled widely. 'We'll sort something out.'

The rest of the day passed quickly. Stanford said a few words to celebrate Spencer and Olivia's special day, food was eaten, drinks drunk and the room was filled with chatter and laughter. Neighbours came and went as some finished work while others went to start their shifts.

Larry came to shake Spencer's hand and give Olivia a kiss. 'We've got to go. Our night shift starts soon, and we need to go home and change into our pit clothes.'

'Thank you for making our day extra special by hiring this room,' Olivia said. 'I shall never forget it.'

'It's what neighbours do, isn't it?' Larry beckoned his three sons who had all been talking to Lachie. Colin, the Hobson's youngest son, was Lachie's good friend, and they'd missed each other.

Stanford came alongside. 'I should be getting our young soldier back to camp. Do you want to go and say your farewells while I say goodbye to Ralph and Mildred?'

Saddened, Olivia nodded. She crossed the room to Lachie as the Hobson men left. 'It's time you were going as well.'

For a second he hung his head but then straightened. 'I'll be back soon enough. We get a couple of days leave before they send us out.'

'Good. I'll see you in the new year then.' She hugged him, not wanting to let go. 'Behave yourself. Stay out of trouble and be careful.'

'I'm not five years old, Liv.'

She raised her eyebrow mockingly. 'What have I always told you? You'll always be my little brother, no matter what age you are.' She kissed his cheek. 'I'll see you soon.'

Stanford and Spencer joined them. Olivia also gave her new father-in-law a kiss on the cheek. 'Thank you for bringing Lachie here for the day. I can't describe how much it has meant to me to have him. It was very thoughtful of you.'

'You are very welcome, daughter.' He faltered. 'I can call you that? Or would you rather I called you Olivia?'

'I miss my father enormously, to be called daughter again would be comforting.'

He squeezed her hand. 'I shall write to you both soon. Goodbye, son.' Stanford shook Spencer's hand with tears in his eyes. 'Stay safe over there.'

'I'll try, Father. Thank you for everything you have done for us today. We appreciate it enormously.'

'You are my first born and my last child to be married. I wanted to give you a day to remember. Your mother would have approved of everything.' Stanford straightened his shoulders. 'Goodbye everyone,' he called out to the remaining guests. He was liked and respected and they sent him off with a chorus of goodbyes and waves.

Spencer wrapped an arm around Olivia's waist and watched them leave in the motor car.

Soon everyone was coming out of the back room and heading to the square, all commenting on what a lovely wedding it'd been.

'I don't want this day to end,' Olivia said to Tess and Sadie.

'It doesn't have to,' Sadie replied. 'We can have some drinks at your place.'

Parky rubbed his hands together. 'I like the sound of that, but unfortunately, I'm due back in London.'

'You are leaving now?' Spencer said with disappointment as Ralph and Mildred joined them.

Parky nodded with regret. 'It is a long drive, and I have stops to make along the way. I shall drive as long as I can and then stay at a hotel somewhere and finish the journey in the morning. Enjoy your leave, my friend. I might catch you in France in the new year. There is a slim chance I might be sent to Paris at some stage. I will do my best to find you.'

'Search the trenches and you will find me,' Spencer retorted, an edge to his voice.

'Just keep your head down, Captain.' Parky slapped him on the back and then bent over Olivia's hand like a knight. '*Madame*, it's been a pleasure as always.'

'Thank you for coming, for everything.'

'Write to me any time.' For a moment his joking manner dropped, and he squeezed her hand. 'I am always at your service,' he said seriously, his glance flicking to Spencer and back to her.

She knew what he meant. Should something happen to Spencer she could call on Parky for help.

'We are leaving as well, brother,' Ralph said. 'We can catch the last train to Darton and then a hansom to the village and home.'

Spencer nodded. 'I know I thanked you before, but it was very good of you to marry us when you have such a busy time of it within your own parish.'

'We wish you could both come and spend Christmas with us,' Mildred said. 'Of course, it's difficult with the limited time you have, Spencer.'

'One year, I don't know when, Mildred, we shall all be together and celebrate Christmas as families do,' Spencer promised, embracing her.

'Write to me.' Mildred gripped Olivia's hand. 'Stay well.'

The short winter's day turned chilly, urging them home. Spencer and Olivia walked arm in arm, letting the neighbours go ahead of them.

'Did you have a nice day?' Spencer asked as they drew close to the square.

'The best day of my life,' she answered truthfully.

'Good. I feel the same as well.' He stopped and kissed her. 'And we have the night to look forward to.'

Her skin tingled at the thought of them sharing a bed. She longed for it. She wanted Spencer with every ounce of her being.

She stared up at him, still not quite believing she had married Spencer Middleton, the Broadbents' grandson, the handsome gentleman whose family she had worked for as a housemaid. She'd always been a blacksmith's daughter, now she was married to Captain Middleton and her life would never be the same again.

'Shall we all get some drinks from the pub?' Gerry called, his arm around his wife's Sadie's shoulders.

Tess stood outside of her front door. 'Are you tired, lass?' she asked Olivia. 'Or want a bit of peace?'

'Yes, that would be nice. Would anyone mind if we didn't join them?' Olivia really wanted to spend all her time with Spencer. So far, they'd not had any time alone.

'Go on inside. I'll tell the others to leave you be. Come around for Christmas dinner tomorrow, but if you can't be bothered, I'll understand.' Tess grinned wickedly. 'Don't wear the poor man out, lass.'

'Tess!' Olivia blushed and then laughed.

Inside the front room, Spencer collapsed onto the sofa and flung his cap off. 'I have no idea why I am so tired. I feel as though I've done a ten-mile march.'

'It's been a big day. Emotional.' She unpinned her veil and walked into the kitchen only to stop on seeing a large wicker hamper on the table. 'Spencer. Come and look at this.'

He stepped into the kitchen and wrapped his arms around her waist from behind. 'A hamper?'

A note was sticking out of the lid. Olivia read it aloud.

. . .

'To the newlyweds.
I assumed you would not want to cook.
I had this hamper prepared for you.
Parky.
P.S. As a thank you for my consideration,
you may name your first son after me.'

SPENCER LAUGHED. 'No chance am I naming my son Orville, after Parky.'

Olivia relaxed back into his arms, loving the feel of him holding her and still not yet used to it. 'I'm very pleased you said that!'

'I'm starving though.' Spencer nibbled her ear.

Desire ran through her, and she swivelled in his arms to face him and kiss him passionately.

He groaned deep in his throat. 'My wife…'

In one swift move he swept her up off her feet and climbed the stairs, carrying her to the bedroom.

Gently he laid her on the bed. 'This is your room I hope?'

'Yes,' She grinned. 'Lachie's is the next one.'

Spencer took off his greatcoat, his tie and sat on the bed to pull off his riding boots. He crawled up beside her, amused that she watched him. 'You have a certain look in your eyes, Mrs Middleton.'

'Do I?' she asked huskily, finding him so attractive she couldn't catch her breath. That he called her Mrs Middleton made her suddenly feel very much a woman, a woman who could freely give in to her desires with this man who made her heart race.

He untied her cape and then ran his hand over her satin and lace dress. 'Have I told you how beautiful you looked today?'

'I'm not sure. Tell me again.' She reached for him and pulled him down for a kiss. There was a fire in her groin, and she knew only he could ease it.

After a few minutes of kissing, Spencer lit the fire in the small grate and fed it sticks and coal to warm the room.

By the bedside, Olivia lit a candle instead of putting on the gas light. A soft golden glow threw shadows across the room and with the fire's flames flickering, the bedroom grew cosy and intimate.

Slowly, they undressed each other, exploring the other's body, kissing and caressing, learning the little pleasures the other enjoyed.

'My body is demanding I go fast but my mind is telling me to take it slowly, to savour every moment, every inch of you,' he murmured, his tongue stroking her naked breasts.

She arched under him, aching for some release she didn't understand. 'Spence…' She opened her legs, lifting her hips for him, a hunger for his body taking over her.

He gathered her close, supporting his body weight on his elbows as he entered her gently, kissing her, swallowing her moans of surprise. 'Are you hurting?'

She shook her head, unable to explain her feelings, or the sensations whipping through her body for the first time. It was strange at first but as he started to move, she felt her body take over, carry her onwards.

Olivia gripped his back, his buttocks, delighting in this moment when they were properly joined. This was what she'd been waiting for. This was all that mattered.

He was hers and she was his.

CHAPTER 6

When Olivia woke the next morning, she had to blink a few times to take in the man sleeping deeply beside her. She stretched slowly, aware of a slight ache in her hips and that brought a smile to her face. Last night had been an adventure, a magical night full of new awakenings, new discoveries of not only her body but Spencer's as well. She familiarised herself with the shape, smell and taste of him. Savouring each tender moment, each little smile, every gaze. They made the most of their first night together, whispering their love, their needs and desires, sharing intimate secrets that only a couple in love can do without fear or embarrassment.

She gazed at his beloved face and for a fleeting moment, an intense fear gripped her. How could he leave her and go back to the war, to the prospect of being killed? How would she bear it? But then she became rational, tossed back that fear and buried it. She could bear it because Spencer had to, and she'd never let him see how frightened she was of the future. He didn't need that from her. He needed her love, her commitment, and her dreams of a happy life together and that's what she'd give him. He deserved no less.

Silently, she climbed from the bed and wrapped her dressing gown over her naked body and went downstairs. The fires in the front room and in the kitchen had long gone out, and the rooms were icy cold.

Late last night between bouts of lovemaking, Spencer had come down and raided the hamper, returning with pâté and wafers, a box of chocolates and a bottle of wine. It had satisfied them enough, but she was hungry now and knew Spencer would be when he woke up.

She placed the kettle on the gas stove to boil, eager for a cup of tea. She took out a loaf of bread and sliced it, then grabbed a tray from the sideboard and loaded it up with items from the hamper. Little jars of jam and marmalade, a wedge of cheese, ham slices wrapped in wax paper, a container of boiled eggs and lastly a small basket of scones with a bottle of thick cream. From the larder she added the butter dish. On another tray she made the tea.

It took two trips to take it all upstairs. Spencer still slept, so she added more coal to the dwindling fire and stoked it up to heat the room. The noise jerked Spencer upright, his hand reaching for something, his face full of puzzlement. 'Stand to!' he shouted.

Olivia jumped at the shout. 'Sorry! I didn't mean to startle you.'

His hands stopped searching and relaxed, focusing on her. 'I didn't know where I was. I thought it was an attack. I couldn't find my pistol.' He rubbed his eyes, blinking. 'I had a dream…'

She felt dreadful. 'I'm so sorry. I didn't realise the noise would shock you like that…' She put the poker on the stand and stood at the end of the bed, not knowing what to do or say.

He let out a breath in a whistling sound. His gaze fell away to the trays on the bed. 'Breakfast.'

It was obvious he was still a little shaken. Olivia waited.

Spencer looked up at her and smiled. He held out his hand. 'Don't be upset. Come here.'

She went to him and held his hand.

He pulled her closer. 'Kiss me.'

Sitting on the edge of the bed, she hated the uncertainty she felt as though last night had never been.

'Darling. Look at me.' He brought her chin up with a finger. 'Everything is fine.' He kissed her tenderly. 'You weren't to know that sleep isn't something I do naturally anymore. It comes in fits and starts and usually ends with a bad dream.'

'I'm so sorry.' It was all she could say.

'There's nothing to be sorry for. It's not your fault. You weren't to know that I am always on edge. We all are. We have to be. Even when we are out of the trenches, at rest well away from the battles, we are still on alert. We cannot let our guards down.'

'That sounds exhausting.'

'It is.' He traced her lips with his thumb. 'Being here with you feels like a dream. One that is too good to be true.' He kissed the base of her neck. 'I still cannot believe you are finally mine, my wife.'

'Nor can I.' She cupped his cheek, feeling the bristles.

He grinned. 'I need a shave.'

She shook her head. 'Later.'

'This looks good.' He indicated the two trays. 'I'm ravenous.'

'Let's eat.' She poured out two cups of tea while Spencer buttered slices of bread.

They ate breakfast each in their own thoughts until Olivia decided that talking would be better than her imagination going mad wondering what Spencer was thinking.

'I've never had a cheese and ham sandwich for breakfast before,' she admitted. 'I really should have cooked you something hot. I've already failed as a wife.'

Spencer chuckled. 'After more than a year soldering, I can tell you this is a banquet.' He munched on a boiled egged. 'I don't need you to cook for me. I just want to spend every moment with you until I have to go.'

Voices rang out from in the square wishing neighbours a merry Christmas.

Olivia stared at Spencer. 'It's Christmas Day! I forgot!'

He laughed. 'So did I!' He leaned over and kissed her. 'Merry Christmas, wife.'

'Merry Christmas, husband.' She smiled and the tense atmosphere was broken and they both relaxed. 'Did you want to go over to Tess and Larry's later for Christmas dinner? We don't have to, of course.'

'I think I'd like that. Normality is important. I want to build memories to take with me to remember when I'm away from you.' He gave her a saucy grin. 'But we won't stay long. We will need an early night, we didn't get much sleep last night and I don't plan on getting much again tonight.'

She tingled all over at his suggestions. 'Suits me just fine.' Then she frowned. 'I've not got you a present. I sent it to you a few days ago hoping it'd reach you before Christmas Day.'

'I haven't received it, but I've been travelling. It'll be waiting for me when I return. Thank you, though.' He climbed carefully from the bed to not topple the trays.

Olivia admired his lean naked form. He was manly and gorgeous, and she wanted him again desperately.

'I bought you something from a shop when we were waiting to board the ship to cross the Channel.' From his greatcoat pocket he took out a small box before climbing back into bed. Side by side they stared at each other as he gave it to her.

She opened it and gasped at the delicate gold necklace. It had a pendant of sapphires and diamonds. 'It's so beautiful, Spencer.'

'I saw it and thought it looked similar to your engagement ring. I had the jeweller add a little gold plate to the back of the pendant.' He turned it around for her to see.

It was inscribed, *My love 1915*

Tears came to her eyes. It was overwhelming that he loved her so much. What had she done to deserve such a man? 'Thank you. It is wonderful. I'll treasure it always. Can you put it on for me, please?' She turned and held her long hair out of the way so he could clasp it around her neck. He followed the movement with a kiss, then another kiss along her shoulder, his hands coming around to cup her breasts and she moaned with longing and leaned back into him.

Breakfast was forgotten, and they gave into the rising passion that consumed them, and nothing existed beyond their embrace, their desires.

Much later, they finally dressed and laughing like naughty children with too many secrets, they knocked on the Hobsons' front door. Olivia carried items from the hamper to share, a jar of chutney, a jar of pickles, a box of candied fruits and a tin of shortbread.

'Well, this is a surprise. I thought we wouldn't see you.' Tess winked.

'We took bets you wouldn't make it here today,' Colin told them as they walked in.

Olivia raised an eyebrow at the three Hobson brothers, Colin, Jonnie and Jules. 'Really?'

'I won,' Jules said smugly. 'I said you would, that you'd have worked up an appetite! And that—'

'Jules!' Larry cut him off with a warning look and the boys fell about laughing.

'You lot are too cheeky.' Olivia took the food through to the kitchen where the smell of roast beef wafted.

'That smells good, Tess.' Spencer gave her a kiss on the cheek and handed a bottle of champagne from the hamper. 'Merry Christmas.'

Tess blushed. 'Merry Christmas, Captain.'

'You can call me Spencer, you know?' he joked.

'I certainly will not.' Tess looked offended. 'You're a captain in our great army and earned the title.'

'Want a beer, Captain?' Larry asked from the front room. 'Leave the champers for the ladies.'

'What ladies?' Jonnie quipped and earned a cuff around the ear from his father.

'A beer would be great, thank you.' Spencer joined the men in the front room.

'You needn't have brought this lot, lass.' Tess admired the gifts.

'As if I'd come empty-handed. Mr Parkinson gave us an enormous hamper to save us cooking. It's only right that we share.' Olivia donned Tess's spare apron. 'What needs doing?'

'I'm about to put the veggies in the oven to roast. Mix that Yorkshire pudding batter.' Tess paused. 'I hope the captain will not think badly of me for serving plain fare?'

'Don't be silly, Tess. He's happy to be accepted. He might be an officer, but he mixes with all ranks.'

'Aye, I remember you reading to me some of a letter once where he said he'd been playing football with the lads, normal privates and the like, when they were out of the lines.'

Olivia nodded as she mixed the batter with a wooden spoon. 'Yes, and one of his lieutenants, Dawes, didn't approve of Spencer mixing with the lower ranks. Not that Spencer cares much for Dawes's opinion.'

'How was last night, lass?' Tess asked seriously, lowering her voice. 'Any concerns?'

'No, none. Your wise talks over the past months have helped me. I wasn't scared of my first time at all. Spencer was loving and tender and everything I imagined it to be and better.'

Tess sighed in relief. 'That's brilliant. I was worried it might not be as... *comfortable* as it could be. For some women it's painful.'

Olivia couldn't stop smiling. 'It was very... *comfortable,* Tess.'

They both burst into laughter.

* * *

THAT NIGHT, Spencer undressed Olivia, taking his time, his movements light, deft and sensual. When he'd finished, she undressed him. Disregarding his uniform, piece by piece, removing the soldier and revealing the man.

They made love leisurely, enjoying the exploration, the whispers of pleasure, the sighs and moans of yearning.

Afterwards, sated and their lust satisfied for now, they lay in each other's arms, the bedsheet tangled about their waists. They chatted about the day, the good food Tess cooked with Olivia's help, the light-hearted talk around the table as though all had instinctively agreed that nothing serious was to be mentioned. They had raised a toast to the two Hobson boys, Lance and Simon, serving overseas, and to Lachie, and all the other men working towards ending the war. Some of the neighbours called in to wish them a merry Christmas, Sadie stayed for a glass of champagne. The Hobson's little house was heaving, yet it was the best Christmas Day Olivia had experienced in many a year.

Snuggling into Spencer's shoulder, she sighed contentedly.

'Are they all my letters?' Spencer pointed to the ribbon-tied bundle of letters on top of the set of drawers.

'Some. The others are downstairs. I re-read them constantly. I feel close to you when I read them. I hear your voice.'

'I feel the same when I read yours.' He kissed the top of her head. 'My letters don't alarm you, do they?'

'Sometimes, but you mustn't ever stop telling me the truth of what you're going through. I need to know, to understand.'

'It's impossible to tell you everything, you realise that?'

She turned to look at him. 'You keep things from me?'

He ran a finger across her shoulder. 'I possibly keep them from myself. To put some of the true horror into words would finish me. I must use distance when I can, mentally. Does that make sense?'

Rising up onto her elbow, she gazed at him. 'It makes sense, though it saddens me that you are put through such torment.'

'Words cannot describe it at times. I do not want to describe it sometimes.' He shrugged. 'Then there are other times, when we are marching in the sun and one of the men starts singing and the others join in, or when we play a game of football or cricket, and we're actually enjoying ourselves... then the fear fades somewhat. It's those times that keep us sane, together, fighting... believing.'

'When it gets too bad, I want you to think of me, of us, of this room and how close we are right at this moment.'

He nodded and pulled her close. 'I will.'

'I can't accept all that will face Lachie when he gets there.'

'He told me at the wedding what regiment he's been assigned to.' Spencer played with a long tendril of pale blonde hair.

'He did? He didn't tell me. What regiment is it?'

'The King's Own Yorkshire Light Infantry. I will write letters to the commanders of the regiment he's assigned to, informing them of his real age, but also his pledge to re-enlist under a false name were they to send him home. I will ask them to engage him in occupations that may keep him from the front lines. They may not listen, but it is worth a try.'

'Thank you! I'm so grateful.'

'It might not work, darling. Be prepared for him to be in the trenches the same as any other man.'

She rested her cheek against his chest, hearing his heartbeat under her ear. 'I understand, but I can hope they will take heed of your letter.'

'I see you still have the little bird from Grandmama's house?' He grinned, eyeing the bird on the bedside table.

'I say goodnight to it every night,' she confessed.

'I don't do that with the tiger. The men would think me mad.'

'You have it with you?'

Spencer shook his head. 'No, not now. It was in immediate danger of being broken. I sent it home to Father not long after retreating from Belgium. It's safer there at Father's house than in my luggage that is carted all around northern France. I should have sent it here... I don't know why I didn't. If I remember rightly, I was writing to Father, and the tiger fell out of my kit. I decided to wrap it up and put it with the letter. Father must have been surprised to see it arrive.' He chuckled.

'We'll reunite them both one day. The bird and the tiger together again.'

He kissed her. 'Absolutely we will...'

* * *

TWO DAYS LATER, Olivia kept busy in the kitchen, washing up the things they'd used for breakfast. Upstairs, Spencer was shaving and packing his belongings. The time had gone by too fast. She dreaded the moment they'd have to say goodbye, but it had to be done. It'd been four fantastic days. A whirlwind of activity with the wedding, Christmas and then yesterday they had their photograph taken in a studio in town. Spencer had obviously worn his uniform, they were his only clothes, but she had worn her wedding dress to mark the occasion of their marriage.

She heard his footsteps on the stairs and her heart grew heavy. Drying her hands on a towel, she pasted a smile to her face. 'All set?'

'As I will ever be.' He didn't summon a smile.

'I'll get my hat.' She walked past him into the front room, but he pulled her into his arms.

They held each other tightly, no words needed.

Eventually, they pulled away, each with their own sad thoughts. They knew they had to go and reluctantly Olivia donned her coat and put on her hat. She couldn't look at him as she pulled on her gloves and picked up her bag.

Outside it was grey and miserable. She was pleased when the Hobsons came out to say goodbye to Spencer. He shook their hands warmly and kissed Tess, who held onto him for a split second before letting him go.

'You come back to that girl, do you hear me?' Tess said in a stern whisper, but Olivia heard her.

'I will do my very best to, Tess,' Spencer promised. 'Take care of her for me, won't you?'

'Aye, lad, of course I will.' She sniffed and took two steps back.

Some of the other neighbours came out and wished him well. Giving him a cheer and a wave as they walked out of the square and into Norton Street.

Spencer cleared his throat. 'That was kind of them,' he said with slight emotion.

'Yes.' She swallowed back the tears burning hot in her eyes. They held hands walking along towards the train station with Spencer carrying his leather portmanteau.

'Now I can picture you in my mind of where you live and your friends.'

She nodded, knowing he was trying to lighten the situation. Only, it was too difficult to converse about anything normal when her chest was constricted with such despondency.

'I will make certain my details are updated at HQ. I will inform them I have married you and you will receive a percentage of my wage. Also, in the case of my death, a pension.'

'Don't. Don't say that.'

'We have to talk about it, my love.'

'I refuse to,' she said stubbornly.

He let out a breath. 'Well, I will have it sorted. You are my next of kin now.'

She glanced at the passing shop windows, anything to distract her from his words. Just days. That's all she'd had with him. Just days. It wasn't enough, and she wanted to rage against the world for taking him from her again. They should be planning their future, not discussing details in the event of his death!

The train station was crowded with people leaving after

visiting family and friends for Christmas. Soldiers finishing leave also added to the throng of people squashed onto the platform.

Spencer showed his ticket and was directed to the first-class carriage of the waiting train. He turned his back on the open door and hugged her to him so tightly the air was trapped in her lungs. 'Do not cry, my love. I could not bear it.'

'I won't...' She bit her lip to stop the tears.

'Liv? *Liv!*' They both turned as her name was shouted along the platform. A soldier came running over to them.

'Lachie!' She hugged him like someone drowning.

'I'm home early for a few days.' He grinned like a monkey, full of youthful excitement. He saluted Spencer.

Spencer answered the salute.

Olivia looked on in awe. Her brother was a fine-looking solider, completely kitted out in khaki and carrying a kit bag.

Lachie shook Spencer's hand. 'Good to see you again, Captain.'

'And you, lad.' Spencer managed to say before the train's whistle blew shrilly. He stepped closer to Lachie. 'Don't be a hero over there. You need to come home. Olivia doesn't want a letter from the king and a medal in your place, understand?'

'Yes, sir,' Lachie said, all trace of humour gone.

The train started to move forward, and Spencer quickly embraced Olivia to him in a desperate final moment. 'I love you more than anything on this earth.'

'I love you!' She kissed him hard on the mouth and in the next instant she was without him as he had hopped aboard the train that gathered pace down the platform.

He was gone.

Lachie put his arm around her shoulders. 'It's perfect timing that I've come home today. You won't be alone tonight.'

She nodded, however, words were hard to come by.

'Come on, let's go home. Shall we go to the cinema tonight?'

CHAPTER 7

Late December 1915

Olivia returned to work the same morning Lachie left for the train station. They said their goodbyes at the house even though Olivia said she could walk with him to the train station, but Lachie refused. He wanted to say farewell in their front room as though it was an ordinary day.

Only three days after saying goodbye to Spencer, it proved tough to wave another loved one on their way to war. Now, she truly was alone. She thanked the fates that had sent her to the square though for her neighbours rallied around her and Tess was her main support.

Entering the Rochdales' kitchen after taking off her outdoor clothes in the scullery, Olivia lifted her apron from the peg. 'Good morning, Mrs Wilmott. Did you have a nice Christmas?'

'You're late this morning,' was the sharp reply. Mrs Wilmott darted from range to larder and back again. Breakfast preparations adorned the kitchen table. 'You know the first morning of them being back from Manchester is the busiest.'

'I'm on time instead of being early as I usually am. I'm not late.' Olivia wasn't in the mood for the cook's cutting manner this morning. She grabbed her cleaning box from the scullery, some old newspapers and a bundle of kindling.

'What's that?' Mrs Wilmott pointed at Olivia's hand with a scowl.

'My wedding ring? I got married on Christmas Eve.' Without further explanation, she left the kitchen to begin her duties.

In winter her first duties were clearing out the fire grates and relighting new fires. She did that in all the downstairs' rooms. Each room was as cold as the previous one. No fires had been lit with the Rochdales being away over Christmas and the chill made Olivia shiver.

While the fires burned, slowly warming the rooms, she collected the newspaper from the front doorstep and set the dining table for breakfast and reluctantly went back to the kitchen.

'Got married then?' Mrs Wilmott stated, setting the butter dish on the tray.

'Yes.' Olivia gave her no encouragement. The woman's unfriendliness wasn't tolerated today. She concentrated on filling one tray with the tea service.

Mrs Wilmott placed bacon in the frying pan. 'Your captain had leave then?'

'He did.' She took the first tray into the dining room. Taking her time to set the tea service on the table. The old couple weren't due downstairs for another five minutes.

'Good morning, Olivia.' Mr Rochdale came in unexpectedly, dressed in one of his best suits that he wore when going into town.

'Good morning, Mr Rochdale.' Olivia's eye widened as his wife followed him in because normally Mrs Rochdale gave her husband a good twenty minutes alone to read his newspaper before she joined him for breakfast. 'Good morning, Mrs Rochdale.'

'Oh, Olivia, good morning.' Also dressed for town, Mrs Rochdale's gaze barely met Olivia's. The old woman seemed unhappy as she took her place beside her husband.

Hurrying into the kitchen, Olivia filled the next tray. 'They are both down early,' she told the cook.

'You're jesting!' Mrs Wilmott fumed. 'I'm not ready. I've the eggs to cook yet.'

'I'll take the toast out.' Olivia cut the toast into triangles and placed it in the little silver rack on the tray along with jars of jam and marmalade.

'This is a great start to the first morning back.' Mrs Wilmott tutted.

'They're dressed for going out as well,' she threw over her shoulder as she went into the hallway.

In the dining room, the Rochdales stopped talking as Olivia entered.

The mistress folded her hands in her lap. 'Ah, Olivia. Could you put the tray down and go and fetch Mrs Wilmott, please? Mr Rochdale and I need to speak to you both.'

'Yes, Mrs Rochdale.' Intrigued, Olivia fetched the cook, who looked discomforted to be out of her domain of the kitchen and in the dining room.

'Good... Good.' Mrs Rochdale glanced at her husband and then back to them. 'As you are aware my sister, Mrs Dewhurst, Alma, is ill, has been for some years, which is why we go and stay with her and her husband every week...' Mrs Rochdale's voice faltered.

Mr Rochdale cleared his throat. 'While we were there over Christmas, Alma took a turn for the worst. The doctor has declared that she may only have three to six months left to live.'

Mrs Rochdale made a little noise and stared down at the table.

'I'm very sorry to hear of such sad news, sir, madam,' Olivia said.

'Thank you, Olivia.' Mr Rochdale waited for Mrs Wilmott to speak but when she didn't, he continued. 'Therefore, due to this terrible news, my wife and I have decided to go and stay with Alma, and her husband, permanently, until the awful day comes when Alma is no longer with us. Consequently, this means we'll be closing down the house for the next few months.' Mr Rochdale swept a hand over his balding head.

'If this house is closed up for months, what about us?' Mrs Wilmott demanded to know.

'Well, we will have to let you both go,' Mr Rochdale said. 'You will be paid for next month in compensation, and we will be in touch with you both when we come home so you can return to your positions once more.'

'One month's pay!' Mrs Wilmott gasped. 'What am I to do if you're gone for more than one month as you expect to be?' Her face had lost all colour.

'We are utterly sorry to have to give this news to you both,' the old man said.

'So, we are out on our ear then?' Mrs Wilmott barked.

'We are preparing to leave by tomorrow night. We'd like you to stay until then.'

'No bloody chance!' Mrs Wilmott snapped. 'I've got to find another job.' She marched out.

Mrs Rochdale looked crestfallen, Mr Rochdale resigned.

Olivia glanced at Mr Rochdale. 'I'll talk to her, sir.'

'Thank you, Olivia.'

In the kitchen she found the cook untying her apron and yanking it off, loudly cursing.

'Mrs Wilmott, calm down.' Olivia took a step towards her. 'If you leave now with bad feeling, you won't get a month's pay or be invited back on their return.'

The older woman turned on Olivia her face twisted in anger.

'Do you reckon one month's pay is enough for me? I have an ill sister, too. One I've been caring for and providing for since I was fifteen, for over forty years it's been! My sister is a cripple and without me she'd have been in the workhouse or dead long ago. My wage keeps us both alive, *just!* Where am I going to get another job at my age, hey?'

'You're bound to find something.'

'Really?' Mrs Wilmott scorned. 'You're married now, you've a husband to care for you. I don't have that luxury.'

'I have a husband who is in France fighting. I wouldn't call that a *luxury*,' she tossed back, annoyed.

Suddenly, Mrs Wilmott grabbed her big black bag that she kept in a cupboard under the sideboard and began stuffing it with the silverware on the Welsh dresser.

'What are you doing?' Olivia gasped, alarmed at what she was seeing.

'They owe me. Years I've worked for them!' The cook rammed a silver platter into the bag, as well as silver candlesticks and a silver coffee pot.

'Stop! Stop!' She ran to grab the bag from the cook. 'You're stealing.'

Mrs Wilmott pushed her hard, and she fell against the table. 'I'm taking what I'm owed. I can pawn this lot and pay my rent until I find another job.'

'You don't need to stoop this low, honestly. The munitions factories are always taking on women.'

'And turn yellow from the chemicals?' The cook snorted in contempt. 'No thanks.'

'And going to prison is a better option?'

Mrs Wilmott opened a drawer and took out the housekeeping money and put that in her bag. 'Are you going to turn me in?'

'The Rochdales will.'

'I'll have this lot pawned within the hour. It takes that long for the old bats to get ready to leave the house. I'll take my chances.'

She headed for the scullery door but turned swiftly to sneer at Olivia. 'If you go to the police, I'll make sure you pay. I know where you live. People who've crossed me in the past have lived to regret it.' With that parting comment, Mrs Wilmott flung open the door and dashed out.

Slightly shaken by the confrontation, Olivia walked into the dining room. Mr Rochdale chewed on a piece of toast while Mrs Rochdale sipped her tea.

'We heard raised voices, Olivia,' Mr Rochdale said. 'Do I need to speak with Mrs Wilmott? Is there something I can do to calm her down?'

'She's gone.'

'Gone?' Mrs Rochdale repeated. 'Where?'

'To pawn the items she's stolen from you.'

'Stolen?' Mr Rochdale jerked up from his chair. 'What did she take?'

Olivia told them everything that had happened.

'Good gracious!' Mr Rochdale sat back down. 'There's no point going to the police. A few silver pieces will easily be sold on, and if they are known to be stolen, they'll be moved on the black market quicker than it takes for me to file a report.'

'George, that's our silver she's taken. It belonged to my mother.' Mrs Rochdale had tears in her eyes.

'Yes, I understand, my dear, however, we don't have the time to deal with a police investigation if you want to be in Manchester by tomorrow night.'

'I cannot take much more, George. To close up the house and go live in Manchester to care for Ada until…'

'I know, my dear.' He rose again and went to comfort his wife.

'What can I do for you both?' Olivia asked, feeling terrible for the whole situation.

'Will you stay on until we go tomorrow?' Mrs Rochdale asked her. 'I need help to get the house closed up.'

'Of course.' Olivia gave her a small smile. 'I won't leave until you do.'

'I appreciate that.' Mrs Rochdale took a deep breath. 'We might as well get started.'

'My dear, maybe you should rest a little longer?' her husband prompted.

'No, George. Olivia and I have much to do.'

'Shall I get you some breakfast first?' Olivia asked.

'I would like some, yes.' Mr Rochdale sat at the head of the table once more. 'Ida, you should eat.'

'I will later.' Mrs Rochdale stood and walked to the door. 'I want to check how many dust sheets we have for the furniture. If we're short, I will get some in town when we go out shortly. I must make a list of all the businesses to contact to cancel our orders, your newspaper, the baker, the butcher, the laundress, the window cleaner, the gardener, we must visit the post office and have them redirect our mail. Goodness, there is so much to do in two days.'

'And we will accomplish it all, my dear,' her husband soothed.

Olivia cooked breakfast for Mr Rochdale, still surprised at Mrs Wilmott's actions. It was strange to find herself working in the kitchen without the other woman's domineering presence.

Once the Rochdales had gone out to conduct business in town, Olivia had instructions to strip the spare beds in the two other bedrooms that were never used. Once the beds were stripped, she closed the curtains in each of the rooms.

Downstairs, she began packing away ornaments from the cabinets. Mrs Rochdale didn't want anything on display in case the house was broken into while they were away.

Wrapping figurines in newspaper reminded her of counting the ornaments at Hawthorn Manor with Spencer in the innocent summer of nineteen fourteen. They'd laughed and joked and started to feel the ties that began to bind them as they took stock of his grandmother's collection in readiness for auction. Spencer had given Olivia the porcelain bird, which sat on her bedside, and he kept a tiger as a keepsake of that day.

It saddened her that she would no longer work for the Rochdales, but it wasn't the wrench she suffered losing her position at Hawthorn Manor when it sold.

Leaving the manor had coincided with her brother Stu's leaving, her father's death and losing their cottage. If she could survive all that upheaval and loss, she could survive being out of work again. Besides, she was a married woman now and a portion of Spencer's army pay would come to her, and Stanford gave her a generous allowance as well.

In fact, she didn't need to work at all, but sitting idle in the house all day didn't appeal either. It would give her too much time to dwell on Spencer and Lachie.

The Rochdales returned home mid-afternoon. Olivia helped them off with their large coats.

'It's beginning to snow, Olivia,' Mrs Rochdale informed her. 'We don't want you walking home in that in the dark. You set off now.'

'What about your evening meal?' She hung up the two coats in the tall cupboard by the door.

'Is there something cold we can have that I can quickly put together?' Mrs Rochdale shrugged. 'I'm not terribly hungry, anyway.'

'No, but I am,' her husband replied going into the sitting room.

Mrs Rochdale shook her head at him as she followed him.

Olivia stood in the doorway while the older couple warmed themselves in front of the fire. 'Why don't I stay and make you both a stew? It can simmer for a few hours and will be ready by this evening. All you'll have to do is ladle it into bowls. There's fresh bread to go with it that was delivered an hour ago.'

'Excellent. But don't take too long making it. The snow is

staying on the ground.' Mrs Rochdale tilted her head and stared at Olivia's hand. 'Are you wearing a wedding ring?'

'Yes, madam. Spencer came home unexpectantly, and we were married on Christmas Eve.'

'Oh, my dear girl. What happy news!' Mrs Rochdale came to her and grasped her hands. 'How fortunate you were to spend Christmas together and to get married at the same time. What a true blessing.'

'It was.' Her heart soared remembering her special day again.

'To hear some good news is a welcome distraction, isn't it, George?'

'It is, dear. Congratulations, Olivia.'

'Thank you, sir.' Olivia left them to make the stew. She found vegetables and meat wrapped in paper that Mrs Wilmott had bought on her way to work that morning. It seemed mad to think it was only this morning when Lachie had left and Olivia had arrived here to Mrs Wilmott's sharp tongue. What a day it had been.

An hour later, the meat and vegetable stew simmering on the stove, Olivia went through to the front room to tell the couple she was going home.

Mr Rochdale was at his desk, writing, while Mrs Rochdale was at her desk on the opposite side of the room packing away her stationery into a leather satchel.

'I'm going now, Mrs Rochdale.'

'Oh, very good, Olivia. Thank you for staying. You've been a tremendous help.'

'The stew is simmering. It only needs to be transferred into a tureen and brought into the dining room. All you need to do is ladle it into bowls, which I've set out on the table in the dining room, along with bread and butter.'

'Wonderful, thank you.' Mrs Rochdale stood and took a parcel from a small table by the sofa. 'Mr Rochdale and I want to give you a wedding gift.'

'A gift?'

Mrs Rochdale gave the parcel to Olivia. 'Don't open it now. We wanted you and Captain Middleton to have our silver cutlery set. It was bought for us on our wedding day. We don't use it much, as we have the other set that belonged to my husband's grandmother. We thought you might get some use out of it. It's still in its box.'

'My dear, wouldn't it have been nice for Olivia to see the gift before you told her what it was?' her husband lightly admonished.

'Nonsense.' His wife waved away his concerns. 'Olivia is a practical girl.'

Olivia didn't know if that was a good or bad thing. 'Thank you very much.'

'I thought that since you have risen in your circumstances, by marrying into a notable family such as the Middletons, that a good cutlery service would be ideal for when you entertain.'

'You're very kind, Mrs Rochdale.' Olivia hadn't spoken much about Spencer's family, but when she had first been interviewed by Mrs Rochdale, she'd shown her the references she'd received from Mrs Broadbent, mistress of Hawthorn Manor and Mrs Hewlett, the housekeeper. Olivia was inclined to think that Mrs Rochdale had done some investigating of the family, especially when Olivia became engaged to Spencer, not only a Middleton heir but the Broadbents' heir as well.

'Every decent household needs a silver cutlery service.'

Olivia thought of the plain bone-handled knives, forks, and spoons she used at home that had belonged to her mother and which she'd brought with her from their old cottage.

'I expect you will not be returning to us when we come back to Wakefield?' Mrs Rochdale returned to her desk. 'It is only natural that Captain Middleton will want you, as his wife, to stay at home. I'm surprised you have returned here at all.'

'He's at war, as is Lachie. I don't really have a home to keep, and I wouldn't have let you down by not coming to work.'

'But you are not in need financially?'

'No…' What was with all the questions? She'd never known Mrs Rochdale to be so inquisitive.

'Then you must step aside and allow others to fill the position you would take. You are a married woman now.' Mrs Rochdale looked out of the window where a grey dusk shadowed the freshly fallen snow. 'It seems the snow is a few inches deep. Be careful how you go.'

'I'll manage. I'll be back in the morning to cook your breakfast.'

'Don't stop to buy any food. We'll be gone by tomorrow night. Just use up what we have, and we can donate the rest of the food to a charity,' Mrs Rochdale said.

'Yes, madam. Good night.' She left them and pulled on her coat hat and gloves in the scullery.

Tucking the gift under her arm, she let herself out of the back of the house and in the darkness and falling snow walked around to the front. Waiting for her by the gate stood Colin.

'Colin? Is everything all right?'

'Oh, aye. Mam told me to come and walk you home as it's snowing and dark.'

'That's kind of you to think of me and to be out in this weather. I would have been fine to walk home alone. I've done it many times before.'

'Aye, but you know what me mam is like. She thought you'd be missing Lachie today. Let me hold that for you and we can link arms.' He took the gift from her. 'That way if one of us slip, the other can stop them falling.'

'Or we both land on our backsides together.' She grinned.

He gave her a cheeky smile.

They walked along quietly for a while, concentrating on their foot placings. It'd gone five o'clock, and the streets were quiet, the snow and cold winter night sending people indoors.

'You were on day shift today?' Olivia asked him.

'Aye.' His gaze dropped. 'I don't know for how much longer though.'

'What do you mean?'

'I've joined up.'

Olivia jerked to a halt. 'Oh, Colin! You're not eighteen yet.'

'I lied, like Lachie did. You can't mention it to me mam, I'll tell her once I've received my papers for the training camp.'

'Tess is going to be furious. She'll not let you go. She was counting on it that you and your brothers were in a reserved occupation. You're needed at home.'

'While other men fight? I'm no coward.'

'It's not cowardice! You're doing work that keeps the country going. Coal is so important, the country wouldn't run without it.'

'I don't want to miss out on it, Liv. Imagine once it's all over and the other fellas come back full of stories of adventure and I've got to spend the rest of my life listening to it, knowing I could have been involved but I stayed home, never left Wakefield. Imagine the experiences Lachie is having. He's in France, a different country, the same as Lance and your captain. Simon is on the open sea somewhere as well.'

'This isn't a holiday, Colin. Our lads in France face a powerful enemy, are shot at, bombed. Simon's ship could be sunk at any moment. Tess won't allow you to go. You're only seventeen.'

'Mam can't stop me.'

'Listen to me, after the war is over, then go gallivanting about and see other places. Don't consider that this war is anything other than a living hell.'

'It's done now.' He shrugged as they turned into the square. 'Promise you won't tell me mam?'

'I promise because it's not my place to tell her, but yours.' She felt sick at heart thinking of another young man facing the enemy.

Once inside her front room, she found mail on the mat by the door. Downhearted at Colin's news and entering a chilly, silent empty house, she couldn't be bothered to do anything but make a cup of tea and a sandwich. The hamper had been depleted, but she had some cold bacon left over from Lachie's breakfast and made a sandwich. She kept her coat on, not bothering to light any fires downstairs.

She spent a moment admiring the silver cutlery set in its red velvet case, however, the icy house made her shiver, and she took her tea and sandwich and the small bundle of letters upstairs.

After lighting her bedroom fire, then having a wash, she changed into her nightgown and climbed into bed with her pile of mail.

A longing for Spencer filled her as she recognised his handwriting on one envelope and opened it to read first.

My dearest darling,

Happy New Year!

We have landed in France, and I am attending lectures at HQ before being sent to rejoin my regiment.

I miss you.

All I think about is those magical days we spent together. They seem a beautiful dream, really. Especially now that I am surrounded by everything military once more.

All my adult life I have been a soldier, in places far from home, and although I have missed England and my family at times, it is nothing compared to the ache of missing you.

In those five days with you I experienced a short time of complete love, the type of which I have never known. Thanks to you.

Our days together gave me a sweet taste of what life would be like when all this madness is over and I am enthusiastic for the future, for a time when we are together.

This leave has given me much to think about and has reinforced my decision to resign my commission once the war is over. The soldiering life is no longer what I wish for now you are in my life.

Father, as you know, wants me to join his businesses, which would perhaps mean living in London. He has expanded greatly recently and has offices in New York and Paris and wants to open one in Sydney, Australia. Places we could move to if we chose. I also thought it would be a good opportunity for Lachie to join us as well and become involved in the businesses?

Obviously, this is a discussion for us to have another time. Only, I wanted to mention it to you so you could think about it. Whatever is decided it must be a joint decision between us.

I must sign off now, my love, as I am being summoned to another training session on the updated new model gas masks being issued.

Oh, and before I forget, you are now my legal next of kin. You will be contacted by the War Office with the details of my army pay, etc. I have also rewritten my will and sent it to my father's solicitor in London.

One last thing. I have been promoted to major. It was offered before, but I refused as I wanted to stay with my men. This time I was not allowed to refuse it. However, I only accepted it on the proviso that I could stay with my men and not be sent way behind the lines to sit at a desk for the rest of the war. Thankfully, my commander values me more at the front line than signing paperwork, so it was agreed.

Give my good wishes to Tess, Larry and all the neighbours.

To you my heart, I send you all my love.

Spencer. XX

Olivia read the letter twice more, as she was wont to do with Spencer's letters on first receiving them. She was married to an army major now. A small part of her wished he was sent far beyond the enemy fire, but she understood that would never suit Spencer's nature.

She touched the letter reverently. He was talking of their future, beginning to plan for it. It worried her to think of a time after the war. First, they had to live through it and Spencer and Lachie had to survive it.

Next, she read the letter from Stanford, telling her he was staying in London for the next few months, and should she need him for anything, she must not hesitate to contact him at his Mayfair address, which he listed. Once more he told how happy he was to have her as a daughter.

Smiling at his loveliness, she opened the next letter to find it was from Spencer's sister Anthea in Paris.

Dear Olivia, or I should write, dear sister-in-law?

My brother has written to us to tell us the delightful news of his marriage to you on Christmas Eve.

Olivia paused, remembering how on Boxing Day Spencer had written to his sister and grandparents about their wedding day. They had posted his letters on the way to the photography studio the following day.

She wondered how Anthea and his grandparents took the news. They knew of Spencer's attachment to her, their engagement, but they were now linked by marriage to their former housemaid. Olivia imagined that many a discussion would have taken place about that news.

Continuing the letter, she sipped her tea.

I must say on behalf of my husband, my two children and my grandparents that we are all so very pleased that Spencer has found someone who makes him utterly happy.

My father, Stanford, has also written to me that he is completely enamoured by you and the happiness you bring to our beloved Spencer. Added to that was a letter from my brother, Ralph, and his wife, Mildred, both who sang your praises.

We are sorry we could not make the wedding. The short notice made it impossible. As much as I would have truly enjoyed witnessing your special day, I could not leave my children and husband at Christmas.

Also, my grandpapa, with whom you are acquainted, is in poor health. My grandmama needs me at this time. Therefore, I cannot make plans to visit you in England any time soon.

However, you are most welcome to visit us in Paris at any time you wish. My address is at the top of this letter.

I wish you and Spencer every joy and happiness in your married life.

With fond regards,

Anthea.

OLIVIA WAS both delighted that Anthea had written and surprised at the kindness of the letter. She hoped the sentiments written were heartfelt. Truth be known she was a little intimidated by Anthea. When Olivia worked as a housemaid at Hawthorn Manor, Anthea visited her grandparents often as a girl. She was only a little older than Olivia, but obviously their worlds were wildly different. Anthea wore the finest of dresses, her every movement watched over by her governess. But Olivia remembered her tinkling giggle, and that she was everyone's favourite. Anthea had married young. By the age of eighteen, she'd wed a rich French gentleman and gone to live in a glamorous apartment in Paris.

Olivia would reply to the letter in a few days, she'd have to carefully construct her wording. She wanted to be accepted into Spencer's family but that wouldn't be an immediate transition. They wouldn't meet until after the war and Olivia wasn't born a lady. Meeting Spencer's family would never be on an equal footing. She'd always feel like the housemaid in their presence. She'd felt that way when meeting Ralph and Mildred on her wedding day, as nice as they were.

She'd been a servant all her life. How was she to conduct herself within that family without embarrassing everyone? They knew her past just as she knew most of their secrets. Servants heard and saw things that was never spoken about outside of the house.

She sighed and put the letter aside. She'd married Spencer because she loved him, he meant the world to her. Only, she'd never really stopped to think of how their future would look. Spencer being a career soldier meant they had been apart more than they'd been together. His idea of leaving the army would throw her into a world where she was no longer a servant, but in a position to employ servants. It was amazing to think of it. She only hoped she could handle the transition.

CHAPTER 8

January 1916

'So, lass, yesterday was your last day as a servant then.' Tess rolled pastry out on her kitchen table.

Sipping tea, Olivia nodded. 'My last day working for the Rochdales, yes. The house is all closed up, and they have gone to Manchester for several months. I felt so sorry for them. Mrs Rochdale is going to nurse her dying sister. What a task. They were a lovely couple to work for. I'm sad to leave them.'

'You did strike it lucky with that old couple.'

'It's interesting, really. Most housemaids stay with one family all their lives, or at least until they marry. I've now worked for three separate houses and I'm not yet twenty-four. Mrs Rochdale has written a reference for me, though she again spoke of me having no need of it because I'm married. I don't think Mrs Rochdale will write to me when they return to Wakefield and open the house up again. She will choose an unmarried housemaid.'

'Don't worry about it. Finding another housemaid position is no longer your problem. You're a lady of leisure for the first time in your life. Fancy that,' Tess joked.

'Hardly. I'll find something else.'

Tess stopped rolling. 'Nay, lass, that's your working life over with now. You're a married woman, and not just any married woman, but you're a Middleton. Your father-in-law is a very wealthy man. Hell, the whole family is upper middle class.' Tess gazed around her tiny, cramped kitchen. 'Very different from what we have.'

Olivia played with her teaspoon. 'Spencer mentioned in his last letter that after the war he is definitely leaving the army.'

'Who can blame him? He's done his bit. Been fighting for and protecting this country for years.'

'He says he'll go into business with his father.'

Tess put down her rolling pin and wiped the flour off her hands on a towel. 'You do realise, lass, that once this wretched war is over, you'll be gone from here, don't you? This square will no longer be your home. Spencer will want you living somewhere grander than theses old, terraced houses in Wakefield.'

Olivia nodded. 'I know. Spencer mentioned the idea of us not even living in England, but to run one of the business offices in another country.'

'You must be excited?' Tess asked with false brightness.

'I am.'

'You'll be with your lovely husband and going on a new journey. You've often said you'd like to see other places.'

'True, but I'll miss you terribly.' She dreaded the day she'd have to say goodbye to Tess.

'It'll be such an adventure. You'll enjoy every moment of it. This life you have now will soon be forgotten. You're destined for grander things, lass.' Tess winked. 'I've always said it. With your beauty and cleverness, you'll do well wherever you go.'

She made a wry expression. 'I'll try and remember those

words when I'm sitting face to face and drinking tea with Spencer's grandparents, my former master and mistress.'

'Are you ready for that?'

'No. Not at all. The minute the tea is brought in I'll want to get up and pour for them.' She made a joke of it, but it wasn't far from the truth.

Tess chuckled as she sprinkled more flour onto the table and began rolling the pastry again. 'Aye, well, let them serve you for a change. From what you've said, they've fallen in position within their society. Went bankrupt and fled to Paris. They aren't so high and mighty now, lass. You'll have the money to wear fine clothes, to travel around in a motor car, own a wonderful house and fill it with grand furniture.'

'They'll never forget I'm from the working class, that I once was their servant. I'll still be below them in their minds. I'm not from a noble family. Spencer has married beneath him.'

'Those old landed-gentry families need new blood bred into them. You'll be a breath of fresh air blown into that family, clear out some cobwebs. God knows most of them need a good dose of muck in their gardens!'

Olivia laughed. 'You are a tonic, Tess.'

'I aim to please. Now, pass me that baking dish.'

Olivia passed her the shallow dish and saw the pan of water boiling on the stove and got up to take it off the heat. A job she'd been doing for the last twenty minutes, Olivia took the pan of hot water outside and tipped it into the tin bath in the yard which the Hobson men would use to wash off the coal dust.

Inside she refilled the pan with water and set it on the gas ring to heat. Steam rising from the copper boiler in the corner of the kitchen caused condensation to run down the kitchen window. 'It looks like more snow might fall later.'

'Hopefully not before Larry and the boys get home from their night shift.'

'Have you heard from your Lance or Simon?'

Tess placed the meat and potato pie in the oven. 'We got a letter yesterday from Simon. Posted weeks ago. He was in port, but couldn't say where, obviously. He's doing well. Nothing from Lance, naturally.' Tess rolled her eyes. 'The boy doesn't know which end of a pen to use, never mind writing home to his mam!'

The front door opened, and Larry walked in covered in coal dust, having just walked home from the pit. Even under the covering of coal dust you could see the fury on his face.

'Larry Hobson, get out of my kitchen. What possessed you to walk in here and not go around the back first and have a wash?'

'Because of *your son,* Tess Hobson!'

Tess stiffened. 'Oh, aye. *My son,* is it now? Which one and what has he done?'

'Colin! Your favourite, your baby!'

Tess stiffened at his anger. 'Colin? What's he done?'

'He's only gone and enlisted!' Larry fumed. 'Well, you can have words with him because he won't listen to me!' Larry jerked open the back door and went out into the yard.

'I'll go home.' Olivia rose, not wanting to intrude on a family matter.

Tess held up her hand for her to stay put as Colin came into the kitchen wearing a defiant look on his dirty face. The other Hobson sons, Jules and Jonnie, could be heard in the yard with their father washing the muck off them and cursing about the cold weather.

'Right…' Tess stood hands on hips. 'Enlisted, have you?'

'Aye, Mam.' Colin sucked in a deep breath as though ready for battle.

'Why?'

'Because it's the right thing to do, Mam.'

'You're underage.'

'So? Everyone's doing it.'

'Are they just?' Tess's clipped words fell into a tense atmosphere.

'Mam...'

'Don't you dare *Mam* me, Colin Hobson.'

A knock on the door interrupted what Colin was about to say next.

'I'll see who it is.' Olivia quickly escaped to the front room and opened the door.

The uniformed messenger bowed his head. 'Mrs Hobson?'

The warmth drained from her face as she stared at him. 'No, she's inside.' She held out her hand for the telegram he held. 'I'll take it to her.'

'Many thanks, madam.' He bowed his head again and walked away.

For a fleeting moment, Olivia watched him stride along the square. What a terrible job he had to do. She closed her eyes. She held information that would cause her dear friends' heartache, and it was difficult to close the door and face it.

Out in the square Ezra was returning home from his night shift. He looked at her quizzically. She raised the telegram to show him and finally closed the door.

In the kitchen she found it empty. The whole family were in the yard arguing over Colin.

Taking a deep breath, Olivia opened the back door and stood there, the words stuck in her mouth.

Larry dried his face on a towel, wearing only his trousers, his chest red from the hot water and cold air. He glanced at her. 'Lass?'

She held out the telegram.

Tess, Larry, Colin, Jonnie and Jules didn't move.

'Read it, lass,' Larry said, pulling on a clean shirt.

She looked sadly at Tess, who nodded.

Olivia read the telegram silently first, her fears confirmed.

'Which one?' Tess whispered.

She read aloud. 'Regret to inform you...'

'Which one?' Tess demanded.

Olivia lowered the telegram. 'Lance.'

'Wounded?' Larry asked hopefully.

'Killed in action. December thirty-first.'

'Five days ago,' Jonnie murmured.

Like a ghost, pale and silent, Tess walked past Olivia and took the telegram as she went. She closed the back door on them all.

'What can I do?' Olivia asked Larry.

'Nowt, lass, thanks. Tess will need you tomorrow, but today she'll want to be by herself.' He turned to his sons. 'Lads, get away to bed, try and sleep. I'll go to your mam.'

Olivia kissed each of their cheeks in turn. Without words the Hobson men went inside and Olivia tidied Tess's kitchen until the pie was ready to take out of the oven. She heard crying from upstairs.

Lastly, with the kitchen tidy, she put fresh tea leaves in the teapot and filled the kettle with water ready for it to be put on the heat.

Outside she gathered all the filthy clothes the boys had shed and shook off the worst of the coal dust before taking them inside and plunging them into the hot water in the copper. The pie was cooling on the table, and knowing no one would eat for a while, she turned off the heat to the simmering vegetables. Usually, the Hobson men would have a meal on their return but not today.

She went around to her own yard and entered her kitchen. She wanted to write to Spencer, but first she went upstairs and rummaged around in her basket of ribbons and lace until she found a length of black ribbon that she'd worn in her hair when her father died.

Downstairs, she knotted the ribbon into a bow and then went outside to fix it to the nail on Tess's front door. The sign of a death would alert the neighbours and respect would be shown.

She added coal to the small blaze in the kitchen and to the fire in the front room. The temperature had dropped in the last hour.

Sitting at the kitchen table, she took a piece of paper out of her stationery box and began to write a letter to Spencer.

My dearest love,

By the time you receive this letter you'll have left HQ and be with your men again.

This morning brought the awful news that Lance Hobson, Tess and Larry's oldest son, has been killed in action in France. I never met Lance, he has been gone the entire time I've lived in the square, but seeing the pain in Tess's eyes is something I never want to see again.

On top of that, Colin has enlisted, which I feel will only add to that family's distress. I don't know how to act or what to say to Tess. Everyone has loss at some point in their lives, I've experienced it by losing both parents, but for a parent to lose a beloved child, that must be the most painful of all. How will they bear it? How do others bear it? All the mothers and fathers up and down the country receiving such telegrams?

In other news, I have finished working for the Rochdales as of yesterday. Tess said I should get used to not working again now I am your wife. I fear that will take some getting used to. I don't know what to do with my time.

I received a letter from your sister, Anthea, which was full of kindness and good wishes. I shall write to her shortly. I have heard nothing from Lachie as yet, but I expect a letter soon once he's settled in France.

You mentioned in your letter about leaving the army when the war is over and working in your father's business. I want you to know that I fully support your decision. As long as we are together, I will live anywhere. In fact, I'm excited at the prospect of a new adventure and our future. Your generosity towards Lachie and offering him a position within the business shows what a thoroughly wonderful man I have married.

I shall post this letter now. I need to do some shopping in town, and I want to get there and back before any snow falls. It's terribly cold here today. I will buy food for Tess as she will not want to face going out for a few days.

I shall write again in a day or two, my love. I miss you terribly, but I'm grateful for the precious days we've had together and the memories we made.

Stay safe and well and warm.

I love you deeply.

Your loving wife,

Olivia. XX

IT TOOK her little time to ready herself for town and as she was locking her door, Winnie came to her.

'Tess has had a death?' She nodded to the black ribbon on the nail next door.

'Yes, Lance. Killed in action.' Olivia kept her voice low and walked with Winnie, pulling up the collar of her coat. It was bitterly cold outside.

'Aww, he was a nice lad, was Lance. Not seen him for years like but we grew up together.'

'I'm going into town to buy some food for them. Tess won't want to cook.'

'Is there owt I can do?' Winnie asked, the face powder she wore barely covered the bruises on her neck, a regular occurrence from the beatings her husband gave her.

'I don't think so.' Olivia patted Winnie's arm. 'Maybe tell the others in the square? Tess wouldn't want people knocking on her door wanting a chat, not for a couple of days at least.'

'No, course she wouldn't. I'll let them all know. Shall I go and tell the vicar? He might call round?'

'That's a good idea. See you later.'

Olivia spent the afternoon shopping, taking her time, despite the cold weather. Tess's words came back to her. A lady of leisure. She was a Middleton now. Her life was changed forever.

Stopping in front of the large window of a women's clothing boutique, she studied the fashions on display, an elegant evening dress, a sable coat, a thick woollen tweed skirt and jacket.

Olivia glanced down at her black coat, one she'd owned for years. It was showing the signs of wear. It would never pass inspection from Spencer's family.

Impulsively she entered the shop. She had money, more than she'd ever had in her life thanks to the allowance Stanford sent her and the money Spencer gave her before he left. She had her own bank account. Perhaps it was time to spend some of it and begin to feel more of a Middleton? She needed new clothes, new boots, shoes, hats and gloves.

'May I help you, madam?' The shop assistant gave Olivia a quick up and down look and didn't seem pleased with what she saw.

Olivia understood the assistant's thoughts. She assumed Olivia didn't belong in such a high-end dress shop such as this. But Olivia had lived and worked amongst wealthy people for years. She knew how they acted and what they bought.

'Yes, you may help me.' Olivia raised her chin slightly, as she'd seen Spencer's grandmama do often, and spoke like her previous mistress. 'I am in need of new clothes.'

'I see… and you wish to purchase something in this establishment?' The woman looked unconvinced. 'Our prices are—'

'I am aware of your prices,' Olivia cut in sweetly. 'My husband's grandmama once used to frequent this salon.'

'Indeed, madam, and her name would be?'

'Mrs Seraphina Broadbent.'

'Mrs Broadbent?' The thin woman's eyebrows rose alarmingly. 'Yes, she certainly was a valued customer here. I understand she has gone to live in Paris now?'

'She has.'

'And you are married to her grandson?'

'I am. Mrs Olivia Middleton, wife to Major Spencer Middleton.' Olivia held out her hand for the woman to shake.

'A pleasure to meet you, Mrs Middleton.'

'Shall we get started?' Olivia found she quite liked this play-acting.

'Certainly, madam. Would you care for some tea or a cup of hot chocolate?'

'Hot chocolate would suit me perfectly, thank you.' Olivia grinned. She couldn't wait to tell Tess about this. It might bring a small smile to her face amidst her grief.

CHAPTER 9

Northern France

Late March, 1916.

In the pouring rain, Spencer led his men on a march to their next destination. They were heading east after months of small skirmishes against the enemy in little villages that no longer existed after days of shelling. Ground was fought over, lost, won and lost and won again in a never-ending game of chance.

His orders were often simple. Find the target area, take it from the enemy and then hold it until relieved by another unit or the Germans fought to win it back again. He did this on repeat.

Winter had been cold, harsh living in an open area with little protection. The men succumbed to illness, frostbite and low morale. Yet, with spring's arrival and the weather warming, the men had started to cheer up again, as much as one could in war. They had rest periods in villages attended to by kind French women who for a few francs would do their washing, allow them to bathe in horse troughs and feed them any spare food they could muster. A few days, a week, in the company of good people, away from the conflict calmed shattered nerves, lessened the nightmares and boosted the men's moral enough that they were ready to march to the next hell hole.

'Major Middleton.' Dawes came alongside him studying a map. 'I have identified the next ridge as—'

The bomb that exploded seventy yards away dropped Spencer, Dawes and the whole column of men to the ground in an instant.

Spencer's ears rang. 'Take cover!' he yelled, blowing his whistle.

Another shell landed closer, vibrating the ground, showering them with dirt and mud. The smell of gunpowder filled his nose.

Spencer jumped to his feet and, grabbing Dawes by the shoulder, hauled him up. 'To the trees!'

A hundred yards behind them they'd passed a sparse wood. Spencer shouted orders to his officers to spread out, to stay low, to find any cover available.

An upturned cart, long broken and left abandon hid Spencer and Dawes as they caught their breath from the mad dash.

'You said the enemy was still two miles away, sir,' Dawes accused Spencer.

'That's the information that was relayed to me, Lieutenant. This area had been routed last week by the French.' Spencer took out his binoculars and lying flat on his stomach on the saturated grass, he peered out from around the side of the cart. He focused the binoculars on the ridge. Low grey cloud made vision difficult, then he saw it. A puff of smoke. Artillery.

'Incoming!' he screamed back at the men.

The shell landed closer to the wood and like a punch to the gut, Spencer flinched as several men were blown up into the air. The ground shook, the blast splintering trees like kindling. 'We are sitting ducks here.' He scrambled to his feet, waving his arms above his head. 'Retreat!'

He ran as fast as he could bent over, dragging men to their feet as he passed them. 'Retreat!'

Another shell landed twenty yards away, the explosion knocking him off his feet. He opened his eyes to the grey clouds above and the rain hitting his face. Dazed, winded, he crawled on the wet grass. His ears buzzed with a tinging sound.

'Get up, sir!' His batman, Private Bishop, grabbed his arm and pulled him along.

Gathering his senses, Spencer started running, blowing his whistle. The rain continued to pour. The men slipping as they ran.

They needed backup artillery. Spencer stopped and scribbled on his notepad their location and action required. He shouted for a sergeant to give the message to a runner to take to HQ.

Fleeing with his men to take cover in a shallow ditch that edged a field, Spencer shouted the order for the men to 'Stand-to.'

As one, the men readied their rifles and flung themselves along the wall of the ditch to face the enemy if they came.

'You think there will be a charge, sir?' Sergeant Matlock asked, his gaze on the fields in front of them as more shells fell, decimating the wood.

'If they are sensible, the Germans should charge. They have us on the run. We have no answering artillery until our runner gets to HQ.' Spencer surveyed the horizon with his binoculars. 'No movement.' His stomach churned with nerves. He hated the waiting.

It took an hour for the artillery cannons pulled by horses to be brought up. Spencer and his men watched the horses drag the cannons into place in front of them. Spencer spoke to the unit's officer and plotted the distance of where he suspected the German guns were positioned.

The roar of their answering cannons shattered the surrounding countryside. With the artillery unit in control of the situation, Spencer pulled back his men to count the dead and wounded.

'Three dead, sir,' Matlock reported back to him. 'Two injured but not severely. A day at the casualty clearing station for some stitches and they'll be back with us.' He handed a sheet of paper to Spencer with the names and ranks.

'Thank you, Sergeant.'

A horse and rider came galloping towards him, the rider jumping down to hand him a note.

Spencer read it and wrote an answering note in reply for the messenger to take back to HQ.

'Sir?' Lieutenant Dawes enquired of the note.

'We are to advance under the protection of the artillery. Spread the word and wait for my signal.'

'Advance?' Shocked, Dawes hesitated.

'That's what I said. Go, Lieutenant.' Spencer winced as the boom of the cannons hurt his ears. He looked at the ridge in the distance. Their objective. A German held ridge that also had artillery attached to it. They would face a pummelling to reach it.

He approached the officer in charge of their artillery. 'We are to advance. I need you to blow the hell out of that trench and ridge before we get there.'

'Yes, sir. We'll do our best.'

By evening as the rain finally eased, Spencer and his men had taken the German-held ridge and captured the German trench, but the toll had taken four more men to their graves and badly wounded another twelve.

They spent an uncomfortable night in heavy fog, the trench waterlogged at the bottom. Food wasn't possible to bring up from HQ, so they made do with their rations of bully beef and hard biscuits.

As the night wore on, the rain returned, hammering down, soaking their boots, and dampening their uniforms under the waterproof sheets they used as capes, Spencer inspected the troops, resting the best they could in the trench. Sentries kept watch, the downpour making visibility and hearing a difficult task.

At dawn, the men grumbled, weary from lack of sleep, cold, wet and hungry.

Spencer received orders to abandon the trench and march two miles east to join up with another unit.

'What the bloody hell was all that for then?' Spencer overheard one private say to another.

'What is any of it for?' the other private replied.

Spencer kept walking, the question lingering in the air. What had it been for? The ground they fought and won was abandoned. In twenty-four hours, he'd lost seven men and fourteen were wounded. And as the sun rose again between wispy grey clouds, he knew with a sinking feeling they'd have to do it all again soon.

When they reached the next hamlet, it pleased Spencer to see a base camp had been set up. His commanders had given permission for the village to be the resting place behind the front-line trenches. He gave his men time to wash, find dry clothes from the stores that had been brought up in wagons and to eat some warm food.

'Spence!' Albert Dunbar called to him from across the crowded village green.

Spencer shook his hand. 'I didn't expect to see you here.'

'Only just arrived.'

'Do you know what is planned?'

'Not much. Waiting on orders. I do know the French have been hit hard to the east.'

'Poor blighters.' Spencer tiredly rubbed his face.

'Heard you had a day of it yesterday as well.'

'Oh yes, fun and games as usual,' Spencer replied sarcastically.

'When I heard you were on your way here, I managed to get

you a cot next to mine. We're in the church. The largest building, a barn, is the hospital.'

'They have a hospital here?'

'It's been here for a while. The French have been fighting in the area for months. We're probably four miles behind the front line, but of course, that line keeps forever moving back and forth.'

'So, if the Germans break through, they will head this way.'

'Quite possibly.'

They fell into step and headed for the stone church at the end of the green. Spencer noticed other regiments, a Highlander company, their men easily distinguished by wearing kilts, and a French company resting by the blacksmith.

'Something must be planned for us all to be here,' he said quietly.

'No doubt. This hamlet is the only place for miles. We're surrounded by fields. I suspect we are to rest here for a few days before being sent closer to the front.' Albert glanced at him. 'You look like hell.'

'I didn't sleep last night. I fully expected the Germans to return and retake the trench.'

'Funny how the Germans never do what we expect them to do,' Albert said.

'Well, that would make a very dull war, would it not?' Spencer said with a wry smile.

'Did you hear that the new conscription act back home is proving unpopular?'

'I did.' Spencer nodded. 'The men here are not happy about it either. They say they do not want to fight alongside men who have been forced to come over and fight.'

'It has to be done.' Albert shrugged. 'More men are needed. It is that simple.'

'Is anything about this war simple?' Spencer sighed. 'I have a pile of paperwork to do. I had better get started on it.'

'I'll leave you to it, friend. Shall I come and fetch you in a couple of hours for some food?'

'Yes, good.' Spencer nodded his thanks. He called to his batman and told him of his lodgings. Bishop ran to the wagon that brought up the men's larger kits and fetched Spencer's kit.

Inside the church, the coldness made Spencer shiver. He admired the stained-glass window at the end of the nave depicting Jesus and his disciples before spotting two army issued cots erected behind the altar that Albert mentioned.

Bishop soon had the area more comfortable. Bishop's knack for procuring items of comfort came in handy as Spencer washed and shaved with warm water for the first time in days. Bishop made him some black tea and, as the afternoon wore on, Bishop worked his magic to find from somewhere in the village a pillow and crocheted blanket for Spencer's cot.

Spencer sat in one of the pews and wrote in the company diary, copying most of it into his own personal diary. He then wrote seven letters, one each to the next of kin of those men who died the day before.

The task of informing next of kin about their loved one's bravery moved him deeply. Naturally, he couldn't write the truth. No family wanted to hear the news their boy died crying for his mother or moaning in pain from his injuries. No wife wanted to hear that their husband's body would never be found because the shell had blown him to pieces.

Bowing his head, Spencer closed his eyes. Even in a church he found no solace to his ragged thoughts. Did he even believe in God anymore? Why would any God allow this carnage to happen?

A discreet cough from behind him raised his head.

Bishop held out an envelope.

With a sinking heart, Spencer took it but brightened on seeing Olivia's neat handwriting. He tore it open.

. . .

My darling love,

I hope this letter find you in good health.

I received your letter on March 15th with the news that your grandpapa has passed away. How you must be suffering his loss keenly. I know how much you admired him.

Spencer lowered the letter. The death of his grandfather earlier in the month had been a great shock. His sister had written to him urgently as his grandpapa lay dying, and he'd replied instantly, telling her that he would try and get leave to journey to Paris. His commander had granted the leave but by the time Spencer had travelled to Paris, his beloved grandfather had passed. He spent four emotional days with his grandmama in her apartment, helping her to arrange the funeral and grandpapa's affairs.

Unfortunately, the time elapsed so quickly, he was saying goodbye to them all too soon. However, it had been good to see his grandmama, Anthea, her husband and children and his father. Ralph and Mildred hadn't made the journey.

He remembered his grandmama holding his cheek as he said goodbye.

'You must survive this war, Spencer,' she demanded. 'And when I see you again, I want you to bring Olivia. She was a good girl at Hawthorn Manor. Very pretty as I remember. No wonder she turned your head.'

He'd smiled and kissed her papery cheek. 'Olivia makes me very happy, Gran. I want you to be pleased for me and to accept her.'

'Does she love you just as much in return?'

'She does. In every look and word and action I see the love she has for me.'

'Then she will always be welcome in this family, my dear boy. I would have no woman love you less.'

Sighing at the memory, Spencer continued to read Olivia's letter.

I HAVE HEARD *from Lachie several times in the last week. He's been moved to another company that needed their numbers building up, but he is well pleased as he is working with the horses in the supply units. Perhaps your letter to his regiment's commander worked?*

Tess's Colin arrived home yesterday from training camp. He departs for France in a few days. I don't think Tess has fully forgiven him for enlisting, but she's putting on a brave face about it. Though Jonnie and Jules have been warned that if they do the same, she'll disown them. She wouldn't of course.

I've heard from Mildred a great deal recently. She tells me her health hasn't been very good lately, though the doctor can't seem to find what is wrong with her. She writes that her one remaining family member, her brother, died some days ago. She sounds very low in spirits.

Your father also wrote to me, a letter I received yesterday. He still resides in London and wishes me to visit him there and spend some time with him in the summer or I could go to him at Christmas. I thought that such a kind offer, but I'm unsure whether it will be possible for I have some news.

Spencer you are going to be a father!

I am with child.

SPENCER LEAPT to his feet in surprise. 'A baby?'

He looked around the church, which was beginning to fill up with junior officers claiming pews as beds.

'Sir?' asked a sergeant from a different company. 'Are you all right, sir?'

'My wife... she's with child...' Shock filtered through his brain. 'I am going to be a father!'

A cheer went up from the officers and the five of them eagerly came over and shook his hand.

'What's all this?' Albert walked down the aisle. 'Spence?'

'Olivia writes that I am to be a father, Albert.' Spencer felt an array of emotions flip through him in a matter of seconds. Happiness, surprise, excitement, then worry for Olivia, for the future.

'I am thrilled for you, Spence. It is fabulous news.' Albert shook his hand. 'This is a celebration. A cause for a drink!' He took his hip flask out of his pocket. 'When is this little Middleton due?'

'Ah...' Spencer continued to read the letter.

I DIDN'T REALISE it until I started feeling sick when I woke each morning. Then Tess was cooking onions the other day, and I embarrassed myself by being sick all over her newly washed floor tiles.

Tess declared me to be pregnant.

I saw Doctor Whittaker on Stanley Street yesterday and he confirmed it. I am three months gone. Obviously, conceived at Christmas when you were here.

I hope you are excited?

Doctor Whittaker tells me the baby will be due in September.

I truly hope this is happy news for you, my love.

Myself, I'm in shock but also terribly happy.

ABERT THRUST the flask into Spencer's hands. 'You've gone a bit pale, Middleton. Have a drink.'

Spencer took a long swig of the brandy that burned its way down his throat. He coughed and wiped his mouth.

'Better?' Albert grinned.

'Christ, Dunbar, I will be a father in September.' It still wouldn't sink into his brain.

'And a great one you'll be as well.' Albert winked. 'Cheers to the exciting news!'

More officers entered the church, chatting away about sleeping on pews and joking about being closer to heaven.

Spencer folded Olivia's letter and placed it in an inner breast pocket of his uniform. He would finish reading the letter later when everyone was asleep.

'Shall we go and get some food?' Albert asked.

He didn't know if he'd be able to eat. His stomach was in knots at the news of his impending fatherhood. He wanted to be pleased, to be deliriously happy about it, but would that tempt fate if he was?

CHAPTER 10

July 1916

'OH, THIS HEAT!' Olivia complained to Tess as she hung out washing in the small yard. 'It's too early in the day to be this hot. It's not cooled down since yesterday. I couldn't get any sleep last night.'

'Being pregnant in the summer is worse than being pregnant in the winter in my opinion,' Tess replied from over the fence where she hung out her own washing. 'Still, it gets our clothes dry quicker.'

The baby moved as Olivia bent down to get a wet piece of clothing to hang out. 'Are you going to the market this morning?' she asked Tess.

'Aye, once I've done this lot. Do you want to come with me?'

'Yes, I think I will. I don't need much being on my own, but I've run out of a few things.'

On Olivia's other side Sadie came out with her basket of washing. 'Great minds think alike,' she said in a way of greeting.

'Day off, Sadie?'

'Not quite. I'm off to the mill once I've pegged this lot out. I worked overtime all week, and the gaffer said I could come in an hour later as a reward.'

'One whole hour?' Tess tossed her head. 'They work you to the bone at that place.'

'We've a lot of big orders to get out.' Sadie shrugged. 'I don't mind working late. I'd only be sitting around the house all evening by myself.'

'How are you coping without Gerry?' Olivia asked. Sadie's husband Gerry had enlisted the week before and gone off to training camp. Sadie had raged that the conscription was void if you were in a reserved occupation, such as mining, but Gerry had ignored her pleas to stay home and gone anyway.

'I'm fine.' Sadie shrugged. 'Gerry is only at the training camp. I'll worry once he's sent overseas. I know he wants to do his bit. At the camp, he's sharing a tent with Mr Muldoon. How fortunate is that to be placed with a neighbour?'

'I spoke to Mrs Muldoon yesterday,' Tess told them. 'She's frantic that she won't cope on army wages. Mr Muldoon earned well as a printer.'

'She has all those children to feed,' Olivia commented. 'We'll need to help her when we can.'

Sadie pegged out a petticoat. 'Winnie has begged her Norman to accept his papers, but he won't. He's been called up and been sent several letters about it but refuses to agree to go and he's now saying he a conscientious objector.'

Tess leaned over the fence dividing her and Olivia's yards. 'Conscientious objector my backside! Norman Briggs is nowt but a coward, letting other men fight for him. Winnie could do with the break from him and his fists.'

Olivia pegged the last item of washing on her line. The baby kicked, and she rubbed her round stomach.

'I can hear the postman,' Sadie announced.

The three women stopped to listen. Mr Thacker, the postman, always whistled to let the people on the square know he held no bad news such as war telegrams in his satchel that day. Any time he had a letter from the War Office, Buckingham Palace or the army council, he remained tight-lipped.

'He's whistling,' Olivia said gratefully.

The three women entered their houses and opened their front doors at the same time, all standing on their doorsteps as Mr Thacker approached.

'Good morning, ladies.' He bowed his head. 'Nothing for you, Mrs Watson,' he said, walking past Sadie.

'Two letters for you, Mrs Middleton.' He stopped before Olivia and handed the envelopes to her. 'And one for you, Mrs Hobson.'

'It'll be our Colin,' Tess said happily. 'He writes every week. What a good lad. I hear nothing from Simon.'

'Well, I'll head to work then. See ya both later,' Sadie said.

In her front room, Olivia opened Lachie's letter, and a piece of white lace ribbon fell out.

Dear Sis,

How are you? Are you getting fat now?

I'm well. Was involved in a bit of do yesterday. I was bringing up a wagon of ammunition towards the lines when random shelling began. It scared the horses, and I had a time of it trying to control them and calm them down. They bolted for a hundred yards, and I feared the ammunition load would go off at any moment, but I managed to talk to the horses and settled them enough to walk.

When I got to the supply area where I was meant to be, I got down and led the horses in, talking to them the whole time. The shells did some damage but stopped after ten minutes. That was the closest I've been to any action. I'm not in a hurry to repeat the experience.

Did you know that Colin has joined my company in KOYLI? I

couldn't trust my eyes when I saw him. It's been a right laugh having him here with me. I've been showing him the ropes. He's useless with the horses but he might not stay in my company and instead be transferred to another, with other miners, but while he is here, we're making the most of it.

I'm in good health, but if you could send me new socks and some food treats, I'd appreciate it. Oh, and a safety shaving razor if you can. I nearly severed my own head using the cutthroat the army supplies. A safety razor would be just the ticket.

I hope you and the neighbours are all well.

I bought the lace ribbon from a farmer's wife. I thought you might use it for a bit of frill on one of the baby's clothes.

Sending much love,

Your brother Lachie.

Olivia smiled at the lace. She would use it to edge a bonnet she'd knitted for the baby. How kind of Lachie to send it.

Tess came in, waving a letter. 'Did you hear? Colin is with Lachie! What are the chances of it?'

'Well, they are in the same regiment.' She grinned, happy that Tess was smiling.

'And Lachie is never near the fighting, is he?' Tess said with conviction. 'Lachie just does the supply runs and so that's all our Colin will be doing. The pair of them are nowhere near a German. I'm so relieved.'

Olivia didn't mention Lachie's experience with the shelling. No one close to the battlefields were ever completely safe. Spencer had told her that repeatedly. Lachie and Colin could, at times, be in as much danger as any other soldier on the front line when shelling happened. Spencer had mentioned that the Germans had dropped bombs on them from biplanes when they were at rest well behind the lines. Bombs had even been dropped on British soil so was anywhere really that safe?

'Imagine the escapades those two lads will get up to!' Tess chuckled. 'They'll be in trouble before we know it.'

'Most likely. Lachie sent me this lace ribbon for the baby's clothes.' Olivia folded the letter away and showed Tess the ribbon.

'That's lovely that is. A bit of French lace.'

A knock on the door interrupted them. Olivia opened it to reveal Ezra. 'Ezra! This is a nice surprise. You've returned from training camp.'

'Aye.'

'Come in, lad.' Tess freely invited him in for there was no difference between her house and Olivia's, both were shared homes.

'How long are you home for?' Olivia asked.

'I'm leaving now.'

'But you've only just arrived?'

'I actually got home yesterday, but I had to meet with the landlord about my house. I've paid the rent upfront for three months and I'll continue to do that until I'm back home from the war. I also had to meet with the pit manager. He assured me I'll have a job to return home to once the war is over. Also, I've cancelled everything I can think of, my milk and bread deliveries. My gas is turned off. I've closed the curtains and packed most things away…'

'You're such an organised man,' Tess complimented him.

'I came to ask a favour though of you both.' He looked uneasy.

'Of course,' Olivia prompted.

'I have no next of kin and I wondered if I could put your name down, Olivia?'

'Yes, absolutely.' She was honoured he'd chosen her.

'Thank you. And, Tess, if anything was to happen to me, I'd like you to sell all my belongings or give them away to a charity.'

'Aye, lad. I'll get it done, but nowt will happen to you,' Tess said stubbornly.

He gave Olivia a bank book. 'I've spoken to the bank manager and your name is attached to my account. I have money in this account, not a lot, but should I be killed, I'd like you to distribute the money between the families in the square. After all, they have been my only family for years.'

'Oh, Ezra…' Olivia cradled the bank book to her chest. 'That's a generous thought.'

'Not that we'll need to do it,' Tess snapped. Since Lance's death she had refused to consider another person she cared about would die in this beastly war. 'You'll be home safe and sound, just like the rest of the square's men.'

Ezra smiled sadly at her, then took Olivia's hand. 'Thank you. May I write to you?'

'I insist that you do,' she replied.

Ezra embraced Tess. 'Goodbye, Tess.'

'God bless, lad. Stay safe.'

He kissed Olivia's cheek. 'Take care, Liv. I wish you all the best with the baby.'

'Thank you, Ezra.' Olivia and Tess stood together as he left without looking back.

'I hate this bastard war!' Tess said harshly, flinging open her own front door. 'I'll go and get my hat and bag, and we'll go to the market, lass.'

Olivia placed the bank book in the dresser drawer in the kitchen. She was seven months pregnant and tired of being alone, of worrying. She wanted Spencer home, and Lachie. She wanted to plan for their future.

Another knock on the door brought her head up. Was she to speak to every neighbour today?

When she opened the door, the last person she expected to see was her sister-in-law, Mildred Middleton. 'Mrs Middleton!'

'Dear Olivia.' Mildred embraced her.

'Come in. How wonderful to see you.' Olivia closed the door.

'I beg your forgiveness for not sending word of my impending arrival. I made a most impulsive decision yesterday to come here, and I travelled on the last train to Wakefield last night, but it was terribly late, so I rented a room at a hotel near the cathedral and walked here after breakfast.'

'Oh, you shouldn't have worried about how late it was last night. You could have stayed here with me and saved your money.' Then she blushed. Why had she mentioned saving money with a Middleton?

Mildred glanced down at Olivia's swollen stomach. 'I truly acknowledge that I am being a most inconsiderate and selfish person landing on your doorstep without prior warning.'

'Nonsense.' Olivia smiled and took her hands to ease her concerns. 'Please, don't think of it again. A visit from you is a lovely surprise.'

Suddenly Mildred burst into tears, covering her face with a handkerchief.

Shocked, Olivia led her to the sofa, her legs as wobbly as jelly. 'Do you know something about Spencer that I don't?'

'Oh! No!' Mildred gasped, gripping Olivia's hands tighter. 'No, nothing like that. Please forgive me for worrying you. What a senseless thing for me to do, arriving here all upset and worrying you in your condition.' She sobbed harder.

Tess walked in and stopped, alarmed at seeing Mildred crying into her handkerchief on the sofa. 'Shall I put the kettle on, lass?' she whispered.

Olivia nodded and when Tess had gone into the kitchen, she gently squeezed Mildred's hands in comfort. 'Are you able to tell me what is causing you such torment?'

'It's Ralph… He's gone. Gone to France. Just like that.' She snapped her fingers angrily. 'He paid no attention to my thoughts and needs.'

'He's enlisted?'

'As a vicar he told me it is his calling to give comfort to those men that need him. Ralph has talked of it often in the last few months. I begged him to stay. He refused to listen to me. He said he had a duty, but what of his duty to me, his wife?'

'I understand your frustration.'

'Frustration and fear. I've read the newspapers. I know of the battles and now there is this great Somme offensive! So many men have died. Ralph could be in the midst of shelling and bullets...'

'Perhaps Stanford could write to his contacts and have Ralph sent to one of the hospitals in France? A vicar working in a hospital would be very welcomed, I'm sure. Spencer told me there are hospitals along the coast, away from the fighting.'

'Our father-in-law Stanford has helped Ralph enough in this endeavour,' she spoke harshly. 'I understand Stanford called in favours for Ralph to go wherever Ralph feels he is most needed, and no doubt that is the front line!' Anger brought out spots of red on Mildred's cheeks. 'Ralph sailed for France four days ago and I've been inconsolable since.'

'I'm so sorry you're upset.'

Mildred sniffed and wiped her eyes. 'I could not stand being alone in that house for another minute. I didn't know what to do. Then, just as I was leaving for the train station last evening, a new vicar arrived with his wife to take over the village services and has come to live in the vicarage. *My house!* I could not stay and live with them. How was that even possible?'

'You've lost your home?' She was alarmed by the news.

'With Ralph no longer overseeing the church services and the needs of the parish, he's been replaced, which means the rectory is no longer my home.'

'Goodness. No wonder you're so upset.'

'I'm furious with Ralph. He has gone and I must deal with all this mess he's left behind. Never in my life would I think him capable of treating me so undeservedly.' She started crying again.

Tess brought in a tea tray and silently placed it on the small table by the sofa. 'I'll leave you to it, lass.' Tess patted Olivia's shoulder as she went out.

Mildred jerked back. 'Have I interrupted something you've planned?'

'Only a trip to the market,' Olivia reassured her. 'I can go there later. It's not important.'

'I am so sorry for bringing this problem to your door. I can leave.'

'Nonsense. We are family, aren't we?'

Mildred nodded tearfully. 'I could travel to London and stay with Stanford or even go and live by myself at his home in York. He is hardly there, apparently, preferring to be in London while the war continues. However, instinctively I knew this was where I should come, to you, dear Olivia. Did I do the right thing?'

'Absolutely.' Olivia poured her a cup of tea. 'I know this little terrace house is far from what you're used to, but I'd be very happy for you to stay here with me if you chose to.'

'You wouldn't mind?'

'Not at all. You could sleep in Lachie's room.' Olivia glanced around the small front room, the second-hand furniture. Although clean and tidy, the place always smelled of damp. 'I would understand if you'd prefer the luxury of Stanford's homes though.'

'To be honest with you, I feel a little intimidated by Stanford.' Mildred sipped her tea.

'You?' Olivia was surprised.

'Like you, I was not brought up in their world.'

'You were closer to it than I ever was.' Olivia laughed. 'I was a servant at the manor, and you were their daughter-in-law.'

'As you are now.' Mildred patted Olivia's hand. 'Do not sell yourself short. You are just as deserving to be a Middleton as I am. My father was a vicar, a gentleman, I suppose, but on a very poor scale. My father was the fourth son and was sent straight into the church. My grandfather spent all his wealth before he died, and poor Father received very little. I was brought up as a young lady but without the means to live amongst that society. The vicarage where I grew up was a sweet house but needed much money spent on it, which we didn't have…' Mildred sipped more of her tea.

'Then you married Ralph,' Olivia added.

'It was my wedding anniversary yesterday which is why I was so upset on top of everything else.' Mildred glanced at Olivia's round stomach. 'I'm so mad at Ralph, yet I feel guilty for being so when he is going into danger.'

'We all feel like that, Mrs Middleton.'

'Oh, please call me Mildred. I have begged you repeatedly in my letters to do so. Can we not be sisters?' Mildred looked ready to cry again.

'Yes, yes, of course, Mildred.' Olivia would try harder to call her by her first name.

Sighing deeply, Mildred placed her cup and saucer on the tray. 'I shall go to the hotel and collect my luggage. Are you certain I can stay with you?'

'I insist.' Olivia stood as Mildred did. 'Though are you sure you want to stay here? I have no servant like you do, I live simply. I cook and clean and the neighbours are in and out of the house all the time…'

'And I shall enjoy it.' Mildred smiled. 'Truly, I will.'

'Well then, let us fetch your things.'

'Thank you for taking me in.'

Olivia pinned on her hat. 'I'll enjoy the company. I've realised I don't like living on my own at all. Though Tess is never off the doorstep.' She chuckled.

'Mrs Hobson is a character, isn't she? But a kind soul.'

'She lost her son not long ago. Killed in action. She has two more serving. She's doing very well at pretending to be brave, but I know she's fearful of more bad news arriving.'

'The poor woman, to lose a child…' Mildred slipped her bag over her arm. 'I shall help you keep her spirits up.'

'The square has grown quieter with some of the men gone, a new face around will be refreshing. I'll introduce you again to the neighbours soon. Though you met them all at our wedding.'

'Thank you. I look forward to getting to know them. I hope they will accept me into their square.'

'They are kind people. I have no doubts they will soon treat you like one of their own.' Olivia wondered how Mildred would cope living cheek by jowl with poor people. It was one thing to be a benevolent vicar's wife in a village and quite another to hear every argument, every baby's cry, every child's running footsteps right outside of your door or on the other side of a wall.

CHAPTER 11

August 1916

Sitting on a chair outside her front door, Olivia pulled her straw hat down lower to cover her face from the sun. She cradled a glass of lemon cordial on her stomach. She'd just finished writing letters to Lachie, Stanford and Anthea and had come outside to sit in the sun to write to Spencer.

The warm summer weather had brought the neighbours out into the square on a lazy Saturday afternoon. Despite the war, everyone seemed happier when out in the sunshine. At the far end of Norton Road, and behind the square, old men were busy digging in their allotments and further beyond the allotments a game of cricket was being played with much cheering and the crack of the ball hitting the bat. If Lachie had been home, he'd have gone and watched the game like he used to before he went away.

It was strange that the country continued to go on when across the English Channel, and other places, shells were exploding, men were dying or getting wounded, families being displaced from their homes. In the waters around England ships' sailors faced dangers as hidden submarines lurked beneath the water and ships were sunk. Yet, in towns and villages people still shopped for food, walked in the parks, cleaned their houses, went to work and all the while men were killing each other. None of it made sense to Olivia.

She sighed and rubbed her belly where the baby lay awkwardly, pushing against her ribs. 'Can you move, little one? I need to write to your father,' she murmured.

It gave her such joy to be carrying Spencer's child. She hadn't expected to fall pregnant from the week they had together at Christmas but was thrilled it had happened.

After losing her parents, and she had no clue of Stu's whereabouts, having this baby gave her comfort that she was growing a new member of their family. The baby would be her focus as she waited for Spencer and Lachie to return. It amazed her how much she loved the baby already. She and Mildred had spent many a night recently knitting little outfits, booties, caps and blankets. They were so tiny and sweet, and she couldn't imagine her own baby would soon be wearing them.

She picked up the pen and started writing.

My dear darling husband,

I hope this letter finds you well. Your last letter arrived two days ago, and I will try and answer all your questions.

It has now been four weeks since Mildred arrived and as I have mentioned in my previous letters since then, she has settled in well. I thought living in the square would be a shock to her, being so close to the neighbours, but she has given me no indication that she is unhappy with the arrangement.

Your father wrote to her two weeks ago offering her either of his homes to live in while Ralph is away, but she has decided to stay with me, and I am grateful she has done that. Her company is a great benefit to me. I would miss her if she was to go.

It took a few days for Mildred to calm her anger and disappointment in Ralph's decision to go to France, but being amongst the square, having Tess and Sadie pop in and out of the door, Mildred soon realised that her resentment hindered her ability to find enjoyment in other things, or so she told me.

Mildred and I live together quite harmoniously. We clean and cook together, go shopping and spend our evenings, sewing or reading. Mildred attends St Andrew's with all of us in the square each Sunday. We go to the picture theatre once a week and watch the newsreels of the war before the main event of the moving picture starts. This week we watched The Battle of the Somme. *It brought home to all of us what you brave men face. Most of the women were crying by the end of it. Tess walked out of the theatre. She could only think of her Lance and couldn't bear it. Larry took her home. An injured soldier home on leave sat beside me and he bowed his head and couldn't watch it either.*

It brought home to me, my love, just what you and Lachie and all the men are going through and it broke my heart to see it. I had to watch it all though, right to the end. I needed to know beyond your letters what it is like over there. Mildred and I held hands, lost for words. The images shook us deeply.

As I write, sitting out in the square, Mildred is surrounded by the Muldoon children, turning one end of a skipping rope so the eldest Muldoon girl could jump. It's a world away from what you're enduring. The children of the square adore Mildred. The minute she walks out of the front door, the children gather to her. She is interested in everything they do. The youngest boy from the Berry family is building a cart and Mildred took time to enquire how he was achieving it. The oldest Berry son, Charlie, is painting their front door and soon Mildred was admiring his work. Charlie is the man of the house now his father has received his call-up papers. Another man gone from the square.

Even Winnie's husband, Norman, has gone, not to war, but into hiding. Officials came to take him to Wakefield Prison eight days ago with the other conscientious objectors. Someone tipped off Norman and he packed a bag and told Winnie he was leaving and wasn't going to return. Poor Winnie had suffered a miscarriage from Norman's last beating, so she was heartily glad to see him go. She and little Martha have gone to live with her mother. She's given up her house. I don't know when any new people will move in. Tess has tried to find out but, so far, we don't know if it's been rented. It is the worst house in the square for damp and needs urgent repairs.

I heard from Ezra. He has been assigned to a mining company involved with digging mines under the German trenches. It sounds dreadfully dangerous.

Yesterday, I received a letter from Anthea as did Mildred. Both letters mentioned that your grandmother's health is failing, and that she hasn't rallied from your grandfather's death. Is there any hope of you being able to get some leave and visit them in Paris? I think your grandmother would benefit from seeing your handsome face.

Lachie wrote to me last week. He sounded very tired. He's been involved in some skirmishes recently. I fear he's been carrying supplies to the front line. His favourite horse was injured and had to be shot, and he seems very low over it.

I read the Somme offensive has been declared a success, but how is that possible with the large number of dead and casualties we've been reading about for the last two months?

Tess and the family are well, though it has been a worrying time. Their son, Simon's, ship was struck by a German submarine, but it managed to make it to a port in North Africa. When the telegram arrived, I thought Tess would faint, but Larry opened it and read that Simon had survived and was in hospital. Simon suffered burns but a few days later, Tess received a letter from him. He wrote saying he was doing well, and the family wasn't to be concerned. As you can imagine, the relief to everyone was great. Tess sent off a package for him filled with a pair of new socks, two handkerchiefs, a tin of toffee and a tin of fruit cake and Larry put in a Wakefield newspaper. I do hope he can soon come home on leave to see Tess and the family.

To answer another of your questions, I am in good health. I know you worry about me, but you mustn't. You have enough to concern yourself with over there. I am fine. The baby is growing and doing well. I continue to see Doctor Whittaker as you instructed, but I also was introduced to the local midwife, Mrs Anderson, who seems very nice, although an old woman, she is wise. Tess had help from Mrs Anderson for the birth of her babies and swears by her.

Olivia put down her pen as Mildred came over and sat in the other chair. 'You look hot.'

'I am.' Mildred poured herself a glass of cordial from the jug placed under the chair to keep cool. 'Who are you writing to?'

'Spencer. He always asks me to give him all the news from the square, but I'm also telling him about meeting Mrs Anderson. He has written before saying he'd prefer for me to have Doctor Whittaker at the birth.'

'And you prefer Mrs Anderson?' Mildred wiped her damp brow with a handkerchief.

'Actually, I'd like to have them both there at the time,' she confessed.

'Are you frightened of the birth?'

'Terrified.'

Mildred patted her arm. 'I'll not leave your side, I promise.'

'Thank you.' She was about six weeks away from giving birth and sleeping was becoming difficult. Tossing and turning all night gave her too much time to think, to worry, not just about the birth but about Spencer and Lachie returning home safe.

Mildred adjusted her wide-brimmed hat. 'Stanford wrote to me asking me to persuade you to come to London and have the baby there. He wants to hire the best doctor, midwife and nannies to care for the child that money can buy.' Mildred tapped her finger on the rim of the glass. 'I replied to him and told him it was your choice where you have this baby, and I would support you whichever choice you made.'

'He wrote to me asking me to go to London.' Olivia shooed away a fly. 'I just don't think I'll be comfortable there, surrounded by strangers, but it was kind of him to offer.'

'He is a good man,' Mildred agreed. 'He is trying to do his best for his children in whatever way he can. Stanford is trying to make up for being an absent father to his own children. When his wife died so young, giving birth to Anthea, he employed nannies to care for his children, many wealthy families do, there is nothing unusual in that. However, his pain from losing her meant the family home in York wasn't full of love, or so Ralph told me.'

'Spencer told me the same.'

Mildred sipped her drink. 'Spencer and Ralph were sent away to boarding school at a young age, then Spencer to the army, Ralph to the church and Anthea married as quickly as she could. All three were striving to find some sort of contentment they didn't receive at home in York.'

'Spencer mentioned to me that their only happy times were spent at Hawthorn Manor.'

'Yes, their grandparents gave them the love they needed.'

'Spencer is amazed at how involved his father has become in all their lives recently. He is grateful for it.'

'Better late than never. Stanford has a lot of making up to do.'

'Have you written to Ralph? I can post your letter with mine tomorrow.'

'No. I have nothing to say to him. His last letter was so… minimal.'

'You both need to be clearer to each other in your thoughts.'

'I've tried. Ralph doesn't listen to me.' Mildred tilted her head at Olivia. 'You and Spencer have spent so little time together, but you talk of him as though you know his every secret, his every thought and dream.'

'I feel as though I do. Our letters sustain us, we have no choice, but when he was here for Christmas we talked and talked, long into the nights and all day every day. It was as though we had to fill each moment telling the other everything in our hearts and minds, knowing time was not something we had. When Spencer returned to France, we continued with our letters. No subject is forbidden. We write as much as we can about all aspects of our days. It draws us closer.'

'How fortunate you are to share such a special bond.'

Olivia sipped her cordial. She had become aware that Mildred and Ralph did not share the same closeness, and they had spent four years married together unlike her and Spencer. She didn't mention it though, not wanting to hurt Mildred's feelings and switched the subject back to the impending birth. 'Do you think I should go to London as Stanford suggests and be cared for by the best doctor and nurses he knows?' Was she making the right decision to stay in the square?

'I think you should do whatever makes you content,' Mildred said diplomatically.

'What would you do if you were me?'

Mildred sighed and watched the girls start to skip again. 'What I wouldn't give to be you right now. I've been pregnant three times and miscarried all three. The last one I managed to get to four months...'

Olivia jerked up in the chair. 'Goodness! I never knew! Oh, Mildred, I'm so sorry.'

'We didn't tell anyone. After losing the first two babies, we decided that the third time we would keep the news to ourselves in case... Well, thankfully we did because it happened again just when I was starting to believe it wouldn't.'

'When was this last pregnancy?'

'I was pregnant at your wedding, no one could tell. Being plump I hid the baby quite easily.' She smiled self-consciously. 'However, on returning home I felt a little tired, and I put it down to travelling and then two days later I started to… well… lose the baby. Ralph called the doctor, but it was too late.'

Olivia grasped Mildred's hand. 'What a terrible time you must have had.'

'Yes, I confess it brought me as low as I've ever been. My body expelled the one thing I wanted most in the world.' Mildred tilted her head back and looked at the blue sky. 'Ralph didn't understand my feelings. He said we could try again another time. It was God's will… Only, Ralph began sleeping in another bedroom and made it clear he wasn't in any hurry to create another child.'

'That must have been so upsetting.' Olivia couldn't imagine Spencer turning away from her.

Mildred inspected a piece of fluff on her brown skirt. 'I couldn't understand why I couldn't carry a child when so many other women can do it easily. I mourned that baby more than the other two times. It was silly to, really, and it caused a… cloud over our marriage. Ralph was confused by my behaviour. We stopped talking to each other, finding ways to not be in the same room together and I think that pushed him towards going to France. With time and distance, I can see that now.'

'People deal with grief in many ways,' Olivia offered gently.

'Oh, I know. I've seen every aspect of grief since I was a child. As a vicar's daughter and then a vicar's wife, I've seen it all. Still, this was *my* grief.' Mildred turned sad eyes towards Olivia. 'Now Ralph has gone for who knows how long, and I must wait even longer to be a mother, if I ever am. Sadly, I feel I've also lost my husband, which is such a self-indulgent thing to say when women are becoming widows on a daily basis. When did I become so selfish?' Her chin wobbled.

'You're not selfish, just distraught, disappointed, confused.' Olivia placed Mildred's hand on her swollen stomach. 'One thing I can say for certain is you're an aunty to this little one and can mother it as much as you want.'

Mildred smiled. 'I pray to God every day for the safe arrival of this baby and you.'

The young Berry boy came over to them. 'Mrs Middleton, will you come watch me drive my cart?' he asked Mildred. 'Our Charlie is going to push me.'

'Of course I'll watch you.' Mildred placed the glass on the ground and smiled at Olivia. 'Finish your letter to Spencer.'

Seeing Mildred with a whole new perspective, Olivia watched as the Muldoon children joined the Berry boys to cheer on the cart's first outing. What a great shame it was that Mildred hadn't become a mother yet. She was the type who'd make an excellent one.

She picked up her pen.

Darling, I must mention to you that Mildred has lost three babies, the last one just months ago, and so if you are able to meet with Ralph or write to him, be aware that they have suffered in silence. Mildred feels Ralph has gone to France to escape her and her grief and yet deals with his own. Mildred shared this with me because I asked her advice about the baby. She still hurts from the disappointment of not becoming a mother. Perhaps it might be something Ralph will discuss with you? I would like them both to be godparents, sponsors, to our little one, I'm sure you'll agree?

Ralph's letters have begun arriving after two weeks of where Mildred heard nothing at all. One letter was sent to the rectory and forwarded here and then last week he wrote to her again—a short formal letter. I worry their marriage is in strife.

Pondering the current gloom of Mildred's marriage, Olivia rose and went inside the house. She picked up the framed photograph of her and Spencer that stood in pride of place on the mantle-piece. She gazed at his handsome face, the wry smile he wore when the photographer had been insistent that they look straight at the camera and not smile or move.

A familiar ache in her heart reemerged whenever she gave herself a moment to think of Spencer making love to her, and of those glorious days and nights together, which had cemented their love, their bond to each other. Their marriage, although only short and spent apart, was far warmer and deeper than Mildred and Ralph's relationship. She was eager for the war to be over so they could start the next phase of their lives together, but she feared Mildred and Ralph would continue to live as polite strangers with each other.

The baby moved, and she rubbed her stomach. 'Soon, little one, soon you'll meet your papa.' She hoped to all the fates in the world that her words would come true.

Suddenly, Mildred hurried in her face full of concern. 'Mr Thacker is coming, and he's not whistling.'

Olivia's stomach swooped, her mind went blank. With mounting dread, she stood by the open door, praying she didn't receive an envelope. A wave of relief as Mr Thacker touched his cap to her in acknowledgement but passed her door made Olivia feel dizzy. Mildred grabbed her arm as she swayed.

Then, in horror, they watched Mr Thacker knock on the Hobsons' door.

'Oh no, not again!' Olivia cried.

Mr Thacker held the official envelope in his hands. 'I'm sorry, Mrs Middleton. I don't like doing this job, delivering bad news day in, day out.'

'Lass?' Tess walked the short distance from Norton Road and into the square. She'd been visiting a relative of Larry's in town. As she saw the envelope in Mr Thacker's hand, her step faltered. 'For me?'

'I'm afraid so, Mrs Hobson,' he told her.

'It can't be Simon as he's in hospital in North Africa...' Tess turned tormented eyes to Olivia. 'It must be my Colin...'

'Shall I read it, Mrs Hobson?' Mildred offered.

'Aye, Mrs Middleton, that would be kind of you,' Tess said woodenly.

Olivia wrapped her arm around Tess supportively.

Mildred tore open the envelope and scanned the letter. 'Colin has been wounded, Mrs Hobson,' she said hastily.

'Not dead?' Tess whispered.

'No, he's not dead.'

'Oh, thank the Lord.' Tess physically sagged and Olivia held her up.

'He's been transferred from a French hospital and will arrive in London…' Mildred looked at Tess. 'The date is for tomorrow. He'll be in London tomorrow where he'll be assessed and transferred to either another hospital or a military command depot. Details to follow.'

'But how badly injured is he?' Tess demanded to know. 'And what's a command depot?'

Mr Thacker shouldered his satchel. 'I've been told, Mrs Hobson, that a military command depot is where they send soldiers who are recovering from their wounds, like a convalescent hospital.'

'Right, he's on his way home to England then.' Tess gathered herself. 'He's hurt, but he's coming home.'

Mr Thacker gave Tess another envelope, not an official one.

'I can't read it.' Tess gave it straight to Mildred.

Mildred quickly opened it and read the letter. 'This letter is from a VAD nurse, Miss Vera Daylesford. She writes that Colin has been in her care for the last two days at Etaples Base Hospital in France. Colin sustained a gunshot wound to the right thigh and some shrapnel penetrations to his chest. Colin begs her to write to you to let you know he is in good spirits. Colin will be shipped to England and asks you to visit him if you can once he's settled.'

'Oh, my boy!' Tess cried, hugging Olivia. 'He's coming home. I can go and see him.'

Mr Thacker nodded to them with a slight smile as though thankful the news wasn't as bad as they feared. He continued on his rounds.

'I shall make us a cup of tea,' Mildred declared as they went inside Olivia's front room.

Tess sat at the table in the kitchen, holding both letters. 'Colin can't be too badly injured if he's talking, can he? He's asked that nurse to write to us. He wants us to visit him.'

'It does sound positive,' Olivia agreed, cutting slices of sponge cake for them all. 'How kind it was for that nurse to write to you.'

'An angel that is what that nurse is,' Tess acknowledged. 'They're all angels, looking after our boys with such devotion, bless them all.'

'It makes me feel guilty for not becoming a nurse and helping,' Mildred said, mashing the tea. 'Unfortunately, I feel ill at the sight of blood.'

'You'd not make a good nurse then, Mrs Middleton,' Tess commented ironically.

'Indeed not, but I do make a very good cup of tea when the situation calls for it.' Mildred grinned and handed Tess a teacup and saucer. 'Milk and two sugars, Mrs Hobson, just as you like it.'

CHAPTER 12

Somme, France
End of September, 1916.

DIRT RAINED DOWN on Spencer's head as he hunkered low in a shell crater while bombs fell around him. The ground trembled as though hell was opening up beneath him ready to swallow him whole.

He and his company had been fighting for two weeks without a rest. Once one objective was taken or lost, they were ordered to another objective, another battle ground. Autumn had replaced the warmth of summer, and the fighting had intensified throughout September.

For the last two days they'd been in the thick of battle, advancing faster than expected, outrunning supplies and sometimes their own cover of artillery. Days and night blended, the will to survive the enemy's onslaught the only focus.

A pause in the shelling gave him a moment to listen. The cries of the wounded filtered across the broken ground, the ping of a bullet hitting a tin helmet was easily heard without the shells bursting. The acid smell of gunpowder invaded his nose. Carefully, he eased his head above the rim of the crater, his face inches from the dirt. Smoke fog hung in the air reducing visibility.

'Major!' Lieutenant Dawes slipped down the back of the crater. 'Are we to stand ground here, sir? Shall I get the men to dig in?'

Spencer slid back down to join him at the bottom. 'No, Lieutenant, we are to advance.'

'But that's madness. We have no artillery cover.'

'Our orders were to take the Transloy Ridges, and that is what we will do. We have Major Dunbar's company on our right flank and a company of New Zealanders on our left. We support them and they support us.'

Suddenly, a grating roar came from behind them. Confused, Spencer scrambled to the backside of the crater and peeped over the edge, Dawes joined him.

'Christ, what is that?' Dawes said with a tinge of fear as smoke blurred the surroundings.

Spencer smiled to himself, staring at the shadow of the huge steel monster that crawled over the uneven ground. 'That is a tank, Lieutenant.'

'A tank, sir?'

'Isn't she magnificent?' In awe Spencer watched the first tank he'd ever seen, only having heard about them in dispatches, slowly creep forward like a giant menacing turtle.

'I've not seen one in action, sir.' Dawes sniffed disparagingly. 'I don't think they'll be successful. Too slow. Too cumbersome.'

Spencer rolled his eyes. Dawes pessimism drove him to despair at times. 'The Germans don't know any of that though, do they? Come on. We can't let that have all the fun, can we?' Spencer blew his whistle, alerting his men to advance, and to prevent any further conversation from Dawes.

Scrambling up the slippery sides of the crater, Spencer spotted his men doing likewise from where they took cover, and they ran across the undulating holey ground which resembled the top of a crumpet.

In and out of shell holes, Spencer ran across No-Man's-Land, stopping often to help a man up who'd tripped.

They reached within the range of the German gunners, and a hail of bullets burst from the enemy trenches.

Bullets zipped into the dirt around them, some catching the soft flesh of soldiers. The men dropped to the ground, taking what little cover they could find.

Once more Spencer found himself in a large hole. At the edge of it, a dead German soldier lay staring blindly up at the sky.

Sergeant Matlock fell into the hole beside Spencer, breathing heavily from the run. 'Is this the original German line, sir?'

'I assume so, Sergeant.' Spencer checked his maps quickly as rain began to fall.

'Their trenches have been decimated, sir.'

'This front line has, yes, but the Germans will have only fallen back to their next line behind.' As if to prove Spencer's point, a fresh onslaught of enemy shells fell from the sky. 'Take cover!' Spencer yelled.

In a pause of shelling, Spencer quickly wrote on his notepad and tore off the top page, leaving the carbon copies underneath. 'Select a runner. This needs to reach HQ giving them our position.' He gave the note to Matlock who crept out of the shell hole and crawled crablike to another hole where several men took cover.

The shelling continued in earnest, pummelling the ground, sending up sprays of dirt like brown fountains. Spencer watched soldiers from the right flank advance. Abruptly, a burst of gunfire cut them down like ducks on a pond. They were Alfred's men. His gut clenched.

As the rain lessened, Spencer rose to his knees and blew his whistle. Alfred needed his help. 'Advance!' He kept blowing his whistle as the bombs exploded around him. 'Advance!'

He sprinted out of the hole through the drizzling mist towards the gunners. Along the line Spencer saw more men being hit and dropped, but he kept going, expecting a bullet at any moment. He shouted orders, blew his whistle and fired his pistol at any movement in front of him. Gaining ground, he saw the pointed helmets of the Germans above the trench.

He fell to his stomach, took aim and emptied his revolver at the helmets. Other soldiers landed beside him, and they put up a strong fight. Blasting the trench with everything they had.

'Grenades!' Spencer ordered, reloading his revolver before kneeling up to throw the first grenade into the trench. A bullet zipped into the dirt next to his legs, another cut through his sleeve, missing his arm.

'Get down, sir.' A private pulled him to the ground as more bullets pinged into the dirt nearby.

The drizzle turned to rain once more as the men threw grenades into the trenches. Spencer noticed one of the German machine guns had jammed. The German soldiers around it where doing all they could to make it work again. Taking advantage of their distraction, Spencer charged the gun post, jumping down into the trench. He kicked the first soldier closest to him in the chest, pushing him backwards and then shot him.

Alerted, another German soldier scrambled for his rifle. Spencer shot him in the head. The two gunners raised their arms above their heads. 'No shoot! Tommy! No shoot!'

Spencer indicated with his gun for them to move away from the machine gun.

Matlock jumped into the trench beside him, his rifle on the two Germans. 'They're surrendering along the line, sir.'

One by one his men clambered down into the German trench, their rifles poised in readiness for a counter-attack. Rain dripped off their tin helmets.

'Sergeant, have a detail round up the prisoners,' Spencer ordered. Dawes was further down the trench reading paperwork from a dugout. 'Lieutenant!' Spencer marched up to him, furious. 'Now isn't the time for reading!'

'We could learn the enemy's movements,' Dawes defended.

'You can read German, can you?' Spencer snapped.

'No, but there are maps, sir.'

Snatching the papers from Dawes, Spencer struggled to keep his temper. 'Secure this trench. I want sentries every ten yards. Select men to guard the prisoners. The dead and wounded need to be listed and cared for. Do your job, Lieutenant!'

Spencer spent the next five minutes writing notes for runners to take to HQ. They'd outrun all artillery and were low on ammunition.

'Sergeant Matlock, tell the men it's rations only until further orders,' Spencer told him as he made an inspection of the captured trench.

'Aye, sir. Some of the men have found a bit of German food, sausages and the like which has cheered them up.'

'Drink?'

'A few bottles of wine, some of rum, sir.'

'Have it all brought to me. I'll not have the men drunk.'

'Yes, sir.'

'I want the wounded assisted.'

'Do you wish for a burial party to be organised?'

Sadly, Spencer shook his head. 'We've no time for that. We have to be ready for a counter-attack or fresh orders. Have the wounded collected and made comfortable until medics arrive.'

Spencer stared out at the ground they'd covered and the number of dead men littering the fields. He turned away from the sight as the rain came in waves across the landscape in a grey curtain.

'A runner, sir.' A private on sentry indicated to the runner coming from the right flank.

Spencer went to meet the soldier. Suddenly, a shell dropped

just behind the trench. He swore. The German artillery was attacking. 'Take cover!'

Crouching low in the trench, the runner made it to him, panting and from his pocket pulled out a note.

Spencer took it and noticed the blood smear on the corner. 'Are you injured, private?'

'No, sir. The blood is from Major Dunbar. It's his note.'

Spence

I'm done for
Bullet to the chest
Wanted you to know
Valued friendship,
Alfred

Spencer's stomach constricted. He closed his eyes momentarily. 'Where is Major Dunbar?'

'We have him in a dugout, sir. He's handed control of the company over to Captain Woods.'

'Will he survive until the medics arrive?' Spencer asked hopefully, having to shout as more shells burst close to the trench and mud fell on them.

'I doubt it, sir. I'm surprised he didn't die on the spot. A machine gun got him as he led the charge. Dropped him like a log.'

Emotion burned inside Spencer, but he couldn't give into it or even acknowledge it. Not yet.

Spencer quickly wrote on his notepad.

Do not give up!

Medics on their way.

Buy you a drink!
Friendship valued.
Spence

SPENCER THRUST the note into the private's hand. 'Go, be as quick as you can. Stay low.'

Within the hour, orders from HQ came fast. They were to hold their positions and defend any counter-attacks.

Just before midnight, sitting in a dugout cold and damp, Spencer tried to get some sleep. He'd been awake for twenty-four hours for the fourth time in seven days. A similar pattern repeated from the week before. Exhaustion was eating away his strength, physically and mentally. The shelling had stopped, but like his men he was wet, tired and hungry. He also knew that come morning the shelling would begin again. The battle was far from over.

'Sir.' Bishop, his batman, entered the dugout. 'A runner just brought this.' He gave the note to Spencer.

Without enthusiasm he read it.

MAJOR ALFRED DUNBAR died at 20:08 hrs.

SPENCER THANKED Bishop and folded the note into his pocket. He stood and donned his waterproof cape.

'Sir?' Bishop enquired.

He stepped out into the muddy trench. 'I shall take a walk, Bishop, check on the sentries.' He didn't have to do the task, he had officers to do it, but since sleeping now was impossible, he might as well show his face to the men and give them a word of encouragement.

For as long as possible he had to put off accepting Alfred was dead.

Alfred, his army friend since the Boer War.

Alfred, who'd always managed to make him laugh, or to see sense, or offer him a drink from his hip flask.

Alfred, who'd rushed the German trench just as he'd done.

Alfred, who'd taken the hit that could have easily been his...

Suddenly the whine of an incoming shell broke the silence of the night. It exploded in the field just beyond the trench, showering mud and stones over the men.

Spencer reached for his whistle as another shell burst further along the trench blowing up several men stationed there. Bodies went up into the air and landed in pieces like scattered confetti.

Spencer ran, whistling, shouting to the men to take cover. More shells landed, rocking the ground, jolting him to his knees. He staggered up and was hit by a flying arm torn from a soldier in a blast. Another shell struck the side of the trench just yards from where he'd originally been sitting. Then he heard the roaring. In the darkness, the advancing Germans yelled as they charged. 'Stand to!' Spencer shouted until his throat hurt, flinging himself against the trench wall, his pistol aimed into the gloom of the night as the enemy bore down on them.

CHAPTER 13

Feeling irritable, Olivia cursed under her breath at the dropped stitch she'd just done. The scarf she knitted for Lachie was straight forward enough, but her mind wasn't on knitting.

She'd not heard from Spencer in two weeks. The longest she'd ever gone without a letter from him. Mildred told her not to worry, that he just might be in an area where the post doesn't reach frequently. There was bound to be a simple explanation, but none of Mildred's sensible words soothed Olivia's frayed nerves.

Also, the baby hadn't arrived, and it was now the first week of October, past the due date Dr Whittaker told her of late September.

She was tired of having a large stomach, of not being nimble on her feet, of every chore taking so long to do. She was used to rushing about, getting things done quickly and moving onto the next task. She was tired of waiting!

Mildred stood in the doorway between the front room and the kitchen. 'I've hung the washing on the inside rack. It looks like rain outside. It's grey and miserable.'

Olivia nodded, feeling the same as the weather, totally miserable. She adjusted her position on the chair by the fire, the constant ache in her back driving her slowly insane. No matter how she sat or where she sat, there wasn't any relief from the ache. Even in bed at night, she tossed and turned uncomfortably, unable to settle into a position that eased the ache in her lower back.

Mildred added more coal to the fire in the front room. 'I'm deciding whether to go to the post office now or wait and see if the rain starts. Although we do need a few things from the market. We are low on tea, sugar and soap.' Satisfied the fire was glowing adequately, Mildred straightened and turned to Olivia. 'Can you think of anything else we need? I thought we could have fish and chips later? Or I could see if the butcher has some pork chops?'

'I don't mind. Fish and chips are fine. You enjoy them.'

'Well, yes, I admit I do. I've never had them until coming to live here. We didn't have such a shop in the village.'

'I don't feel like cooking today.' Olivia put her knitting aside, fed up with it.

'And I'm dreadful at it, to my shame.' Mildred laughed. 'I wish I had learnt to cook though. It's a convenient skill to possess. My father always had a cook and Ralph employs one…'

Voices outside made Olivia push herself up off the chair just as the door opened and Tess walked in. 'Tess! You're back!'

'Aye, lass, I am. I thought to check in on you first to see if that baby has arrived, but I can clearly see it hasn't.'

'No, I don't think it's ever coming out! You've been gone for six days. I thought you'd only be gone for three at the most.'

'Aye, that's what we thought but Colin's hospital is not far from the sea, and he was recovering so well they gave him permission to come with us for a couple of days and we stayed in a hotel right on the seafront.' Tess looked happier than she had for some time. She had colour in her cheeks and her spirit was high.

'How is your son, Mrs Hobson?' Mildred asked.

'Oh, he's doing really well, Mrs Middleton. He's hobbling about on crutches, but the doctors are happy with the way his injuries are healing. I'll tell you all about it in a minute. I'll just go next door and take my coat off. Larry and the boys are off to the pub.' Tess went out again.

'I'll put the kettle on,' Mildred said to Olivia.

The pain in her back forced Olivia to bend over and rub her lower back. It was maddening how the simple act of standing straight seemed impossible to her right now.

Mr Thacker's whistling had her scurrying to open her door. He posted a letter through Sadie's door, and still whistling merrily, nodded to Olivia but didn't stop. She watched him carry onto Mrs Muldoon's house.

Worried that something wasn't right with Spencer, she paced the front room, wondering what she could do.

Tess returned minutes later, holding a small brown paper bag. 'I've brought you and Mrs Middleton some sweets from the seaside, lass.'

'Thank you.'

Tess frowned. 'What's wrong, lass?'

'Another day of not hearing from Spencer, that's what's wrong,' she said, angrily. 'Something isn't right.'

'He's still not written?' Tess came closer. 'I've been gone a week. I thought for sure he'd have written by now.'

'Two weeks, Tess! Two weeks of silence.'

'I'm sure that's normal,' Mildred said, carrying in a tea tray.

'It's not normal, not for Spencer and me. Two letters a week I've had since the start of the war, sometimes three letters if he was at rest and had plenty of time to write.' Olivia continued to pace, bent over, getting more scared and angrier by the minute. 'It's so frustrating not knowing what is happening.'

She stopped pacing. 'I need to send a telegram to Stanford. He'll find out what's going on, and maybe one to Mr Parkinson as well. Mr Parkinson knows everyone and everything.'

'Nay, lass. Steady on.' Tess held up her hand. 'If there was owt to report, Mr Middleton or Mr Parkinson would have done so by now.'

'I've told her that repeatedly,' Mildred said quietly. 'We went to the cinema last night and saw a newsreel, which mentioned the current battles being fought. Spencer might be involved in those.'

Olivia turned on her. 'Or he could be dead somewhere, his body blown to pieces.'

Mildred and Tess gasped.

'Or he could be knocked senseless and in some foreign hospital or he could be a prisoner of war!' she shouted. 'We don't know!' She tried to pace the room, but her legs felt stiff, her back spasming.

'Lass, calm down.' Tess's gentle tone had the opposite effect.

'I don't want to calm down, Tess! I want to rage and scream. I want my husband here, with me! We've had just days together! I don't want any more letters from him, I want him *home* with *me!*' she raged, not understanding the violence of her feelings at the moment.

'Aye, lass, course you do.' Tess took her arm. 'Come and sit down.'

'I don't want to sit down!' Suddenly, water seeped between her legs, soaking through her drawers and petticoat and skirt. 'Oh!'

'Aye, I thought so.' Tess nodded wisely. 'You weren't being yourself. It happens to some women, they go a little mad when they are about to give birth. Some clean like the very devil, others go quiet and then there's those who act totally unlike themselves.' She raised her eyebrows at Olivia.

Olivia didn't know what to say or do next.

'Dearest,' Mildred stepped to her, compassion on her face. 'Shall we go upstairs and get you into bed?'

'I'll fetch Mrs Anderson,' Tess said.

'And Doctor Whittaker,' Mildred suggested.

A pain wrapped around Olivia's stomach like a vice. She sank to her knees with a guttural groan.

Mildred squeaked.

'I'll stay and help you get her up to bed,' Tess said to Mildred. 'We need to strip it and then cover the mattress with newspapers and an old sheet. Have you been saving the newspapers like I suggested?'

'Yes, Mrs Hobson. I have.' Mildred nodded. 'They are under the kitchen sink.'

'Then we're going to need towels and some warm water and soap.'

Another pain gripped Olivia fiercely from the inside, drawing her chin to her chest at the force of it.

'Lass, stand up now.' Tess took one elbow and Mildred the other.

'I don't think I can,' she murmured, panting. Another pain came quickly, and she smothered a moan.

'Christ Almighty, her pains are close together.' Tess hauled Olivia up. 'Come on, lass. Up the stairs.'

Olivia shuffled a couple of steps before she felt something heavy and low between her legs. She stiffened in fear. 'I can't, Tess! I can't walk!'

'All right now,' Tess soothed gently. 'Just stay calm, that's it, my lass. Nice and calm.'

'What's happening?'

'You're having a baby, lass,' Tess joked. 'How long have you been having pains for?'

'I haven't, not really. Just lower back pain for days.'

Mildred rubbed her back in soothing strokes. 'Olivia has been terribly uncomfortable since yesterday. Unable to sit still.'

'She was in labour,' Tess declared.

Another contraction sent Olivia to her knees again. She cried out in agony.

'Sweet Jesus. She's going to have this baby down here.' Tess burst into action. 'Mrs Middleton, help me get her onto the floor.'

They laid Olivia down on the rug in front of the fire.

'Run to a neighbour and get them to find Mrs Anderson. She lives on Jacob's Well Lane,' Tess told Mildred. 'Hurry!'

Olivia gripped the edge of the rug as another pain ripped through her.

'Let's get these clothes off you, lass.' Tess found a folded blanket on the sofa that Olivia and Mildred shared over their knees while knitting at night. Tess undressed her, taking off her wet drawers, the petticoat and her skirt and left her shift, pregnancy corset and blouse on. She covered her lower body with the blanket. 'Right, lass, I'll just go and get the newspapers to put under you.'

Olivia didn't care about the newspapers. The intense urge to push took over and her body made all the decisions. She brought her knees up and pushed, growling deep in her chest. She rested a moment, eyes closed.

Tess rushed back in and put the newspapers under her bottom as Mildred re-entered the house.

'Mrs Muldoon wasn't at home, but Mrs Berry has gone to fetch the midwife and Doctor Whittaker.' Mildred panted as though she'd run a mile. 'Oh, goodness.' She knelt down beside Olivia and took her hand. 'You look in so much pain, dear Olivia.'

'Aye, that's what childbirth is all about, Mrs Middleton,' Tess said in her no-nonsense way. 'It's painful and undignified. Brutal. There's nowt pretty about it.'

Needing to push, Olivia put all her strength into getting the baby out.

'That's it, lass. God above, I can see the head already.' Tess knelt between Olivia's legs, her face full of concern.

'Tess?' Olivia didn't like the look on Tess's face. 'What's wrong?'

'Nowt, lass. It's just that I've never done this before. I've always been at your end, not this end.' Tess gave her a wink of reassurance.

Olivia held onto her legs and pushed as another pain seemed to tear through her groin. She strained, feeling the heat in her face.

'Shouldn't we wait until the midwife arrives?' Mildred asked innocently.

Tess chuckled. 'There ain't no baby in this world who'll wait patiently for a midwife. Babies come when they come.'

Olivia felt a hot burning pain and cried out. 'It hurts!'

Mildred started crying silently. 'She needs help, Mrs Hobson.'

'No, she needs this baby out.' Tess concentrated on the baby. 'Steady now, lass.'

Olivia strained, pushing hard. Abruptly, she felt a release, a wash of fluid and the pressure was gone and replaced by the wail of a baby.

'It's out!' Tess crowed, frantically wiping the baby with a towel.

'You've done it, Olivia!' Mildred cried more tears. 'Oh, thank you God and all his angels.'

'Is it all right?' So many emotions circled Olivia's head as the pain receded slightly.

'Aye, he's a fine handsome little man. Let me see to his cord now.' Tess tied the cord with thread from the sewing basket and cut it. She swaddled him in a towel. 'Here you are, lass.' She handed him to Olivia.

She took the bundle to her chest and gazed down at the little pink face and the blood-matted hair. 'A boy?'

'He certainly is.' Tess knelt back, her expression one of relief and joy. 'Well done, lass.'

In awe, Olivia stared down at her son and saw a glimpse of Spencer and her heart ached.

Mildred wiped her tears. 'He is such a miracle. A precious gift.'

Olivia gently touched her son's cheek with a finger. 'He's actually here. Thank you both for everything. I was so scared.'

'You and me both!' Tess declared with a grin.

'I'm very grateful.' Olivia squeezed her hand in thanks.

'How about a cup of tea, Mrs Middleton?' Tess asked Mildred.

'Yes, absolutely.' Mildred smiled and kissed the top of Olivia's head. 'I'm so proud of you.' She rose and stepped into the kitchen.

'Well, lass, you did a magnificent job for your first time. Clever lass.' Tess patted Olivia's knee. 'There's the afterbirth to deliver, but it can take a little while.'

As she spoke the door opened and Mrs Anderson walked in carrying her bag. 'Ah, I've missed all the excitement!'

'You did, Mrs Anderson, you did.' Tess grinned.

'And you've done me out of my fee, Mrs Hobson.' Mrs Anderson smiled good-naturedly.

Tess gripped the arm of the chair and hauled herself up off the floor. 'There's the afterbirth, Mrs Anderson. I'll leave that in your capable hands.'

'I'm too old to be getting down on the floor. Happen we might take Mrs Middleton upstairs to bed?' Mrs Anderson suggested.

'Aye, good idea. I'll fetch me husband, Larry, from the pub and he can carry her up.'

Olivia wanted to protest she could walk but the thought of getting up seemed nigh on impossible at that present moment.

'Let me have a look at your baby, Mrs Middleton. I'll give him the once over for you.' Mrs Anderson held out her arms.

She looked down at her son, not wanting to part with him. She felt a twinge low in her pelvis and grimaced.

'Ah.' Mrs Anderson sighed. 'Happen we'll sort out this afterbirth first after all.'

Mildred brought the tea tray in just as Mrs Anderson delivered the afterbirth. Mildred turned a pale shade of green at the sight of it and hastily made a retreat back to the kitchen.

Olivia closed her eyes, tired and exhausted, while Mrs Anderson cleaned her and rolled up the bloodied newspapers which she put straight into the fire.

Tess returned with Larry and Mildred once more ventured into the front room with the tea tray.

'A little fella then, Liv?' Larry asked, wearing a wide grin. 'Congratulations. Does he have a name?'

'He does. In Spencer's family the first-born son is named after the maternal grandmother's surname. So, this little one is to be called after my mother's family name.' She beamed down at his sweet little face. 'Meet Bailey Spencer Middleton.'

Tess pulled a face. 'Bailey? Different I suppose.'

'It's a fine name,' Mildred murmured tenderly.

'And Bailey's godparents are Mr Parkinson, our Lachie…' She turned to Mildred. 'Mr and Mrs Mildred Middleton and…' She glanced at Tess. 'Mrs Tess Hobson.'

Mildred started crying once more while Tess beamed as though she'd found a treasure chest.

'I ain't ever been a godparent before,' Tess admitted.

'Nor I.' Mildred wiped her eyes with a handkerchief.

Olivia smiled, contented to have brought them such happiness. 'A telegram must be sent to Spencer, and Stanford, and Spencer's family in Paris and Mr Parkinson.'

'I'll do it all in the morning,' Mildred said, glancing at the clock. 'The post office will be closed now. It's past six o'clock.'

'As lovely as all this chatter is…' Mrs Anderson picked up her bag. 'It's time mother and baby were made comfortable. Mr Hobson will you carry Mrs Middleton up to bed for me, please? And could one of the godmothers organise a bath for Master Middleton?'

Mildred swooped on the baby faster than Tess. 'Come along,

my little sweet godson. Aunty Mildred will hold you while Aunty Tess fills up the sink so we can give you a bath and freshen you up.'

'Oh, I'm doing the donkey work, am I?' Tess protested with a laugh. 'I'll be lucky if I ever get to hold this one. He's got two mothers it looks like.' She grinned at Olivia as Larry carried her past.

'Then he's a lucky boy indeed,' Olivia replied sleepily. She was desperate to write to Spencer, but tiredness won, and she rested her head against Larry's chest.

'You all right, lass?' Larry whispered, climbing the stairs.

'I am. Just tired and a bit sore.'

'You get some sleep then, lass, and let those two downstairs take care of the baby. He'll be wanting you soon enough.' Larry laid her on the bed.

Snuggling into the pillow, she heard Mrs Anderson bustling about her, making her comfortable and telling her about breast-feeding. The old woman's words became muted and then there was nothing but the blankness of deep sleep. Her last thought was of Spencer and how happy he'd be to know Bailey had arrived safely and that both she and the baby were fine. He should have been here to celebrate…

CHAPTER 14

November 1916

Carrying Bailey in one arm, Olivia put away the food that had arrived in the hamper Stanford sent. In the four weeks since Bailey's birth, Stanford had sent a hamper of food each week and to celebrate the safe arrival of his grandson. Stanford had also sent an array of baby products he bought and arranged to be delivered a few days after Bailey was born.

In amazement, Mildred had come up to Olivia's bedroom and told her what had arrived. An expensive pram so big it only just fit through the door and it filled the small front room, a wooden cot, mattress and sheets, a large selection of baby clothes in varying sizes, a dozen napkins and safety pins, a silver hairbrush and comb set, a small baby bath, white soft towels and a glass feeding bottle with rubber teats and a can of Nestlé milk powder in case Bailey couldn't feed properly at the breast. It was all very thoughtful and a little overwhelming.

From Egypt where he was on official war business, Parky had

sent a small gem-incrusted silver box lined in blue velvet with Bailey's initials engraved on the lid. While Olivia's former mistress and Spencer's grandmother, Seraphina, had sent a parcel of finest lawn baby garments and ten pounds with a letter of congratulations written in a shaky hand. Anthea had sent a similar letter and a gift of French lace and a knitted bonnet and booties.

'Here, let me do that.' Mildred came into the kitchen and took the jar of orange marmalade out of Olivia's hands.

'I can do it. There's washing to hang out.'

Peering outside through the window, Mildred shook her head. 'It's starting to rain. I'll hang the washing up on the racks.' She spoke of the drying racks suspended from the ceiling in the kitchen.

Sitting at the kitchen table, Olivia fed Bailey at the breast. The glass bottle and milk powder sat forgotten in the cupboard unused. Little Bailey drank his mother's milk well and slept soundly after each feed. Doctor Whittaker told Olivia that Bailey was doing splendidly, and that's what she reported to Spencer in every letter she sent.

However, in the four weeks since giving birth, she'd only heard from Spencer twice. One letter had crossed hers with the news of the birth and so it was the second letter she received from him which made her cry. Spencer's love poured out with every word. He was so proud of her and couldn't wait to meet his son. But that letter had arrived last week and nothing since. She was beginning to worry at the length of time between letters.

Mildred took a box of candied fruits out of the hamper. 'As much as I appreciate Stanford sending us these hampers, I do wish he'd put more useful things inside for us to eat. I'd much prefer a pound of tea, or flour, or a sack of potatoes, a few turnips and a string of onions.'

Olivia laughed. 'You're sounding like one of the housewives on this square. When did you become so working class?'

'When I had to learn to cook and clean as we do.' Mildred huffed. 'I'm no longer a lady of leisure with servants.'

'Do you regret coming here?'

'Not at all. How could I when I have such a wonderful relationship with you? You are like a sister to me, and then there's this sweet darling boy, whom I adore.' Mildred shook her head. 'No, coming here saved my sanity and gave me perspective that I was lacking, despite thinking the opposite. It's one thing to visit the poor, totally another to live amongst them.'

'When Ralph comes home, and you return to your parish duties, you'll have a new viewpoint to how others live and work.'

'Absolutely.' Mildred didn't sound enthusiastic.

'Ralph will come home. They all will. We have to believe that.'

'I pray for it daily. Did you reply to Mr Parkinson's letter?' Mildred asked, changing the subject and putting a plum pudding in the cupboard.

'I did. I answered it this morning.' Olivia watched Bailey suck. 'I told him that I understood he couldn't make it to the christening, with him being in Egypt.'

'I'll post the letter for you in the morning.' Mildred placed a tin of shortbread on the side near the sugar cannister. 'I wrote to Ralph last night after I went up to bed.'

Olivia gazed at her sadly. Ralph and Mildred's lack of letters to each other was noticeable. She wished she could help them come back together and be happy. Since moving into this house, Mildred had lost weight and looked the better for it. Since Bailey's birth she did all the cleaning, shopping and cooking, but Olivia was starting to help again now she had recovered from the birth.

Last week, at Olivia's insistence, Mildred had bought new clothes to show off her new figure. Mildred always wore dark colours befitting a vicar's wife, or so she thought, but Olivia and Tess had assured her that wearing lighter colours was allowed and encouraged her to pick skirts in the colours of dove grey, soft caramel, sea green and dusky rose. Matched with white and cream lace blouses, Mildred looked younger, slimmer and even allowed Sadie to cut and style her hair in a softer arrangement about her head.

The transformation had been astonishing to the whole square. Olivia expected Ralph would be just as surprised if he was to see his wife now. 'Ralph will be pleased to hear from you.'

'Will he? I've shown you his letters. He writes to me as though I am a friend, an acquaintance he must answer for politeness's sake.'

'I'm sure that's not how he feels at all.' Though Olivia wasn't totally convinced of that.

'When you read Spencer's letters to me, the love he feels for you is in every word. Even when he mentions details of the war, the conditions, he does so in such a way that you are there with him, to share it, to experience what he is going through.' Mildred stared down at the tin of apricots she held. 'Spencer wants you to be a part of his world. Ralph is the opposite. He is so formally polite. He asks after my health. He talks of the weather. He mentions the countryside he walks through or the people he meets as though he is a guide. There is no passion in anything he writes.'

'Do you still love him, Mildred?' she asked bluntly.

'I do, yes.'

Olivia sat Bailey on her knee to burp him. 'Then its time you showed him.'

'How?'

'What did you write in the letter last night?'

'I told him that you are well, and Bailey is growing and is such a beautiful baby. I told him Mrs Hobson's son Colin has returned to France, though not to fight as yet, and that the sermon at St Andrew's on Sunday was most interesting and I told him what hymns we sung. I wrote I was in good health—'

'Gracious me. You're as bad as each other!' Olivia laughed.

'What kind of letter is that to a husband? It's boring. Ralph might be a vicar but he's also a man. He's your husband. You shared a bed, were passionate, surely?'

'Well, yes, in our way.' Mildred's face reddened.

'Remind him of that.'

'Oh, I couldn't.' Mildred turned away. 'I couldn't write such intimate details.'

'Why? Who is going to see it besides Ralph? Remind him he has a wife waiting for him who loves him, needs him.'

'No.' Mildred put the apricots on the cupboard shelf. 'I do not have your talent for such openness.'

'Do you want to exist in a marriage that is polite?'

Sighing, Mildred closed the hamper lid. 'I want what you and Spencer share. On your wedding day you both looked at each other with such... longing. The world around you didn't matter, you only had eyes for each other.'

Olivia remembered the burning desire that consumed her that wedding evening when Spencer undressed her. 'I surrendered to my feelings, Mildred. Spencer was in no doubt of how I felt about him in every way.'

'How lucky you are to be so free with your emotions.'

'You can be as well.'

'You and Spencer have been apart longer than you've been together but your letters to each other fill in the gaps and build a strong bond. I sincerely doubt Ralph and I will ever have such devotion to each other.'

'That makes me terribly sad to hear those words, Mildred. You both must have been deeply in love when you first married?'

'I suppose we were, or at least I was, only, Ralph and I have never been very demonstrative towards each other. We care about the other, but there is a lack of...'

'Desire?'

'Yes, I suppose that is a good description.' Mildred looked at Bailey. 'I was desperate for a family of my own.'

'And Ralph?'

'I shouldn't put words into his mouth, but I expect he was desperate for a warm loving home, something he's lacked because his mother died so young, and Stanford was mired in grief. I provided a comfortable home, and I was as devoted to his causes as he was. A perfect fit it seemed.'

'Except emotions and feelings come into play.'

'And my failure to carry a child.' Mildred touched a fingertip to Bailey's soft hair.

'You mustn't give up.' Olivia clasped Mildred's arm. 'Fetch some paper and pen and we'll write another letter to him. One that shows your love.'

Mildred hesitated. 'I wouldn't know how to start.'

Olivia put Bailey to the other breast to suckle. 'After two years of writing passionate letters to Spencer, I can show you.'

They heard the front door open, and Tess came in, raindrops glistening on her coat. 'I've just heard that Mr Thacker has been sent his papers. He'll not be delivering our post anymore.'

'But I thought he had bad eyesight and that's why he was refused at the beginning of the war?' Olivia laid Bailey on the opposite chair and changed his wet napkin for a clean one.

'Aye, well, the War Office has changed its mind it seems and now they'll take anyone, even those who can't see anything a hundred yards away like Thacker.'

'No more of his whistling,' Mildred murmured.

Olivia adjusted Bailey's clothes. 'Who has replaced Mr Thacker, do you know?'

'Oh, some young Post Office lass,' Tess said dismissively. 'She's the one who told me just now outside.'

'We've not got any mail then?' Olivia's shoulders sagged.

'No, none of us got owt.' Tess took Bailey from Olivia to give him a cuddle.

The front door opened again, and Olivia expected a neighbour. When no one came through into the kitchen, she moved from the table to see into the front room and stifled a scream.

Spencer stood with his hand still on the doorknob as if unsure what to do next. A misty rain fell behind him.

'Spencer?' Olivia made to run to him, but something stopped her. Her heart somersaulted in her chest. Spencer didn't look the same. He'd lost weight, he was unshaven, his skin held a grey hue to it, and he had a weeping wound under his left ear. He was covered in mud, his greatcoat and boots thick with it.

He raised his eyes to her, and they were haunted, dull. Rain dripped off his officer's cap.

Olivia felt Mildred and Tess stand behind her. Mildred gasped.

Spencer held out his hand towards Olivia in desperation.

She ran to him as he collapsed. His weight bowed her down, but Mildred hurried to help her.

'Get him on the sofa,' Olivia said, her arms wrapped about him as Spencer staggered.

'I'll go for Doctor Whittaker! I'll take Bailey to Mrs Muldoon.' Tess ran out with the baby into the rain.

'Spencer needs to be in bed.' Mildred strained to hold him up.

'Yes, yes.' Olivia swallowed her shock, and, with Mildred's help, they shuffled and strained to get him up the stairs and into her bedroom which was warm from the fire that glowed in the grate.

'I shall hold him, while you take off that muddy wet coat,' Mildred instructed, using all her strength to hold Spencer up as he swayed.

Rushing, Olivia shrugged off his greatcoat, took off his hat and pulled back the blankets on her bed. She and Mildred sat him on the bed, and she quickly pulled off his filthy boots and socks. He stank of earth, wet wool, body odour and gunpowder.

'Get his jacket and trousers off, Olivia,' Mildred instructed, untying Spencer's tie.

'Olivia?' Spencer's eyes rolled back and he went limp, falling back on the bed, making the task of removing his trousers even more difficult.

'Is he breathing?' Mildred whispered shakily.

Olivia tensed and leant down to place her ear to his face. Ever so gently she felt his breath on her cheek. She let out a sigh and straightened. 'Yes.'

She pulled the blankets over him and then sank onto the bed beside him to hold his cold hand. 'Rest now, my love. You're home.' She gently kissed his cheek. He didn't move.

'How could they have let him travel in such a state? He needs to be in hospital.' Mildred collected the filthy boots and clothes. 'I'll take these down to clean and bring up a hot-water bottle.'

Olivia sat beside Spencer for the next twenty minutes until Doctor Whittaker arrived. She moved aside so the older man could examine Spencer. He tutted constantly as he inspected every part of Spencer's body.

Finally, he washed his hands in the basin on the chest of drawers and dried them on a small white towel. 'I shall be writing to the medical board about this. The major and so many soldiers like him are returning home in such terrible states. I understand the hospitals are bursting with wounded but to allow fighting men to stumble home barely alive to frighten their families is not to be tolerated.'

'He will live though,' Olivia prompted, barely able to say the words.

'He should be in hospital, Mrs Middleton. But I dare say he will be no better off there in his weakened condition.' The old doctor turned to her with a steely glare. 'Can you nurse him?'

'Yes.' There was no doubt in her mind.

'You have a month-old baby.'

'I have help.'

'Your husband will require around the clock care for days, possibly longer.'

'And he will get it.'

'Yes, I am confident he will, far better than he would in a hospital already stretched to their limits.'

'What exactly is wrong with him?'

'Exhaustion mainly, slight malnutrition, and the hideous effects of war, Mrs Middleton.' Doctor Whittaker exhaled heavily. 'I've been to many a household recently where the son or husband has returned and been in poor health, physically and mentally.'

'What do I need to do?'

'Let him sleep. Sleep will heal his body. When he wakes, feed him good food, don't let him go more than four hours without a decent meal inside of him, plenty of fluids. A bed bath first though to make him more comfortable.' Doctor Whittaker frowned. 'He's likely got lice. It's a plague in the trenches over there. Strip him and wash everything.' He steepled his fingers together. 'I saw no evidence of trench foot. He does have a wound to his neck which I've washed with iodine. He has some cuts and abrasions on his arms, face and chest, be careful of those when you wash him. I'll leave you this bottle of iodine.' From his black bag he took out a small brown bottle.

'Thank you, Doctor.'

'I shall notify the war medical board and other necessary officials. Major Middleton needs to be assessed by them, and they will determine his care and when he can return to his duties.'

Olivia swallowed at the mention of Spencer going back to France. She'd only just got him home.

'I shall call again tomorrow. Send for me should your husband seem to worsen. I don't think he will. He's a strong man, and I imagine was in good health before the war. Care and comfort will see him right again.'

'I appreciate you coming so swiftly.'

At the door, the doctor glanced back at Spencer. 'I wish the major was my only such case, alas, he isn't. Men arrive home silent and fatigued beyond their limits. Usually, the love of family, sleep and good food recover them sufficiently enough.' He shook his head in dismay. 'When will it all end?' He walked out.

Olivia didn't see him out, knowing Mildred would. She sat beside Spencer and studied him properly now the shock of seeing him in such a state had worn off. She would do whatever it took to get him in good health again.

Downstairs she heard voices and Bailey grizzling. She kissed Spencer's lips. 'I'll go down and see to our son, my love, but I'll be back shortly and give you a bath.'

In the kitchen she found Mildred holding Bailey while Tess sponged down Spencer's greatcoat and Mrs Muldoon heated pans of water.

'The doctor said Spencer needs a bed bath,' Mildred said.

'Yes.' Olivia took Bailey and hugged him to her, finding it difficult to accept that Spencer lay upstairs.

'Are you up to doing it, lass?' Tess asked. 'I can help you. He'll be too heavy for one person to turn over.'

Olivia nodded, her mind wandering in different directions. 'I should send a telegram to Stanford and let him know Spencer is here.'

'I'll do it now and I'll go to the shops and buy more food to make broth and wholesome stews for Spencer. Tess will teach me how, won't you, Mrs Honson?' Mildred grabbed her woollen hat and winter coat hanging on the back door.

'Aye, of course. We'll feed the major up!'

'Shall I take the baby back home with me, Olivia?' Mrs Muldoon asked. 'My girls will make a fuss of him when they are home from school.'

'Do you mind?' Olivia kissed Bailey's forehead. 'I fed him about an hour ago. He's not due for a while, but if he gets too fussy, bring him back and I'll feed him.' Olivia went to the baby's clothes basket in the corner. 'Here are some napkins and a change of clothes. He's usually a good baby and normally just sleeps unless he's hungry and then he'll certainly let me know about it.'

Mrs Muldoon smiled, tucking the items under her arm and taking Bailey from Olivia. 'I've had six babies, and, like Tess here, there's not much I don't know about looking after them.'

'Yes, of course.' She gazed tenderly at her son. 'Be good.'

'Right, lass. Let's get your man cleaned up, shall we?' Tess carried a basin of warm water.

Olivia grabbed another basin and followed her upstairs.

In the bedroom, Spencer hadn't moved. The weak daylight highlighted the hollows on his handsome face. His brown hair usually so shiny with health lay dull and flat against his skull. His tanned skin from spending years outside in the hot countries where he served had lost its glow and looked sallow.

'Poor lad,' Tess mumbled. 'What has he been through?'

'I dread to think.' Olivia wanted to cry at the weakened sight of him but dared not. He needed her strength more than ever.

Tess put the basin on a chair. 'I don't think we should wash his hair, it might give him a chill, but we can use the nit comb and kill any lice we see. We can give the rest of him a good scrub.'

'I'll fetch some soap and towels.' Olivia went out onto the landing cupboard to fetch what they needed and returned beside the bed. Tess had pulled back the blankets. 'Stoke the fire up, lass. We don't want him getting cold.'

They worked solidly for two hours, washing him thoroughly, ridding him of the stain of war, the filth of living in the trenches. They cleaned his cuts carefully and then applied more iodine and fresh bandages. Together they rolled him to one side and then the other, cleaning back and front before stripping the bed and remaking it. In all that time Spencer never woke. He was like a rag doll placed where they put him so deeply did he sleep.

At the end of it, Olivia and Tess were tired and went downstairs for a cup of tea. Mildred had returned, baskets bulging with food products.

'I'll start making a beef broth.' Mildred unpacked her shopping. 'Beef broth is always best for invalids. Gentle on their stomachs. It's the one thing I know how to make well, something my mother taught me. When she did her rounds of the parish, as a proper vicar's wife should, she always took pots of beef broth for those who were ill.'

'Did you send the telegram?' Olivia asked, her back aching from bending over for so long.

'I did. The postmaster said he'll send a messenger to us straight away should he receive a telegram in reply.'

Mrs Muldoon came in with a crying Bailey. 'I think he's hungry, Liv. He's slept the whole time but just woke now and I think he wants the one thing I can't give him.'

'Thank you, Mrs Muldoon.' She took the baby from her neighbour and put him straight to her breast which tingled on hearing him crying. Soon, Bailey was sucking contentedly.

'He knows what he wants does that one,' Tess commented, sipping her tea and giving Bailey a wry look.

'I can take him back home again once he's fed, if you want?' Mrs Muldoon offered. 'He wasn't any trouble. I did my ironing while he slept.'

'There's no need,' Mildred said, placing beef bones into the roasting tin. 'I can look after Bailey while Olivia tends to Spencer.'

A little put out, Mrs Muldoon drank her tea.

'But should I need any help, Mrs Muldoon, I'll call on you first,' Olivia assured her quickly to smooth her ruffled feathers and passed her the tin of shortbread.

Satisfied, Mrs Muldoon selected a shortbread.

Eager to return to Spencer, Olivia gave Bailey to Tess the moment he finished feeding. 'I want to check on Spencer.'

'Aye, lass. Go on up. I'll burp and change little master here.' Tess placed Bailey over her shoulder to burp him.

Mildred, busy at the oven, paused. 'Stay with Spencer as long as you want. I'll take care of everything else.'

Upstairs, Olivia sat beside the bed. Spencer had moved position since she left. She took his hand and realised that for all the newsreels she'd watched at the movie theatre, for all of Spencer's detailed letters, none of it brought home the true horror of the war. What the men went through was evident right in front of her. Spencer's exhaustion, the shadows under his eyes and thinner body, pin-pricked with cuts, was the silent toll.

She lightly kissed his forehead and was grateful that for now, she had him home.

CHAPTER 15

In the grey hours before dawn the following morning, Olivia finished feeding Bailey and changed him. He fell asleep in her arms, and she took him into Mildred's room and placed him in his cot. Mildred slept on contently in Lachie's bed.

She snuck back into her own room to check on Spencer. Surprised to find him awake, she hurried to his side. 'Darling?'

'I didn't know where I was at first,' he whispered.

She took his hand. 'You're home with me.'

He closed his eyes and relaxed. 'I don't remember boarding the train...'

She checked the temperature of his forehead with the back of her hand. It seemed normal. 'You were exhausted, my love, but you're here now. That's all that matters. Can I fetch you anything?'

'Don't leave me, not yet.' His eyes closed.

'I'm not going anywhere,' she promised.

'Lie down beside me.'

Shrugging off her dressing gown, she climbed into bed beside him. She lay on her side and faced him. 'Go back to sleep. You need to rest.'

'Olivia?'

'Yes, darling?'

'Will you hold my hand…'

Under the blankets she held his hand tightly, swallowing back the tears. 'Always, my love.'

When she woke, a dull morning light framed the curtains. From downstairs she heard Bailey crying. The little clock on the mantlepiece showed ten past six.

Without disturbing Spencer, she slipped from the bed and quickly donned a dark blue dress, tying her long hair up haphazardly. She added more coal to the low fire in the grate trying not to make a noise.

'Olivia?' Spencer spoke from the bed.

She dashed to his side. 'I'm sorry I woke you.'

His smile was everything. 'I thought I'd dreamed that I was here with you.'

She kissed his dry lips. 'There, do you believe it now?'

'I'm not sure, try again.'

Chuckling, she kissed him again.

'I'm starting to believe it's true.' His green-hazel eyes were full of love.

The jingle of a horse's harness and the clink of milk bottles placed on doorsteps in the square brought the sound of realism into the room, that and Bailey's wails that were grower stronger.

'Our son needs feeding,' she said, bending to kiss him again.

'Bailey.' Spencer tried to sit up.

'No, stay there. You're in no state to get out of this bed.' She gently pressed his shoulders back down.

'I want to see my son.'

'I'll bring him up.' Olivia raced downstairs and into the kitchen.

'Oh, thank goodness.' Mildred handed the baby to her. 'I tried to keep him quiet, but he's hungry.'

'Yes, sorry. Spencer's awake.' Olivia hushed Bailey, and he stopped crying to look at her.

'He is, oh wonderful.' Mildred swung back to the oven. 'I'll make him some boiled eggs. Something soft and light, and toast and tea. The broth needs finishing off, but it'll be ready for mid-morning.'

'Thank you, Mildred.' Olivia climbed the stairs as Bailey set off crying again. 'Yes, little man, breakfast is coming for you as well.'

In the bedroom she sat on the chair next to the bed. She opened the buttons on her dress and soon Bailey was contentedly drinking, and the only sound was the coal shifting in the fire.

Spencer pushed himself up in the bed and stared in awe at his son. 'He has fair hair like you.'

'It seems to get lighter every day.' She gazed lovingly at their baby. 'He's growing so fast, but he's such a good baby. He only makes a fuss when he's hungry.'

For a long while Spencer stared at his son, watching him feed, his tired expression a mixture of joy and something else that Olivia couldn't quite detect, trepidation perhaps? She sensed Spencer was fighting to stay awake, still exhausted but not wanting to miss a moment with the baby and her.

'I am a father. It does not seem real just yet,' he murmured. Shadows bruised under his eyes and grey sprinkled his beard stubble.

Olivia nodded. 'There are times when I sit and look at him and think how did it all happen? How am I now a wife and a mother? Sometimes, I still feel I should be running to the forge to visit my father or polishing the furniture at the manor.'

'Because they were simpler times.' Spencer reached out a finger and stroked his son's face. 'Now we have much more demanding responsibilities.'

'How are you feeling?'

'Tired.' He sighed heavily. 'Tired and too many other

emotions to name, but mostly grateful to have made it back to you and our son.'

'How long are you on leave for?' she asked tentatively, wishing he'd never leave her again.

'Six days, then I have training at HQ in France.' His tone showed his lack of enthusiasm.

Olivia sat Bailey up to burp and faced him towards his father so Spencer could see his face properly for the first time.

'He looks like me!' Spencer said in surprise.

'Indeed, he does,' Olivia agreed as their son burped loudly. 'I see your face every time I look at him and it gives me both comfort that he looks like you and sadness that you aren't here to watch him grow.' She stood and changed his napkin on the bed, allowing Spencer to see his son's healthy little body.

Spencer touched Bailey's palm and the baby's hand closed over his father's finger. 'He's got a strong grip!' He beamed as Bailey gazed at his father's face. 'What a little champion you are, my son.'

Olivia's heart swelled watching the two most important people in her world interact with each other. She dressed Bailey and placed him in Spencer's arms. 'You two can have a chat while I go down and fetch you some food.'

Spencer settled back against the pillows, cradling Bailey in his arms.

At the door, Olivia halted and burned the image of them into her memory. It was something she couldn't take for granted.

After eating Mildred's plentiful breakfast, Spencer slept for most of the day. Olivia kept going up to check on him but knowing he needed rest, she left him to sleep.

Doctor Whittaker knocked as the sun was going down. 'Sorry I'm late, Mrs Middleton. I had two emergencies today. How is the major?' He gave his hat and coat to Olivia who passed them to Mildred. Bailey slept in his basket on the kitchen table.

'He slept all night, ate breakfast this morning and has slept all day.'

'Good. Sleep is a great healer. No fever?'

'No. He seems in good health apart from the tiredness and his thinness.'

'Shall I go up and see for myself?' He smiled kindly and Olivia followed him up.

Spencer opened his eyes as the door opened. He frowned on seeing the doctor. 'Am I ill?'

Doctor Whittaker chuckled. 'You look a sight better than you did yesterday, Major.' He opened his bag. 'Still, I will examine you. I wrote to the war medical board alerting them to the condition you were in when you arrived. I should hopefully hear from them in a day or two.'

'You have wasted your time, Doctor. I am perfectly well enough to return to my duties. I have seen men in worse health go into battle.'

'Ah, perhaps so, Major, however, you are here and in my care, not over there.'

'It will make no difference. Besides, I must return to my men.'

The doctor opened his bag. 'I expected you to say that, they all do.' He shook his head sadly and began to examine Spencer. When he'd finished, he packed away his tools of the trade and closed his bag. 'Visiting you yesterday, I was concerned you might develop a fever, but your lungs sound clear. A good amount sleep seems to have brought about an improvement to your general state. Sleep and eat, Major, and you'll recover quickly enough.'

'Thank you, Doctor.' Spencer shook his hand.

'You do not wish for me to try and extend your leave due to medical reasons?' Doctor Whittaker suggested.

'No, sir, but I thank you for the offer. I must return to my men.' Spencer closed his eyes and sank against the pillows once more.

Downstairs, Doctor Whittaker donned his hat and coat. 'I tried, Mrs Middleton, but men like your husband have a strong urge to do their duty and return to their men. We mustn't condemn them for it.'

Olivia wanted to feel slighted that Spencer was so devoted to his men and wouldn't take up the doctor's offer to extend his leave, but common sense prevailed. She knew Spencer, knew his loyalty to his regiment. The time would come when she had him all to herself, but it wasn't now.

Spencer slept a lot for the next two days. He ate and slept, held Olivia in bed at night and watched her feed Bailey, but he was distant, quiet.

On the third night he started dreaming, twitching in his sleep, murmuring for someone to get down, hold fire, take cover. He winced and flinched, and sometimes he reached for something around his chest and putting it to his mouth, which she realised was the whistle in his pack.

When he woke, she didn't mention his dreaming, not wanting to remind him of painful images that haunted him in his sleep.

He only left the bed to visit the lavatory. At first, he'd been stiff and weak when he stood, pulling on his clothes was an effort.

By the fourth morning, Olivia woke to find him sitting up in bed, holding Bailey who stared at him in quiet contemplation.

'I heard Mildred on the landing. I said I'd hold Bailiey while she dressed,' he explained. 'I think Bailey is getting used to me,' he said, grinning. 'Aren't you, my boy?'

Olivia didn't want to say that Bailey would forget all about him and who knew when they'd see him again. Instead, she smiled and stretched, then stilled, thinking rapidly. 'Bailey slept through the night! I didn't get up to feed him. Goodness. That's the first time.'

'That's because he's a good boy,' Spencer confirmed. 'Here, go to your mama. He'll be hungry now.'

As if to agree with his father, Bailey started to fuss once in Olivia's arms. 'Oh yes, young man, it's coming.'

'While you feed him, I might go downstairs and boil some water. I need to shave.' He touched the short beard that had grown.

'I can do that for you once I've finished feeding Bailey.'

'No, my love. It's time I got out of this bed and joined the world again, as much as I'd rather not.' He climbed from the bed and dressed in his uniform.

Seeing him once more a soldier affected Olivia more than she could say and she bent her head to gaze tearfully down at Bailey. Two more days and Spencer would be gone again.

Knocking on the front door brought a frown to her face. The clock showed just after six. 'Who could it be at this time?'

'Milkman?' Spencer grinned. 'I'll go down.'

She heard male voices drift up the stairs and wished she could go down.

The bedroom door opened and Mildred, still putting up her hair, stepped in. 'Who is here so early? Who is Spencer talking to and why is he out of bed?'

'I don't know who it is. Spencer is feeling better and wanted to get dressed.'

Mildred looked at the empty space on the bed. 'You should have shouted for me, I'd have gone down to save him the trouble.'

'He doesn't want to be spending his last two days in bed.'

Mildred nodded with understanding. 'His leave has gone by so quickly.'

'And he slept through most of it.'

'Poor dear Spencer. He's just recovered only to go straight back into the thick of things.' Mildred placed a final comb in her dark hair and patted it into place before straightening the sleeves of her olive-green dress. 'I'll go down and make a start on breakfast.'

'I'll be down shortly.'

With Bailey fed and changed, and dressed in a clean woollen outfit, Olivia let him kick on the bed while she dressed and tidied herself. She studied herself in the mirror. She wore a white lacy blouse and a dark rust-coloured skirt. She threw a thick woollen shawl of mottled caramel colours about her shoulders. Her hair needed washing and so she'd plaited it and wound it into a knot at the back of her head.

Downstairs, she heard Mildred's voice join those of Spencer and Olivia recognised her father-in-law's deep voice. She smiled entering the kitchen. 'Stanford!'

'Ah, here they are. Sweet Olivia and my fabulous grandson.' Stanford rose from the kitchen table and kissed them both. 'My, he's grown. He's so like Spencer as a baby it's incredible.'

'I am surprised you remember how I looked as a baby, Father. It was an age ago,' Spencer joked, adding sticks of wood to the fire to get it to catch.

'When you're as old as me, Spence, *then* you can say it was an age ago.' Stanford plucked Bailey from Olivia and settled with him at the table. 'There's a hamper in the motor car. Spencer, ask Holden to bring it in, will you?'

'Holden?' Spencer asked. 'A new chauffeur?'

'Aye, and a woman to boot.'

Spencer's eyebrows rose. 'A woman drives you?'

Stanford grinned. 'While the men are away fighting, it's only right that we should employ women.'

'Absolutely,' Spencer agreed, placing pieces of coal onto the flaming sticks. 'In France, there are women ambulance drivers, and the nurses over there are the bravest people I've ever seen. They protect their patients like lionesses.'

'Holden is very good. I've been travelling all over the countryside and the motor car is better than the train at times as I don't have to conform to a station's timetable.'

'Shall I fetch her inside? She'll be freezing sitting in the motor car,' Olivia tutted.

'She'll want a cup of tea,' Mildred added.

'I'll send her to the hotel, and she can wait there.' Stanford jiggled Bailey's little fist. 'I thought to stay a couple of days in Wakefield to see you all before driving on to York. When do you go back, Spence?'

'The day after tomorrow.' Spencer glanced at Olivia and away again. 'I'll fetch the hamper.'

'No, you're just out of your sick bed,' Olivia protested.

'I'm fine, darling. Some fresh air will do me good.'

'Tell Holden to go onto the hotel, will you? She knows which one.' Stanford waited until Spencer had gone out the front door. 'He looks well. Better than I expected. I thought he'd be bedridden or something. In your telegram Mildred you said he was ill. I was so worried. I came as quickly as I could, but your telegram was sent to London, and I was in Southampton organising a shipment. Thankfully, my secretary redirected the telegram.'

Mildred poured boiling water into the teapot. 'When Spencer arrived, he was in such a terrible condition.'

'You'd have been shocked to see him,' Olivia told him. 'He's been sleeping and eating, resting for four days, that's how long it's taken to get him back on his feet.'

Stanford lowered his voice. 'Things are tough over there. The Somme campaign was complete bloodshed. My information is it's been three months of horror. Fierce fighting and the weather has turned the trenches into mud pits. In some areas we're losing more men to trench foot than to bullet wounds.'

'How ghastly,' Mildred murmured.

They all sat up straighter as Spencer came in carrying a large hamper.

'Goodness.' Mildred smiled over brightly. 'You spoil us, Stanford.'

'A few comforts, nothing much.' Stanford glanced around the kitchen, with its steaming windows and moisture running down the walls. 'I wish I could do more.' He looked at Olivia. 'I can get you a better house for a start. Will you not allow me?'

'No, Father.' Spencer shook his head. 'Olivia needs to stay here, where she is surrounded by friends and where Lachie can return home to her.'

Olivia placed her hand on Stanford's arm. 'Thank you for the offer but Spencer is right. Until the war is over, I cannot leave here. This is Lachie's home, and I want to be with my neighbours, not strangers.'

'Very well.' Stanford conceded defeat. 'After the war, we shall talk again.'

Olivia helped Mildred cook breakfast. 'There is one thing I'd like to discuss.'

'Oh?' Spencer sat and took his son into his arms.

'Bailey's christening. After breakfast I want to go and talk to the vicar of St Andrew's and see if he is willing to christen Bailey tomorrow while you both are here.'

'That's short notice, my love.' Spencer frowned.

'But if it's achievable, do you agree to it? After all, doing things with short notice is what we do best,' she reminded him of their quickly organised wedding.

He smiled, his eyes always full of love for her. 'It is a brilliant idea.'

* * *

FORTUNATELY, the vicar was agreeable to the christening being held the following afternoon. Although it was a small affair on an icy snowy Thursday afternoon, the people standing in the freezing church gave thanks that Bailey didn't cry when the cold water was anointed on his head. Spencer looked a little more his old self and, freshly shaven, he stood proudly holding his son at the altar.

Tess and Mildred repeated their vows to care for their

godson, but the Hobson men were working and only Mrs Berry and Mrs Muldoon were the other guests. Sadie was at work and Winnie had moved to her mother's and so with such a small group, they headed back to the square to have a cup of tea and cakes and biscuits all supplied by the Fortnum and Mason's hamper Stanford had brought.

Later that night, Olivia fed Bailey in the bedroom as Spencer undressed and climbed into bed. The day had taken its toll on him and the fatigued look had returned. She worried he wasn't well enough to return to France.

Olivia had observed Spencer all day and noted that sometimes his gaze turned inward, and his eyes would become dull, and his mouth turned down.

Settling Bailey into his cot, she banked down the fire and put the guard around it. Spencer watched her as she undressed and washed in the basin and cleaned her teeth. But, by the time she got into bed, his eyelids were heavy.

'I do not want to sleep, not on my last night,' he said then yawned.

She smiled and snuggled into him. 'It's been a long day.'

'I wanted to make love to you, but I honestly don't think I can perform.'

She raised herself up onto her elbow. 'Having you lying here beside me is more than enough. I gave birth five weeks ago. I don't think I'm ready for it either as much as I'd like to.'

He nodded. 'Then we shall just hold each other.'

She kissed him softly, one hand on his cheek. 'I feel we've barely had the chance to talk and tomorrow you'll be gone.'

'Then we'll talk now.' He cupped the back of her head and brought her mouth to his for another kiss. 'I don't want to go and leave you and Bailey, but I must. You understand, don't you?'

'Yes, I do.' Their faces were inches apart. 'But I can't pretend it's easy to let you go.'

He closed his eyes and kissed her again. 'One day, nothing will part us.'

'I hold on to that.' She rested into the crook of his shoulder, their arms wrapped around each other.

'I cannot return to you until the war is done. Until my men no longer need me to guide them, to see them through the tough days and to celebrate with them the kinder days.'

'They are lucky to have such a caring leader.'

'I am lucky to have them. We watch each other's backs. We suffer through the loss, the destruction together. We bury our dead and we raise a drink to the fates that spared us. In the quiet times, we learn more about each other. We shake a man's hand when he receives word from home that he's a father, or offer him sage advice if he plans on getting married to his sweetheart. We commiserate when a parent dies, or a pet…' Spencer smiled slightly. 'Together we travel the dusty roads, or slog through the mud. We tend to each other's wounds, share our food and ammunition. We sit in the rain together, bake in the sunshine. We are a strange type of family. There are times when they all get on my nerves, and I bark an order for them to just shut up for five minutes. But then there are times when someone will make a joke, and we'll roar with laughter.' His voice broke. 'They are my men, Olivia, mine. I could never turn my back on them.'

'I wouldn't expect you to, that's not Spencer Middleton, the man I love.'

'Then you forgive me?'

'For what? For doing your duty?'

'For not taking a desk position behind the lines as my father wishes me to do.'

She thought for a moment. 'Of course I want you safe, but not at the cost of you being the man that you are.'

He pulled her to him and kissed her with such longing and passion. 'Thank you,' he whispered against her lips.

She ran her fingers through his short hair. 'Return there with my love and support.'

'That is all I need.' He held her close. 'I have to finish this, to see it through, for Albert's sake and all the others we've lost.'

'And I'll be waiting here, with Bailey, for when you come back to us.' She entwined her fingers through his as their son made a little noise from his cot.

CHAPTER 16

France,

April, 1917.

In the warm spring sunshine, Lachie loaded his wagon with rolls of barbed wire, iron stakes and other tools. His two favourite horses, Pippy and Bonnie, were snuffling in their nose-bags for the oats he'd placed in the bottom. They had a long day ahead. He was to make several deliveries today in preparation for an allied advancement at dawn. Supplies had been brought in by train and Lachie's job was to bring the goods from the train station to the holding barns at the edge of the village and then take wagon loads miles to the reserve lines. He wasn't the only wagon team working, several other privates with wagons were making the trips as well.

In the village where he was billeted, a company of Australians had stopped to rest, having been pulled out of the front line at dawn. Their unique accents could be heard up and down the small green in the middle of the village, their laughter, too. They seemed a happy bunch.

In the centre of the green stood a large well and it was the general meeting place for soldiers to sit and chat and eat. Some of the French villagers continued to live in their houses, while others had joined the crowded roads of people seeking a safer place to wait out the war.

'G'day, mate.' An Australian soldier came up to Lachie, the colonials were easily identifiable by their slouched hats and devil-may-care attitude to everything. 'You haven't got a match, have you?'

'No, sorry. I don't smoke,' Lachie replied, tying down his load.

The Australian leaned against the wagon, his slouched hat at a jaunty angle, the sleeves of his army shirt rolled up revealing tanned arms. He squinted in the sunlight, his manner conversational. 'Are you only carrying rolls of wire?'

'Aye.' Lachie nodded, checking the ropes were tight.

'No wine or whisky? Rum?'

Lachie laughed. 'No, stuff like that has a guard to it.'

'Typical. They don't make it easy for us to sneak the odd bottle, do they?'

'I think that's the point.' Lachie grinned. 'How are you finding France? I heard you ANZACs had it rough at Gallipoli.'

'Christ, yer. That place was hell on earth. I don't know how I made it out of there alive. Standing on the beaches, looking up at those cliffs, we knew it was a suicide mission, but still they made us do it.' The fellow stared down at the dirt and scuffed it with the toe of his boot. 'Lost a lot of good men. I suspect France will be just the same.'

'Just not as hot,' Lachie joked.

'I don't mind the heat, I'm used to it. It's the being shot at I can't get used to.' He laughed. He held out his hand for Lachie to shake. 'Walter Lynch.'

'Lachie Brodie.' Lachie shook his hand.

'Scottish?'

'No, just the name is.'

'I didn't think you had the Scottish accent.'

'No, my grandfather was a Scot. I was born in Yorkshire. Heard of it?'

'I have. My mother's family comes from Leeds originally. Settled in Australia when my mother was just a girl.'

'Is that so? I live in Wakefield, not far from Leeds.'

Lynch shooed away a fly. 'Never been to Yorkshire. Never left home Australia until this war.'

'Is it difficult being so far from home? I can be home in twenty-four hours but for you it's a lot more than that.'

'Ah, yer, about six weeks sailing. It's all right I suppose. I'm seeing a bit of the world.' The Australian shrugged. 'I miss my dog.'

'Just your dog?'

'And the beach.'

'The beach?'

'Yer, got meself a little hut right on the water. I fish, hunt for crabs, mend nets. I spend hours combing the beach for driftwood and shells with my dog. It's a good life. I miss it…' His voice drifted away.

'Sounds like a great way to live,' Lachie commented.

'It pretty good.' The Australian shrugged. 'Can't wait to get back to it. I joined up for a bit of adventure, me sister pushed me into enlisting, said it'd be good for me to experience a bit of culture instead of walking barefoot on the beach every day.' He huffed. 'That's the last time I'll listen to her, that's for certain. There's nothing that compares to my beach.'

'My sister, Olivia, and my brother-in-law might go to Australia, Sydney, actually, after the war. She said she wants me to go with them if they do.'

'You should, mate,' Lynch encouraged. 'You'll enjoy it.'

'Though they might pick Paris or New York, or maybe just London.' Lachie wasn't sure of their plans. Olivia had mentioned it in a letter months ago, but nothing had been said since. The idea of travelling to Australia appealed to him, more so than the other places. He'd learned from other soldiers that Australia had a good deal of horses and wide-open spaces. He fancied the idea of owning a small horse farm and perhaps have a little forge as his father had done.

'Choose Australia if you get the chance, mate.' A call from one of his pals brought the Australian's head up. 'I'd best be getting back. We're marching out in a few minutes. Bloody Germans. I wish they'd all go home and stay there. See ya, mate!'

'Good to meet you.' Lachie watched the soldier saunter back to his company who were making ready to march out of the village.

'Hey, Brodie, got any mail to send?' A soldier attached to the army mail walked past him.

'Aye, I've a letter to send.' Lachie pulled out of his pocket a letter he'd written to Olivia. He quickly added a note on the back of the envelope.

Let's go to Australia!

He gave it to the soldier to put in his mail bag. 'Thanks.'

The soldier walked away and Lachie returned to checking his load, whistling a tune.

'Well, I'll be jiggered!'

Lachie swung around at the voice behind him. 'Colin!'

They shook hands and heartily clapped each other on the back, grinning like monkeys.

'I didn't think I'd see you again,' Lachie said to his old friend, having to yell as the Australian company marched out singing a song and saying goodbye to the French people who came out of their houses to wave them off.

Lachie moved around to the other side of the wagon. 'Are you all healed?'

Colin nodded with a cheeky wink. 'Aye, there's nowt wrong with me. I've been back in France a while now but on light duties at various places. I actually think they forgot about me until last week when a commanding officer decided he'd had enough of looking at my ugly face.' Colin chuckled. 'I'd been working as a runner for weeks.'

'So, what are you doing now?'

'I'm on my way to a new company, make up the numbers and all that.'

'You're not staying here?' Lachie tried not to let his disappointment show. He turned away and took the horses' nosebags off.

'Nah. I'm on the next train heading north.'

Lachie frowned, placing buckets of water under the horses' heads so they could drink. 'There isn't a north-bound train today. It'll be the morning train. The only one expected today is from the south bringing men and supplies.'

Colin preened. 'I've got the day off then!'

'You could come and help me.' Lachie nudged him with his elbow. 'Afterwards, I'll show you the local inn where you can get something to eat and a drink of ale. The barkeeper's daughter is a looker as well.'

'I'm sure I could find all that out by myself!' Colin protested with a grin.

'Fine, suit yourself.'

'Oh, all right. Come on then. I'll help you with your delivery. But you're buying the first pint when we get back.' Colin threw his pack in the back of the wagon and climbed up onto the seat. 'Have you heard from home lately?'

Lachie clicked his tongue and flicked the reins to set the horses into a walk. 'I got a letter from Olivia two days ago. Spencer is fighting somewhere in the Loos Salient, apparently. Olivia said Bailey is growing fast.' Lachie paused. His little nephew was six months old now, and he'd not seen him yet.

The morning grew hotter as the sun beat down from a clear sky. The horses plodded along, sending up puffs of dust from the dry road. A farmer brought in a lone cow from a field, and further away the remains of another village lay broken, not one cottage left standing from previous shelling.

Colin pulled his cap lower to shield his eyes from the sun. 'Me mam wrote a few days ago. She said everyone back home was well. Me dad is a foreman now and earning better money. Our Jonnie took his place as a hewer.'

'Really? That's good.' Lachie guided the horses out of the village and into the flat countryside. 'Do you miss the mine?'

'Nah, not at all.' Colin snorted. 'I doubt I'll want to go back to it once this is all over. I can't imagine being stuck down a black hole again after years of being out of it.'

'You and me should go to Australia.'

'Australia?' Colin's voice rose in surprise.

'Aye. I was just chatting to an Australian. It sounds an interesting place to go. Mr Middleton, Spencer's father, wants to open an office out there for his business. There's a chance Olivia and Spencer might go and if they do, we should go as well.'

'Oh, aye, me mam will love that idea!' Colin said sarcastically.

'She let your Lance and Simon go away.'

'Aye and she didn't like it. There's no chance Mam will let me go. I reckon even if I got married, she'd have us all live with her.'

Lachie laughed. 'True enough.'

They'd gone less than a mile when they heard the shelling. Lachie frowned in confusion. 'I was told there wasn't a battle starting today.'

Colin rolled his eyes. 'Obviously the Germans had different ideas.'

'Damn it to hell,' Lachie swore as the shelling grew louder and more frequent. The horses became nervous, jingling their bits in their mouths. 'Steady, girls. You're doing fine,' he calmed them.

'Where are we dropping this stuff off to?' Colin scanned the horizon.

'The reserve trench. They'll take up to the front line.' Lachie noticed the shelling continued along the hill a mile or so ahead.

Plumes of smoke funnelled up into the serene sky, destroying the beauty of the day.

'If that shelling keeps up, there won't be a reserve trench left,' Colin said worriedly.

Lachie clicked his tongue to hurry the horses along. 'I don't understand it. It's meant to be a quiet area.'

'We should go back.'

'I can't. I have my orders.' Lachie concentrated on guiding the horses along the track. 'There's another three loads I have to deliver today.'

'The shelling might stop soon,' Colin said hopefully.

Suddenly they heard the low hum of a biplane. Lachie and Colin twisted in the seat, searching the sky for sight of it.

'There it is!' Colin pointed to the black dot high above them. 'It's coming this way and getting lower.'

'Is it ours or German?' Lachie urged the horses on, but they weren't in a hurry to do his bidding, tossing their heads nervously.

The noise of the plane grew louder as it neared.

'Difficult to tell. It'll be aiming for the trenches if it's German,' Colin stated, watching as the plane flew over them and continued straight ahead. 'It's German. I can see the markings on the wings. I wonder how many hand bombs they're carrying.'

'One too many,' Lachie muttered, flicking the reins.

As they travelled over a slight rise, they saw ahead the marching Australian company.

Suddenly, the biplane changed course, veering for the column of men.

'Oh no!' Lachie stood up in the wagon to see better as the biplane dropped lower and the pilot's passenger leaned over the side of the plane and began dropping bombs on the soldiers.

The call went up, and the Australians fell to the ground, crawling away from the road and into the ditches lining either side.

'Christ Almighty!' Colin stared as the biplane circled back again, clearly outlined against the brilliant blue of the sky. Like a lethal giant bird, it flew back over the Australians, dropping bombs along the ditches blowing men into the air.

Screams cut the peaceful countryside.

Lachie watched in horror as the plane circled once more, dropping lower despite the men shooting at it from the ground and released more bombs.

A bomb dropped a hundred yards from Lachie's wagon. His horses backed up in their harness, jerking the wagon. 'Steady girls, steady.'

'Bloody hell, Lachie, its coming right over us! We're a sitting duck! Jump!' Colin sprang from the wagon.

Lachie went to leap off as well but a blast from the front flung him high in the air. He landed on the ground with a hard thud that took the breath from his lungs. His body collapsed like a limp rag doll.

When he came to, all he heard was screams, yelling, and the torturous sound of a horse neighing in distress.

Struggling to raise his head, a shadow passed over him. The plane flew overhead, and Lachie waited for the next bomb to land. It didn't and the sound of the plane grew distant as it continued on its way.

Dazed, tasting blood and dirt in his mouth, Lachie half sat up, swaying. It took a moment for his brain to understand what he saw. Dozens of dead men blown to pieces and scattered around him. The wagon was on its side. Rolls of wire and tools lay around it. Its wheels were shattered spikes of wood.

Pain gripped his body, torturing him. The madness of the wounded and dead men encircled him. He felt wetness trickle down his chest. He glanced down to see a piece of shrapnel sticking out of his shirt, embedded in his chest. His uniform was cut to pieces and from his stomach a gaping hole bled freely. He swayed in agony. He needed help.

Chaos and noise bludgeoned his senses. Officers were shouting orders, men were calling out for help and a horse kept whinnying, braying in its suffering.

Not just any horse but his horse. Groaning at the effort to move, he ignored the pain tearing at his stomach and crawled on his hands knees towards the wagon and around to the other side. He stopped abruptly on seeing Bonnie's lifeless body torn apart. Further away, Pippy neighed, wounded, striving to gain her feet, but she was missing one leg.

Moaning in anguish, Lachie tried to reach her. 'Pippy, lay still, girl,' he called, crying.

An Australian solider walked up to Pippy and shot her in the head.

'No!' Lachie screamed. Stumbling up onto his knees to reach her, knowing it was too late. Not his Pippy.

Sickened by the slaughter of another of his beloved horses, he sat on the grass, shocked and defeated.

'Lachie!'

He turned, hearing his name. Colin... *'Colin!'* He winced and groaned in pain as he twisted to find his friend. He couldn't find the strength to move.

From around the wagon, Colin staggered towards him, his arm hanging by his side, but as he came closer Lachie stared at the shattered face of his best mate.

Colin fell down next to Lachie, a section of his skull open, his arm nearly torn from his shoulder. 'I found you...' he croaked.

Hot tears burned Lachie's eyes as he laid down next to him, the ache in his chest throbbing so much he felt sick. 'They'll look after us...' he said, reaching for Colin's hand and holding it tightly. 'We'll get a Blighty for this.'

It was agony to draw breath as though a red-hot poker was twisting in his chest. 'Colin... I don't feel too good.'

He turned his head slowly and saw that Colin had gone limp and was staring without seeing.

He refused to accept that his best friend was dead. 'We're going home, Colin,' he whispered. 'Going home to your mam… to Liv…' He stared up at the blueness above him. 'I'm going home to Olivia…'

The pain gripped him in a vice so tight he couldn't breathe. He fought the pain, fought for air, fought to live…

Sometime later, Walter Lynch, the young Australian soldier who'd spoken to Lachie in the village, found them side by side, holding hands. Their eyes open to the pretty sky above.

He smacked his slouched hat against his thigh in anger at the death of two young men who could barely grow a beard. 'Fuck this bloody war!'

* * *

HANGING out the washing in the sunshine, Olivia smiled down at Bailey who sat in another basket playing with the wooden pegs. He was happy now but had kept her and Mildred awake all night with his teething. He chewed on a peg contentedly, only his red cheeks gave any indication of the two little bottom teeth forcing their way through the gum.

Aside from the lack of sleep recently, she wouldn't swap being his mother for anything in the world. Bailey gave her so much joy and her love for this baby consumed her. She couldn't think of how her life was before he came.

Bailey reminded her of Spencer in his smile and the shape of his face, but he also reminded her of Lachie and her father, even Stu. Her son had the fair colouring and blue eyes of all the Brodie family. Everyone who met him commented on what a handsome little boy he was.

Mildred came out of the house into the yard, unpinning her hat. She'd returned from shopping. She bent and kissed Bailey. 'Have you behaved for your mama?' She straightened. 'That's the food shopping sorted for the next couple of days. The market was terribly busy. I bought the newspaper as well. It's full of the news that America has joined the war on the Allies side, thank goodness! Sadie is sitting out the front reading it. I gave it to her as I passed. I said I'd put the shopping away and make a cup of tea for us all.'

'Perhaps with the Americans joining the war, the Germans might turn tail and run back to Germany.' Olivia hoped it would be so, and quickly.

'We can only pray they do.'

Olivia hung the last sheet on the line and grabbing Bailey placed him on her hip. 'I'll take some chairs out the front.'

'I thought we'd have pork chops for our meal later. Mr Keane said the chops were fresh this morning.' Mildred followed her into the kitchen.

'He's a butcher, he's bound to say that.' Olivia changed Bailey's napkin for a fresh one.

'Well, anyway, they looked fresh. From the market I bought a cabbage, potatoes and some onions.'

'Lovely. I'll fry them all up to have with the chops.' Olivia placed Bailey on the rug on the floor so she could help Mildred pack away the items she bought. 'I'll make a rice pudding later. Bailey enjoys a bit of rice pudding, don't you, sweetheart?'

'Bailey enjoys any food you put in his mouth.' Mildred chuckled, bending down to plant a kiss on the top of his blond head. 'Aunty Mildred will give you a bath later while your mama makes us a rice pudding.'

'But first we'll have a cup of tea and a chat to Sadie,' Olivia said.

Outside they drank tea sitting on the chairs from the kitchen table. An old rug was put down for Bailey to practise his crawling on. Toys were scattered around him and Mildred was feeding him small bits of an oatmeal biscuit.

Tess joined them, looking hot and bothered.

'What have you been doing?' Olivia asked her.

'What haven't I been doing!' She huffed, blowing a tendril of grey hair out of her eyes. 'I thought to give the bedrooms a good going over.'

'On a warm day like this?' Sadie chuckled. 'You're mad.'

'Well, our Jonnie has met a lass—'

'Ooh, anyone we know?' Sadie butted in.

'Margy Lewis. She lives on Duke of York Street. Her father works on the railway, apparently. I've not met her, but our Jules told me that Jonnie is really keen on her and been secretly meeting her for months.' Tess's annoyed expression showed her thoughts about that. 'I cornered him about it this morning and told him to invite the lass for tea on Sunday. I ain't having my boy skulking about like he's got something to be ashamed of.'

'Hence the cleaning,' Mildred added.

'Aye. I regret I started it now. My, the bits and pieces my lads have stuffed under their beds defies explanation. There were all sorts under there.' Tess raised an eyebrow. 'Even a box of dirty cards.'

'Dirty cards?' Mildred repeated. 'Why were they dirty? Do they play with them down the coal mine?'

Tess, Olivia and Sadie looked at her and then burst out laughing.

'No, you daft 'apporth!' Tess crowed. 'Dirty as in the cards have naked women on them.'

Mildred gasped. 'No!'

'You can tell Mrs Middleton is a vicar daughter!' Sadie chuckled.

'Aye, and she's also a vicar's wife!' Tess laughed.

Mildred smiled, a little embarrassed. 'I had a sheltered upbringing, you are right about that. I didn't know such things existed.'

They laughed some more.

When the Post Office messenger girl rounded the corner into the square, the laughter stopped.

'I wish she would whistle like Mr Thacker used to do,' murmured Sadie.

They all tensed as the girl headed their way, her young face unreadable.

Olivia placed her teacup and saucer back on the tray her eyes not straying from the girl who opened her satchel and took out two envelopes. She gave one to Olivia and one to Tess without saying a word.

'Nay, there's some mistake!' Tess waved the letter at the girl. 'My Simon is in North Africa fitting out a new ship and my Colin is on light duties behind the lines. So, this isn't mine.' She held it out for the girl to take back.

'I'm sorry, but it has your name on it, Mrs Hobson.'

'There're loads of Hobsons in Wakefield,' Tess snapped. 'It belongs to another family.'

'Shall I read it?' Mildred offered quietly.

Tess thrust the letter at her. 'Aye, go on, read it and we'll soon sort this mess out.'

Mildred glanced at Olivia, who still held her letter. Olivia couldn't look at the envelope, so she stared at her son playing with his rattle and handed it to Mildred as well.

The messenger girl hurried away, and Mildred opened both letters and read them to herself. She closed her eyes.

'Well?' Tess barked. 'It's a mistake, isn't it?'

Olivia felt light-headed. *Please just be wounded and not dead.* 'Who is it?'

'Colin and Lachie,' Mildred murmured.

'You're wrong!' Tess screamed at her.

'Are they wounded?' Olivia whispered, praying for the lesser hurtful option.

'No...' Mildred murmured. 'Killed in action.'

'Not my Colin. They've got it all wrong!' Tess's shouting brought out the neighbours who hurried over.

Olivia walked inside and sat on the chair by the unlit fire. She heard Tess wailing outside, and it hurt her ears. The commotion made Bailey cry, and she knew she should go to him but couldn't. Her body wouldn't move.

Lachie.

Her Lachie.

Her little brother she'd been caring for, looking out for since her mother died.

Gone. Dead. *Killed in action.*

What hateful words they were. Words to tear a family into shreds.

Her chest constricted, paining her heart.

Hot tears blinded her, but she refused to give in to them.

She thought of her mother and father. Lachie was with them now. She had to trust that. They were all together, the three of them, and one day she would join them, as would Stu. A flash of anger hit her hard towards Stu. Why wasn't he here to help her through this? If he'd not left, none of this would have happened. They'd still be in their cottage in the country, Stu and Lachie forging and she caring for them. Spencer would have found her earlier, and they'd have had more time together. Lachie wouldn't have joined a war he wasn't old enough to fight in and he'd still be alive.

All this was Stu's fault, and she'd never forgive him.

A sob broke from her throat, jagged and harsh. She missed her family. She missed her old life. All of them were lost to her now.

Mildred walked in carrying Bailey who was happy again eating an oatmeal biscuit. Mildred sat opposite Olivia, her expression one of sadness. 'I can't express my sorrow, dear Olivia. Lachie was a fine young man.'

'Yes, he was,' she managed to say. 'Why did he have to die? He was behind the lines. Yes, he'd seen a few shells land, but he often told me the only fighting he saw was when the men got too drunk on leave and started throwing fists.'

She jerked to her feet and paced the small room unable to sit still and process her thoughts and feelings. She wanted to rage, to cry, but all she felt was a strange numbness. Why wasn't she wailing like Tess, who she could still hear through the thin walls dividing their houses?

'This little man is falling asleep.' Mildred held Bailey over her shoulder. 'I'll go up and put him to bed.'

Olivia nodded and turned away. She should be doing the task, but the idea of holding her precious child, of feeling any emotion, would weaken and break her.

'I'm going for a walk, Mildred.' Olivia grabbed her hat and dashed outside. She strode out of the square, past faces full of sympathy. She wasn't ready to face anyone, to talk to anyone, to hear their words of comfort. There wasn't any comfort to be had. Her brother was dead.

Head down, she marched away, eager to be lost in the hustle and noise of Stanley Road.

Hours later she found herself at Thorne's Park. All the flowers were gone and replaced with vegetables. Several gardeners were tilling the soil or planting seeds. What once was a beautiful park now resembled a working farm, and the loss of the flowers brought silly tears to her eyes. Was there nowhere left that was pretty?

She collapsed onto a park bench and fought for control. Her chest ached and unshed tears clogged her throat. To give into her grief and acknowledge the agony of losing Lachie scared her. Fear prevented her from breaking down completely. Fear of not ever being able to stem the ache of losing all her family. Now wasn't the time to surrender to the pain. Would there ever be a right time? She didn't know, but now wasn't it. She wouldn't cry until the war was over and Spencer was safe with her.

Straightening her shoulders, she lifted her head, determined not to give into the deep sorrow needling at her. She watched the gardeners labour until an older man lead a small pony and cart out of a shed. The pony was too little to be commandeered by the army as most other horses had been for the war effort and seeing the pony toss its head made her think of Lachie. He'd tell her that pony had a mischievous streak. How he loved horses of all sizes, but he had a fondness of ponies since working with them down the pit.

Hot tears burned behind her eyes as she watched the pony pull the cart, tail whishing. Suddenly, it turned its head and looked straight at her. She gave it a watery smile, her heart in pieces. She hoped there were horses in heaven for Lachie.

CHAPTER 17

Early May 1917

WITH BAILEY ASLEEP in her arms, Olivia gently put him in his cot and tucked the blankets around him. Closing the door slightly, she descended the stairs just as the door opened and Mildred walked in followed by a man wearing a trilby. At first Olivia stopped, thinking it was Spencer, but as Stanford took off his hat, she smiled, hiding her disappointment and embraced her father-in-law.

'How are you, my dear?' Stanford looked keenly into her face. 'I was astounded to hear the news of your brother.'

'Thank you for the basket you sent and the flowers.'

'They were little compensation for the loss.'

'I'll make some tea.' Mildred headed into the kitchen.

'We have fruit cake,' Olivia offered to Stanford.

'Lovely.' He joined them in the kitchen. 'How is my grandson?'

'Growing like a tree.' Olivia grinned. 'He's just gone down for his nap. We didn't expect to see you.'

'I made a short visit home to York after being in Edinburgh and am on my way to London.' Stanford placed his hat on the table. 'I have come to implore you to join me in London.' He held his hand up to forestall Olivia from speaking. 'Just for a week or two. I thought a little time away might be beneficial. We could go shopping, visit the theatres, the museums, walk in the parks and so forth.'

'That is kind of you to think of us.' Olivia brought the cake out of its tin and cut it into three slices.

'Yes, very thoughtful, Father.' Mildred set out the teacups and saucers.

'You do not seem very excited by the idea?' Stanford quizzed. 'Let me explain. I have been considering the future, and as you know Spencer and I have been discussing his role in the business once the war is over. I thought it might be educational for Olivia to visit London and experience the city first hand. Of course, you and Spencer have not yet decided where you want to live after the war, but it might be time to consider where that might be and by visiting London and possibly Paris in the near future you can start to plan as to whether either of those places would suit you.'

Olivia sat down beside him. 'Has Spencer spoken to you about his preference?'

'No.' Stanford accepted a cup of tea from Mildred. 'He tells me in his letters that he'll wait to discuss it with you.'

'I had thought Paris…' Spoken out loud for the first time, she shocked herself at mentioning it. At one time, the very idea of living abroad would have excited her. Now, she didn't know how to feel about it. Planning a future at the moment seemed ridiculous. What future did any of them have while the war raged?

'Paris is an excellent option.' Stanford nodded.

'I could visit Lachie's grave often.' Was that a sensible reason to live in a foreign city? She didn't know. This new life had meant to include Lachie.

'Ah, yes,' Stanford said softly.

'In Paris Spencer would be close to Anthea, and his grandmother. But Lachie's last letter had a message on the back of the envelope, saying we should go to Australia.'

'Did it indeed?'

Olivia looked at him. 'You don't sound convinced?'

'Not me, my dear, but *you* need to be convinced. We are discussing the rest of your life. It must be spent where you'll be the most happiest.'

'I will be content just to have Spencer home and we are all together. Where we live means little to me.' She knew she sounded negative but couldn't help it.

'Understandable after all you have been through.' Stanford turned to Mildred. 'And you, my dear, what are yours and Ralph's plans? In his last letter to me he mentioned his reluctance to return to his old parish and instead feels the need to work in a mission in another country somewhere. He mentioned Africa and also New Zealand. Mission work. That is brave of you both.'

Mildred's face had lost all colour.

Olivia half rose in her seat to go to her.

The teaspoon in Mildred's fingers shook slightly. 'It seems you know more than I do, Father.' A muscle ticked on her left eyelid.

'Ralph hasn't discussed this with you?' Stanford frowned. 'Forgive me, I assumed you had both decided on it.'

'No. To do that would mean we'd have to converse, to write letters to each other regularly. Ralph seems to write to everyone but me, his wife.' Mildred's hard tone matched the brittle glaze in her eyes. 'He is making decisions without informing me…' Mildred stood, tea and cake forgotten. 'If you'll both excuse me.' She paused beside Stanford. 'Forgive me, Father, but I don't feel up to a journey to London. Thank you for the offer though.'

Stanford stood. 'Mildred, my dear. I have upset you.'

'No, you haven't, not at all.' Mildred's chin wobbled, and she placed her hand on Stanford's arm. 'Your son has.' She walked out of the kitchen, and they heard her footsteps on the stairs.

Sighing heavily, Stanford resumed his seat. 'Will you come to London?'

The sound of mail being pushed through the letter flap on the front door made Olivia crane her neck to glance at the envelope fallen on the mat. She'd received a letter from Spencer only yesterday and didn't expect one today and no one else who might write to her had the importance of her rushing to pick up the envelope on the mat.

Shaking her head, Olivia took his hand across the table. 'Thank you for the offer, but I don't want to leave Tess.'

'Tess? Mrs Hobson next door?'

'Yes. Since Colin's death, she's not been herself.' That was an understatement. 'And, honestly, until the war is over, making plans seems useless.'

'We must not think like that, my dear. The war *will* end, and we must be ready to move forward when it does.'

Olivia collected Mildred's teacup and saucer and put them in the sink. 'I am scared to think of the future, Stanford, as I don't know whether Spencer will be with me or not.'

'Do not speak so.' He stood and came to her. 'We must remain positive.'

'I'm finding that difficult.'

'Olivia, I truly feel a trip to London will give you some joy. My home has every comfort and there is a garden where you can sit with Bailey and let him feel the grass under his feet.'

'One day we will visit you, just not yet.'

He hung his head for a moment. 'As you wish.'

The back door opened, and Tess came in a letter in her hand. 'Have you seen this!' She stopped on seeing Stanford. 'Oh, Mr Middleton.'

'Good morning to you, Mrs Hobson.' Stanford bowed his

head to her, his gaze darting to Olivia. 'My deepest condolences about your son, Colin.'

'Er, thank you.'

Sensing his concern, Olivia smiled at Tess, ignoring her state of undress for Tess till wore her dressing gown over her nightwear, her hair, lank and grey, not brushed. All Tess's plumpness had shrivelled away since Colin's death, leaving her gaunt and sickly in appearance. 'What do you have?'

'A letter from Colin's commanding officer.' Tess thrust it at Olivia. '*Read it.* He writes that Colin and Lachie were *together*. They were found together... where... where it happened. Can you believe it?' Tess pointed at the letter. 'They buried them together, side by side they are.' Tears rolled down Tess's pale cheeks. 'Buried together. Our boys.'

Emotion caught in Olivia's throat as she quickly read the letter confirming Tess's words. Lachie and Colin died in the same explosion. She winced, trying not to picture the incident and passed the letter back to Tess.

'Isn't that the best we could hope for?' Tess asked her. 'That they are together? Friends side by side and not alone. My boy wasn't alone. Lachie wasn't alone. They were together.'

Tess's repeated words grated on Olivia slightly and she was ashamed to feel that way. 'It's such lovely news,' she murmured.

'Did you not receive a letter? It came just now.'

'It's probably on the mat.' Olivia picked up the teapot, having no intentions of ever opening that letter and reading those words again.

'And we can visit them.' Tess gripped the letter like a lifeline, her movements jerky. 'In France. We can go and visit them.'

Olivia held up the teapot, relieved her eyes remained dry. 'Will you stay for some tea?'

Tess's face closed down and she withdrew into herself again as she had done since the news of Colin's death arrived. 'No, lass. I'm away home.' She scuttled out of the back door.

Stanford shook his head sadly. 'Gracious me, Mrs Hobson is in a deplorable state, the poor woman.'

'And that's why I can't leave her. Tess has supported me through everything. I can't leave her now.'

'Of course. Another time perhaps. Would it be possible for me to take a look at Bailey before I go?'

'You're going now?'

'Yes. I shall catch the next London-bound train. I was on my way to London when I thought to stop off here to see you all and invite you all to come back with me.'

'Bailey could sleep for another hour but come up and see him and say goodbye to Mildred.'

Stanford hesitated. 'Mildred is unhappy with Ralph.'

'Yes, I've tried to help her to write more affectionate letters to him as Spencer and I do to each other, but Ralph doesn't return the same sentiment. He writes as though she is a friend, not his wife.'

Tapping a hand against his thigh, Stanford appeared annoyed. 'This will not do. I shall write to Ralph and ask him to explain himself.'

'I doubt he'll unburden his husbandly concerns, if he has any, to his father.' Olivia packed away the tea things. 'Ralph and Spencer are so different in that way. I am never in doubt of Spencer's love.'

'No, Spencer is a lot like me. We love to the death whereas Ralph is more reserved. I don't doubt that the feelings are there, he simply cannot express them. His teachings in the church make him even more rigid in his emotions.'

'What can we do?'

'I will write to him and suggest he returns home to his wife before he realises he does not have a wife to come home to!' He fumed, then took a breath and gave her a small smile. 'Come, let me see my grandson. One glimpse of him will restore my good mood.'

Later that evening, Olivia stood and watched Bailey sleep for a moment, also listening for any noise coming from Tess's house next door, but it was eerily silent. Olivia wasn't used to not hearing Tess's laughter, or Larry's voice as he told off one of his sons. Since Colin's death, Tess had barely left her home. The Hobson house had lost all its noise, its laughter. Once, Tess was a constant visitor in Olivia's kitchen, now it was Olivia who regularly went into Tess's kitchen a few times a day to check on her friend.

Outside, the warm night still held a touch of gold from the late sunset, birds twittered not yet fully roosted. Below her bedroom window, the square had grown quiet, everyone indoors after a lazy Saturday sitting out in the sunshine, chatting, drinking tea or cordial, or an ale for the few men left in the square.

Sighing, Olivia climbed into bed and settled the wooden tray on her lap that she used as a portable writing desk. Picking up the pen, she wrote to Spencer.

My Darling.

Your last letter arrived yesterday on my birthday which gave me some small happiness. You mustn't worry that you weren't able to send me a gift. You being safe and well is the only gift I need.

I was very pleased to read that you are now in a quiet section of Northern France, and I pray you stay there until the war ends without ever seeing another battle. Are you looking after yourself? Did you receive the tin of fruit cake I sent?

Bailey is determined to crawl and everything he finds goes into his mouth. Mildred and I need eyes at the back of our heads to watch him. He now has four teeth. Two at the bottom and two have broken through his gum at the top. I'm hoping we can now get some sleep during the night and his troubles ease for a few weeks.

Your father arrived today. He wished to take the three of us to London for a couple of weeks. Mildred wasn't in the mood for it, and I can't leave Tess. I think we upset him with our refusal. Hopefully, he understands. Mildred hasn't heard from Ralph in some time. Do you hear from him at all?

We received a letter from Lachie's commanding officer telling us that Colin and Lachie died together and are buried together. It gave Tess some contentment that they were together when it happened. I could take little comfort from it. We will be notified at a later date where that burial site is so we can visit.

SHE PAUSED, her pen hovering above the paper. Lachie's grave. It was absurd to think of it. It was impossible to accept such a thing existed. Somewhere in France her brother lay beneath the soil. France. If it should be anywhere, it should be next to her mother and father's graves back in the little hamlet they grew up in. Not in France.

Suddenly, she realised she could never live in France. The notion hit her like a fist in the chest. She didn't want to be in a country where battles scarred the countryside like pox marks on skin. She didn't want Bailey growing up surrounded by a foreign language, foreign rules and where families had to rebuild shattered lives and ruined towns and where the enemy was just over the border.

She quickly continued to write.

I HAVE GIVEN our future home some thought and if you agree I wish to rule out Paris as a place for us to settle to run your father's business office. I would prefer any other place rather than France. Please let me know your thoughts on this.

Lachie mentioned Australia. If that was his wish, I feel it's important to consider Sydney.

HARSH HAMMERING SOUNDED on the front door. She jerked in alarm. Scurrying from the bed, she wrapped her dressing gown around her, meeting Mildred doing the same on the small landing.

'Is it our door?' Mildred asked, her brown hair in a long plait.

The hammering came again.

'I think so.' Olivia dashed down the stairs and slid back the bolt on the front door. 'Larry?'

'Is Tess here with you?'

'No. We are all in bed.' It took a moment for her heartbeat to settle and for her to think clearly.

'She's gone, Liv.'

'Gone?'

He looked distraught. 'Aye, my lass, lovely lass, she's packed a case and gone. Her hat and coat aren't hanging up.'

'Did she leave a note?' Mildred asked from behind Olivia.

'No, no note.' Larry's hair stood on end where he'd run his fingers through it. 'I came home from my shift and the house was quiet, but it's been like that since our Colin.' He blinked rapidly. 'I thought she might be in bed, sometimes she doesn't get out of bed all day. You've seen how she is lately,' he rambled. 'But I noticed her hat and coat wasn't on the back door. I thought she'd gone for a walk, or to the market, but it's been hours. It's dark now. Tess hasn't been herself, has she? I'm worried.'

'No, she definitely hasn't been herself,' Oliva agreed. 'If she's gone for a walk, she's probably gone too far and is resting somewhere.'

'Would she have money for a tram?' Mildred asked.

'I don't know.' Larry looked tormented. 'I've been home since six and it's now nearly ten o'clock. Where could she be? Did you see her at all today?'

'This morning, yes. She came to tell me about the letter.'

'What letter?'

'The letter from the boys' commanding officer. Have you not seen it?'

'No.' Larry's puzzled expression worried Olivia.

'Then Tess has it with her. The commanding officer wrote that Lachie and Colin died together. They are buried together.'

Larry closed his eyes in a flash of pain. 'She's not coping with the boy's death, Liv. She's taken it worse than Lance's death. Colin was her baby, the youngest…'

'We need to go out and search for her,' Mildred said.

'Jonnie and Jules are walking the streets already.'

'I'll help. Give me a few minutes to dress,' Olivia said.

Larry nodded. 'I'll wait for you. I'll ask some of the neighbours as well.'

Closing the door, Olivia hurried up the stairs. 'Will you watch Bailey for me?'

'Of course,' Mildred whispered, following her into her bedroom and helping her dress quickly. 'Where could she be?'

'I wish I knew.' Olivia glanced at Bailey as she left the bedroom. 'Sleep in my bed tonight, Mildred.'

'There won't be any sleep happening until you come home,' Mildred said following her back downstairs. 'I'll make some tea and wait.'

Olivia went out into the square where the neighbours, those who could, gathered, but it was a small group with Ezra, Mr Muldoon, Mr Berry and Sadie's Gerry away in France.

Mrs Berry donned her shawl over her head and Mrs Muldoon instructed her eldest child to care for the younger children while she was out. The women split off in pairs, Mrs Berry and Mrs Muldoon, and Sadie and Olivia, while Larry headed for the allotments behind the working men's club.

'What was she thinking going off on her own?' Sadie muttered.

'I don't expect that she was thinking at all,' Olivia replied.

They walked down Stanley Road, past the closed shops, slipping in and out of the streetlamps' glow.

'Where will we head to?' Sadie asked as they passed a noisy pub.

'Larry said he's been to Warrengate where his brother lives, and she's not been there.' Olivia slowed to look down the narrow opening to a row of tenement houses. Several tenement yards run off Stanley Road.

'I don't suppose she'd have any need to be in any of those yards, do you?' Sadie asked.

'We should check them while we're passing.' Olivia peered into the shadowy lane. 'Tess?' she called.

The only movement was a scrawny cat jumping down from the wall to land at their feet and meow for attention.

Sadie pushed the cat away from her skirts with the tip of her boot. 'Perhaps she's in town? Jonnie has gone to the theatre on Drury Lane to check there. Should we try St Andrew's?'

Olivia struggled to think. 'Wouldn't the church be locked now? Besides, the vicar knows Tess. If she'd been there a long time, he'd have sent word by now.'

'True enough.'

'I really don't know where she could be.' Olivia pondered all the usual places she and Tess had gone to since they met, but mostly those places were the shops, or the market, sometimes a stroll around the park before the war started.

Sadie stopped outside of another pub. 'Should we go in and ask?'

'It can't hurt.'

All eyes turned towards them as they entered the busy pub, and the talk quietened.

'Oh aye, what's this then?' One fellow nudged his friend at the table.

'We've got some fine company tonight, lads,' another jested.

'We're looking for a friend of ours,' Sadie suddenly announced to the whole bar. 'A woman called Tess Hobson, from Woodcock's Square. She's gone missing. Today she received a letter with news about her son who was killed in action.'

The teasing and grins on the men's faces altered and became serious. Many shook their heads in sympathy.

'Larry Hobson's Tess?' One man stood up from his table. 'I work with Larry down the pit.'

'Yes, Tess!' Olivia said eagerly.

'I saw her walking down Kirkgate earlier, hours ago.'

'Towards the river?' another man asked.

A deathly quiet filtered over the taproom.

'She's not been herself since Colin's death,' Olivia told them, refusing to accept Tess would harm herself, but the thought lingered that Tess couldn't swim.

'Right, lads!' Larry's friend urged the men in the bar to leave their pints and follow him out. 'We'll search the riverbanks.'

'You'll need lights.' The landlord took several lanterns from the shelves behind him. 'These are filled with oil in readiness for when we have gas problems.'

'When you forget to pay your gas bill more like,' a man at the bar jeered.

The landlord threw him a filthy glare before giving the lanterns to some of the men. 'Take them.'

The tingle of emotion shivered over Olivia's skin at their generous kind spirit, but she shook it off and hurried to join them.

They searched the riverbanks throughout the night and by dawn there still hadn't been any sighting of Tess.

Weary, Olivia and Sadie turned away from the river and

started for home as the birdsong trilled over the rooftops and the sun gave the sky pink and violet streaks.

'Larry will be beside himself.' Sadie held up her long skirts which showed muddy signs of trudging through the reedy banks.

A train whistle cut the morning sounds, loud and shrill. Puffs of smoke billowed into the sky over the train station. Olivia gazed at the smoke, listened to the noise of the train gathering speed. 'The train station!' She began to run, holding her skirts high.

'Liv!' Sadie chased after her as Olivia ran up onto the station's platform.

'Excuse me,' Olivia panted to the porter. 'Did you see an older woman yesterday, grey hair and wearing a black coat?'

'Madam, you've described half the women who come along this platform.' The porter shrugged and wheeled his trolley away.

Olivia followed him. 'Where there any trains last night, late ones?'

'The London express leaves at ten every night,' he threw over his shoulder.

Olivia glanced at Sadie. 'She might have caught the train.'

'To where? London? Whatever for?'

It suddenly occurred to Olivia where Tess might have gone. 'To get to France. To visit Colin's grave.'

'But you said you don't have the details yet of where that is!'

'I know, we don't, but Tess isn't thinking straight. Come on. We need to get back to Larry.'

Once in the square, Olivia noted many neighbours were standing around drinking tea and eating bread and jam provided by those who stayed behind. Mildred had Bailey on one hip, as she offered boiled eggs to those hungry.

'My darling boy.' Olivia kissed Bailey and took him from Mildred. 'Thank you. Did he sleep?'

'Straight through the night until about half an hour ago. He was wet and hungry, so I changed him and fed him porridge. He's happy now.'

'You truly are wonderful.' Olivia clutched Mildred's hand in gratitude.

'He's no trouble. You must be tired though,' Mildred whispered.

'Yes, a little, but I have an idea where she might have gone. Where's Larry?' Olivia looked around the square and spotted him coming out of his house. He wore a tired haggard expression. She went to him. 'Larry. How much money did Tess take?'

'All the housekeeping money in the tin on the shelf in the kitchen and the Post Office savings account book has gone.' Larry's eyes were red. 'She's left me, Liv. After all these years, she's left me.'

'Not quite. At least, she might have left only to travel to France. To find Colin's grave.'

Larry's eyes widened. 'That could be anywhere! We don't know where it is. There's a war on! They won't let her get anywhere near where he's buried. We don't even know where he is!' he repeated.

'I doubt she'll even make it close. She'll be stopped if she tries to board any train heading to northern France, not without official papers. The army doesn't allow people to just wander around battlefields willy nilly.'

He breathed out slowly. 'You might be right. I should have thought of it sooner. She's gone to find Colin.'

'There's nothing much we can do but wait for her to return. I'll send a telegram to Stanford and ask him to see if he can find out any information. He has friends in many high places within the army and Westminster as does Mr Parkinson.'

'Thank you, Liv. I'm so worried about her.'

She rubbed his back gently. 'Go and get some sleep. We'll find her and you need to be strong for when she does come home.'

'And what if she never does come home to us?' his voice was barely audible.

'Don't think that way,' she said with a reassuring smile she didn't feel.

Tess was not in the right state of mind to go travelling to a war-torn country. Olivia was frightened the whole ordeal would be too much for her dear friend and that she would struggle in a foreign country, out of her depth and possibly soon out of money.

CHAPTER 18

For a week, the neighbours in the square searched for Tess just in case she hadn't gone to France. Larry grew more withdrawn and more tired. Olivia and Mildred cooked meals for the Hobson men, did their washing and cared for them the best they could as Larry and his sons spent all their hours searching the town when they weren't working down the pit. The police had been notified, but they also didn't have any answers.

'I know I sound terribly spoiled when I say this, but I do miss not having a maid to do all the ironing,' Mildred said, puffing air out of her red cheeks as she ironed a skirt on the kitchen table.

The kitchen was like an oven. The warm day intensified inside the small kitchen as the copper boiler in the corner sent steam rising to the ceiling as Bailey's napkins soaked within it. A lamb stew was simmering on the stove.

'Have a rest from it,' Olivia instructed from where she sat on a chair polishing her and Mildred's shoes. 'I said I'd do it once I've done these.'

'But I dislike polishing shoes even more!' Mildred declared.

'Take Bailey out for a walk in his pram. He's due for his nap.' Olivia glanced at her son crawling around the rug.

Mildred placed the skirt on the hanger. 'Yes, maybe I will, but first I'll go next door and hang out Larry and the boys' clothes.'

Olivia admired the shine she'd created on one of Mildred's black low-heeled shoe. She could see her reflection on the brass buckle and satisfied, placed it with its pair she'd done earlier.

Bailey sneezed and looked up at her with a smile.

'Was that funny, my darling? Bless you.' She picked up one of her own shoes as Mildred ran back inside. 'What's wrong?'

'Tess. She's returned. She's sitting in her kitchen. She frightened the life out of me. She's just sitting at the table, staring into the fire grate.'

Olivia grabbed Bailey and with Mildred they dashed out of the backyard and around to the next one and into the Hobsons' kitchen. 'Tess!' Olivia stopped in front of her. 'Tess? We've all been so worried about you. Larry, Jonnie and Jules are going to be very happy to see you home.'

'I couldn't find him, lass,' Tess said, without looking at her. 'I tried.'

'You went to France?' Olivia asked gently.

'To find my boy.' On Tess's lap was a small black bag. She still wore her coat and hat. She looked worn out. 'I made it as far as Calais. I was standing on French soil. The same soil that they buried my boy in, but I couldn't find him.'

Olivia passed Bailey to Mildred and knelt before Tess. 'One day, when the war is over, we will go and visit Colin and Lachie's grave.'

'I couldn't find it!' Tess snapped.

'The army, the War Office, will help us.'

'No one *helped* me. Everyone I spoke to told me to go home. No one had the time to help me. I snuck onto a troop train at Calais, but they found me at the next station and put me on a wagon and drove me back to Calais.' She sighed deeply. 'A kind officer said he'd make enquiries and let me rest in a tent. Then he put me up in a hotel near the port…'

'That was good of him,' Olivia said, taking Tess's hand.

'He couldn't find any information. He escorted me to a ship. I didn't catch his name.' Tess stared at Olivia, her face tormented. 'I didn't want to fail.'

'The odds were against you.' Olivia squeezed her hand softly. 'But when the war is over, we'll try together. Yes?'

'Will it ever be over?'

'We must believe it.' Olivia stood. 'Now, how about a bath and I'll wash your hair.'

'I can wash my own hair.'

Olivia raised an eyebrow. 'Let me look after you. You've had a long journey and must be so tired.'

Tess looked past her to the baby. 'How's my precious Bailey doing?'

'He's doing just fine but missed his Aunty Tess.' Mildred placed him on Tess's lap. 'We all have missed you.'

Tess gazed down at Bailey's sweet face and kissed the top of his head. 'I just wanted to find my boy.'

Olivia leaned closer to Mildred and whispered, 'Can you send a neighbour to the pit? Larry needs to know she's home.'

Mildred nodded and slipped out of the back door.

Olivia started filling the kettle with water and some pots to heat up for the bath.

'I've never crossed a sea before,' Tess told her, stroking Bailey's head. 'I've never been out of Yorkshire without Larry to organise it, like he did when we visited Colin when he was wounded. But I managed to find my way to London by myself this time, and from London to Dover and across the water to Calais. Me, Tess Hobson, travelled to another country, alone.' She stared at Olivia. 'It's opened my eyes, lass. There's a whole world out there. So much more beyond Wakefield, beyond England.'

'That's true.'

'Our boys experienced something of life before they died. They saw new places, experienced new things. I take comfort from that.'

Olivia remained quiet, for she didn't quite agree. A place in wartime wasn't normal life. They hadn't been on a holiday to enjoy.

'My Simon has sailed the seas, visited more countries than I can name while I've been content to stay in this town, in this square, never wanting to venture further away.' She glanced down at Bailey and then back to the unlit fire.

'But you've been happy, Tess. You've raised a family.'

'Aye, I have. But I feel stupid for not wanting more, like you. I never understood why you wanted to see other places. When you nearly went to America with Mr Sheridan, I couldn't appreciate the desire to leave your home.'

Tess's face held no expression as she continued. 'Being on that ship, watching the water flow past it was like a dream. Finally, I imagined what it must be like for our Simon.' Tess shook her head. 'I've always resented our Lance and Simon for leaving and going away, for not staying here with me, with the family.' Tess shrugged, deflated. 'What a bad mother I've been to begrudge them for spreading their wings.'

'It was only because you loved them so much and wanted them near you.'

'Two of my boys are dead. Simon prefers the life on the seas, and Jonnie has met a girl, Jules will too one day, and they will move away. I am frightened that when all my boys leave me, I'll have no purpose.'

'Children leave home, Tess. It's natural.'

'But what will I do without my boys?'

'You'll do other things, without being tied to that oven making food, or to that boiler washing filthy pit clothes. You'll have time for yourself.'

'To do what? Being a mam is all I've ever done since I was eighteen years old. And you and Bailey will leave one day as well.'

'You have Larry.'

Tess gave Bailey to Olivia. 'Larry, yes… He will be all I have once you are all gone.'

* * *

November 1917, South of Ribecourt, France.

In the eerie silence of predawn, hidden in a wood, Spencer crouched near a tree, leaning his back against the broad trunk. His men were flanked on either side of him, well hidden. In front, at the edge of the wood, British tanks waited for the signal to advance. The cavalry were in support at the rear. Their objective was Ribecourt village, possibly Marcoing and hopefully Cambrai, one of the main supply centres for the German army.

Spencer felt confident. His men were well rested having spent the last six months in the Loos Salient being involved in only minor skirmishes and mostly staying in caretaker positions away from the serious fighting. However, too much time doing nothing but drilling, training and caretaking gave the men the excuse to squabble, to become lax, and to think of home too much. They all wanted it to be over, and with the Americans soon to be landing in France, bolstering the allies' numbers, then surely a turning point should come soon. He hoped the forthcoming battle was another step in that direction.

Movement made him swing around as Sergeant Matlock knelt down beside him. 'The men are in position, sir.'

'Where is Lieutenant Dawes?' Spencer hadn't seen him for an hour.

'Last I saw he was writing a report on Private Boyle who he claims had severely broken his orders.'

'What orders were they?' Spencer rolled his eyes, knowing that after the battle he'd have to deal with Dawes and his grievances.

'Lieutenant Dawes reckons Boyle defied the order to wear the correct uniform. You know how Boyle likes to wear the feather tucked into his webbing, the one sent to him from his daughter? Lieutenant Dawes threw it on the ground because Boyle didn't salute him and made a rude comment about him.'

'Christ Almighty. I don't need this ridiculous time wasting!' Spencer growled between clenched teeth.

'The men don't like him, sir.'

Spencer stiffened. For months the unsettling reports of the French soldiers mutinying against their commanders had sent shock waves through the British army. They last thing they needed was their own men to do the same as the French. 'Whether they like him or not, Sergeant, they are to follow orders from senior officers.'

Abruptly the quietness of dawn was broken by the booming sounds of heavy cannons firing some distance away and it brought their attention back to the planned battle. To the north the shells from those cannons bombarded the German lines. The battle had begun.

'Good luck, sir,' Matlock said.

'And to you, Sergeant.' Spencer felt the familiar tingle run down his spine as he stood and reached for his whistle. For a second he closed his eyes and thought of his beloved Olivia, of his son Bailey and prayed he'd see them again.

He had his orders, the tanks were to lead the battle, do all the heavy work after the cannons' bombardment. He and his men were to follow behind the tanks and the overhead creeping barrage towards the enemy's lines.

Lieutenant Dawes joined him. 'Why are we not advancing, Major!'

'Because, Lieutenant, our orders are to wait behind the tank battalions. We hold this line.'

'We should follow them, sir!' Dawes urged.

'And outrun the tanks and straight into our own barrage?' Spencer glared at the irritating man. 'Go back to your men and wait for my command.'

Dawes jerked his chin out. 'This is not how I interpreted the battle plan, sir.'

'Then it's a good thing you aren't the commanding officer, isn't it?' Spencer could easily have throttled the fellow's scrawny neck. 'Return to your men, Lieutenant.'

Spencer nearly missed the signal to advance and threw Dawes a vicious look that would make other men obey immediately, but Dawes was too full of his own importance to recognise it. Spencer blew his whistle before turning to Dawes. '*Get back to your men, Lieutenant!*' he yelled above the jarring noise of shellfire and creaking tanks.

Following the creeping barrage, Spencer's company moved as quickly as possible under the fog of smoke. They had a lot of ground to cover and found little resistance until they reached the edge of the village.

Heavy fighting occurred but the success of the tanks directly in front of Spencer's men gave them enough cover to overcome the enemy's positions throughout the village.

As the Germans retreated, Spencer signalled for his men to advance through the streets and cottage gardens.

Hidden behind a sandbagged barricade, four German machine gunners stood up and surrendered.

'Take those prisoners!' Spencer ordered to a nearby sergeant. 'Check them thoroughly.' He walked quickly past the German soldiers to their gun post to search for any hidden enemy. 'Clear! Corporal McDonald, disarm that machine gun.'

Spencer continued through the village, ordering his men to investigate the buildings surrounding them. Explosions from hand grenades thrown into suspicious buildings blasted the streets. He met up with another company's commanding officer, one who'd replaced Albert Dunbar, and they compared notes and sent runners back to HQ with information.

They slowly continued out of Ribecourt, meeting some resistance along the way as the Germans fought minor counter-attacks but as the day progressed, the fighting lessened as the company made for the village of Marcoing.

As they neared the village, Spencer and his men came under intense fire. Finding whatever protection they could, the men fought back with aggressive determination. Spencer barked orders until his throat grew hoarse.

The German retaliations grew fiercer as the Allies pushed the enemy back towards the canal. Some of the tanks began to break down due to German shell fire and mechanical problems and were abandoned.

With dogged determination, Spencer urged his men onwards, routing the straggling German soldiers and securing sections of the village.

Ducking from a sniper's bullet coming from up in one of the large trees by the church, Spencer hid behind a garden wall, Sergeant Matlock joining him.

'Have we lost our tanks, sir?' Matlock asked, panting.

'We have outrun the ones that are operational.' Spencer took a swig of water from his drink bottle, his throat parched. 'We need to hold this village.'

'And not try to make it across the canal, sir?'

'No, the mounted cavalry will lead that charge.'

'But where are they?' Matlock said mostly to himself, looking back to where they'd just fought through the village lanes.

'They should be here.' Spencer flinched as a bullet nicked the edge of the wall, splintering stone chips over his tin helmet that sounded like hail.

Without warning, a group of three of his soldiers burst out

from under cover and ran towards the church opposite. The sniper cut them down one by one. It happened so quickly that Spencer was hardly aware of it before he realised. Lying in the lane the three dead soldiers were the evidence of the madness of breaking cover. In astonishment, he noticed two more soldiers creep closer to make the suicidal run across the lane.

'Stop! Stop!' Spencer sprang up, screaming at them.

A bullet grazed by his shoulder and he ducked down. 'Stop!'

Thankfully, the men hunkered down behind the side of a building, looking at him in confusion.

'Who gave that order to advance!' Spencer yelled across the lane.

'Lieutenant Dawes, sir,' a young soldier called back.

Spencer swore loudly and violently. 'Stay where you are! There's a sniper in one of the trees.' He turned to Matlock. 'Can you see the sniper?'

Matlock crawled further down the wall and peered around the side of it. 'He's not in a tree but on the church roof, sir.'

'Can you take a shot?'

Before Matlock could answer, a shell burst in the lane. The ground vibrated, the explosion hurting Spencer's ears. He flung himself down as dirt and stones rained down on him.

Spencer looked around as more shells landed in the village streets destroying cottages and barns.

'Germans or ours, sir?' Matlock coughed, crawling back to him.

'Germans.'

The sound of hoofbeats echoed along the dusty lanes. The cavalry charge was magnificent to watch as they rode hard and fast past Spencer and through the falling shells.

A shell landed in the churchyard and taking advantage of the smoke, Spencer blew his whistle to advance.

'Get that son of a bitch on the roof!' Spencer shouted to Matlock, following him as they sprinted towards the church.

A bomb exploded to Spencer's right, blowing up the tail end of the cavalry. Two horses went airborne, the riders flung into the sky before falling back to earth. The two horses, killed instantly, lay amongst the rubble of the lane. Spencer ran to check one of the riders and found him also dead. The other rider was lying on his back close to a wall of a small cottage.

Kneeling beside him, Spencer recognised the uniform of the Canadian cavalry. Spencer smiled down at the young man, who was bleeding heavily from a head wound and from his stomach. 'We'll get you fixed up, trooper.'

'Thank you, sir.' The young man's hat had fallen off and blood seeped through his pale blond hair.

'You have the same colour hair as my wife,' Spencer told him, taking the man's own bandages from his pockets and wrapping it around his head.

'Is she pretty?' the soldier joked.

'I've never met any woman more beautiful than my Olivia,' Spencer said truthfully, securing the bandage as the soldier's eyes narrowed on him.

The soldier winced and struggled to breathe.

Spencer looked up the lane. He need to get to his men. 'The stretcher-bearers will be along shortly. Lie still now. Wait for them.'

'Olivia… My sister is called Olivia, and I know your face…'

Spencer froze.

'You're the captain from Hawthorn Manor.' The soldier's blue eyes stared at him the same as Olivia and Bailey's did and a shiver tingled down Spencer's spine.

'What's your name?' he asked urgently, remembering Olivia's other brother.

The soldier's eyes were closing slightly. 'Stu Brodie…'

'Brodie!' Spencer grabbed his shoulders. 'Stu! Stay with me now. Hold on!'

Stu spoke with his eyes closed, the pain pinching around his lips. 'Your friend Mr Parkinson… Fixed his motor… He gave me the money to get to Canada…'

'Olivia thinks you're in America.' Spencer was dumbfounded. 'She'll be so happy that I've spoken with you.'

'Dear Liv…' Stu smiled. 'I wrote. Never heard back…'

'They've left the cottage. She wanted to find you, but didn't know where you went.'

'Canada. Worked all over. Couldn't settle. War sounded like another adventure.' Stu tried to focus, his breathing became laboured. 'Won't survive this one though…'

'Steady now.' Spencer gripped his hand. 'Do not give up. Your sister needs you.'

'Miss them. Father, Lachie…'

Spencer's stomach somersaulted. He wouldn't tell this badly wounded man that his actions of leaving home, and the argument beforehand, gave his father a fatal heart attack, nor would he tell him about Lachie.

'You married our Liv?' Stu's eyelids fluttered.

Spencer pulled out his own bandages and pressed them to the stomach wound. 'I did marry her.'

'Good on Liv. She's like me, adventurous. Married a toff.' Stu tried to grin, but blood trickled over his bottom lip.

Wiping the blood from his mouth, Spencer kept up the chatter, looking around for the stretcher-bearers who brought up the rear. 'We have a son, Bailey. He's just turned one. He has the Brodie pale hair and blue eyes. You're an uncle, Stu. Once they have you fixed up at the hospital, you can go and visit them.'

A weak smile appeared on his face. 'Tell Liv I miss her…'

'I will.'

'I'm going to my mam. She's waiting…' Stu's eyes closed, and his chest stopped moving.

For a moment suspended in time, Spencer held Olivia's brother and cursed the fates that had brought about the death of another young man, but also praised them for allowing him to be the one to find Stu, for Olivia.

Stretcher-bearers came running, and the noise of distant bombings, of machine guns firing, of soldiers yelling brought him back to the moment. The battle was moving on beyond the village and he had to join his men. He searched Stu's pockets for anything personal to give to Olivia but found nothing of note, nothing that she could take comfort from, then he found a small iron bird shaped like a swallow in his breast pocket.

'Sir?' A stretcher-bearer waited by his side holding one end of a stretcher.

'He's gone. My brother-in-law. Stu Brodie.' Spencer didn't want to leave him. Olivia wouldn't want him to, but he had his duty to his men.

'We'll take good care of him, sir.'

He nodded, took a step, reluctant to go. Then he heard Matlock calling him and he turned and ran up the lane to rejoin his men.

The heavy fighting continued into the afternoon as they reached the next village of Noyelles. The Germans counter-attacked, turning on the Allies with vengeance, cutting off the advance. The Allies retreated and by nightfall Spencer found himself back in Marcoing, nursing a sore ankle that twisted under him as he jumped a ditch.

He and the men were exhausted, but they had to remain alert for night raids. Spencer organised for the wounded to be sent back down the line to the casualty clearing stations, and he noted the names and ranks of the dead men under his command.

His batman, Private Bishop, brought him water to wash away the grime and blood of the battlefield as he wrote in the company logbook while his men worked alongside other companies to barricade and defend the village as the countryside descended into a tainted peacefulness.

Orders arrived from HQ that the battle was to be renewed at

dawn. Spencer instructed his men to rest for a few hours, eat their rations and bandage their minor wounds.

Unable to sleep for more than an hour, Spencer took a lantern and returned to the dark lane near the church. Stu's body was gone. Only the blood-stained dirt remained.

He sat down, his back against the wall, his knees drawn up, staring into the darkness, listening to the soft murmurs of the men settling down for the night.

Stu hadn't known his father was dead and likely he'd have put him down as his next of kin. The official letter would be sent to the family's cottage long abandoned and never find its way to Olivia. Spencer knew that he'd have to be the one to write to her and break the news. He didn't know how to do such a task. Oh, he'd written to countless families when his men died. He'd written words of sympathy, of bravery, but how was he to write to the woman he loved and tell her what happened today?

She'd want to know it all, every detail. Suddenly he realised he'd have to write to her now, tonight, for tomorrow he could die in battle and Olivia would never know of Stu's death. Perhaps it was better that she didn't know, that she thought of him being in America and having a good life?

Tormented by indecision, he pulled the swallow out of his pocket and ran a thumb over it. He didn't have the mental strength to write to Olivia tonight. When he wrote the news to her, he needed to word it carefully and that wouldn't be achieved if he took to pen and paper at this moment.

No, he'd write to her after the battle, when he was behind the lines, refreshed and able to concentrate.

Resting his head against the wall, he closed his tired eyes. He recalled the time of that summer when he first met Olivia. When he sat in the yard at the forge, listening to Olivia's father and brothers tell him stories and his beautiful Olivia poured tea for him trying not to be caught out looking at him. How innocent it had all been. It'd been the only time he'd seen them all together.

Their laughter had floated up into the warm summer sky…

CHAPTER 19

December 1917

PAINTING her corner of the front room, Olivia stood on the chair and stretched as high as she could. 'Can you reach, Mildred?'

'Not really. I'm not as tall as you.' Mildred reached higher, dabbing the paintbrush above the front door frame just as the door opened and Tess tried to walk in, banging into the chair.

'What in God's name?' Tess stuck her head around the door. 'What's blocking it?'

'Me!' Mildred climbed down off the chair and moved to open the door wider for Tess to come in. 'The one day you don't come through the kitchen,' she tutted.

Tess raised her eyebrows. 'I see you're in a good mood, Mrs Middleton.'

'I told you we were painting the front room today.' Olivia finished the corner she'd started.

'Aye, lass, well I forgot, didn't I? Shall I put the kettle on?' Tess bent and tickled Bailey under the chin where he stood holding onto the sofa.

Olivia got down from the chair and put the paintbrush on the top of the tin on the mantlepiece. She scooped Bailey up onto her hip and followed Tess into the kitchen. 'I thought you were going to the market this morning?'

'I've been and come back.' Tess put the kettle onto the gas stove. 'I couldn't dally there as our Jonnie is bringing Margy for tea this afternoon and I wanted to make a semolina cake, which I've done and it's in the oven.'

Mildred came in carrying an old box.

Olivia put Bailey on the floor where he took wobbly steps over to Tess and grabbed her skirts.

Tess picked him up. 'There's my clever boy. You'll be running before long, won't you?'

Olivia smiled, watching Tess with Bailey. Since returning from France, Tess had fooled everyone that she was back to her old self, but Olivia, and Larry, didn't believe it. A sadness still lurked in Tess's eyes and her jolly nature had quietened a little. She hadn't regained her plumpness, and her hair was nearly pure white now.

'They seem to be serious, Jonnie and Margy,' Mildred said, sorting through a box of Christmas decorations.

'What have you got that lot out for? Christmas isn't for another three weeks.' Tess frowned.

Olivia knew Tess wasn't looking forward to her first Christmas without Colin, and, if she was being truthful, she wasn't looking forward to it either, not without Lachie, and she wasn't sure if Spencer would make it either. She'd not heard from him for over a week or more and last time that happened he arrived on the doorstep. Could she be lucky enough to have him home for this Christmas?

Mildred held up a coloured paper chain. 'I do know when

Christmas is, Mrs Hobson,' Mildred said with a hint of sarcasm and a wink to Olivia.

'Hark at her,' Tess declared. 'When she first arrived on this square, she'd hardly say boo to a goose and now listen to hear with her smart quips.' Tess grinned, showing no hard feelings.

Mildred brought out another paper chain. 'We are sorting through the decorations to see if we need new ones once the painting is finished,' Mildred explained.

'That's all you needed to say.' Tess looked at the front door as a knock sounded, her face lost all colour. She put Bailey on the floor and edged towards the back door as though ready to flee.

Olivia hurried to open it, praying it wasn't a post office messenger. Instead, a sailor stood in front of her, a kit bag slung over his shoulder.

'Excuse me, madam, but would you know if Tess Hobson will be home soon? There's no one in next door, but there's a cooking smell coming from the oven. So, is she about?'

Olivia smiled at the sailor. 'Are you Simon?' she whispered.

'Aye, are you Olivia?' he whispered back, grinning.

'I am. Come in.' Olivia stepped aside so he could enter the front room. 'Stand over there.' She pointed to the hearth where a good coal fire burned. She went to the kitchen doorway. 'Tess, there's a man to see you about your oven.'

Tess crept back to the table with a scowl. 'I ain't buying owt from no salesman, so he can sling his hook.'

'Go and talk to him.' Olivia folded her arms as though it was none of her business.

'Lord above, I just wanted a cup of tea.' Tess strode into the front room only to stop and stare, then screamed. 'Simon! Oh, my boy! Oh, you're home!' She ran to him and enveloped him into a tight embrace, crying tears of happiness.

Mildred stood beside Olivia, tears in her eyes as well. 'That's lovely, so lovely.'

Olivia went into the kitchen. 'I'll get another cup and saucer.'

Tess brought Simon into the kitchen and made the introductions, her eyes shining with utter joy. 'This is the best surprise. My boy is home.' She hugged her son to her again.

'Sit down, and we'll have some tea,' Olivia invited Simon. She remembered what Simon said about the smell of cooking. 'Tess, your cake! Simon said he smelt it.'

'No! I forgot about it.' Tess hurried out of the back door and around to her own.

Simon accepted the tea from Olivia. 'How is she doing? After Colin? Me father sent me a telegram saying Mam had gone to France.'

'Is that why you came home?' Mildred asked, placing Bailey on her knee.

'Aye. Father said if I could, to come home. I was due some leave, and I took it.'

'How long are you staying?'

'We sailed into Southampton at the end of November and I was meant to be assigned to another ship while ours is getting a refit. But I've managed to get leave on compassionate grounds.' Simon had Tess's eyes and her round face, but his father's black hair and cheeky smile.

'Your father and brothers will be so pleased to see you.' Olivia offered him a plate of the chocolate biscuits she'd made the day before.

'And I them! It's been so long. Everything is familiar yet also feels strange.' He ate a biscuit in record time. 'These are so good.'

Tess walked in with a resigned expression. 'The cake is burnt all around the edges.' She smiled at Simon. 'But what do I care about a cake when my boy is home!'

'When will Father and the others be home?' he asked.

'This afternoon. They've worked a shift and a half. Jonnie is saving all his money at the moment and trying to earn as much as he can.'

'Why?' Simon ate another biscuit.

'He's got a lass. I think they'll be married by the spring.'

'A lass?' Simon shook his head. 'He was just a boy when I left.'

'Aye, that was years ago, lad, you were a boy yourself. You've become a man,' Tess admitted. 'They've all grown up.' Her smile slipped. 'Aye, well, our Lance and Colin won't grow any older…'

Simon took her hand. 'Mam, I was so upset to hear about them.'

Tess nodded and gripped his hand with both of hers.

The sad moment made Olivia nod to Mildred, who understood and rose from her chair with Bailey. 'This little man needs changing. Excuse me.'

'I'll do it.' Olivia stood as well. 'He's ready for his nap.'

'We'll go home, lass, and leave you in peace to get on with your painting,' Tess told her. 'Our Simon might want a rest.'

Simon grabbed his kit bag. 'Thank you for the tea and biscuits.'

'You're welcome.' Olivia watched Tess link her arm through Simon's even though they were only going next door. It did her heart a lot of good to see her dear friend close to being happy again.

Olivia took Bailey upstairs to change him and then put him in his cot for a nap. For a while she sat on the end of her bed and watched him until he drifted off to sleep. He was such a darling baby, her son, and as he grew, she saw so much of Spencer in him, but at times she saw her father and brothers and that gave her a strange kind of comfort.

When she went downstairs to resume painting, she found Mildred was sitting on the sofa reading a letter, her face full of misery.

She hadn't heard the mail delivery. 'Mil? What is it?' Olivia sat beside her. 'Bad news?'

'No, no. It's a letter from Ralph.' Mildred waved the letter dismissively. 'Another one of his dutiful letters to his dutiful wife,' she scorned. 'Only this time he tells me the plans are in place and secure for our future. The plans he organised without even discussing any of it with me.' She looked at Olivia with such anger. 'Unlike Spencer, Ralph doesn't feel the need to talk to his wife about the future or even consider my opinion.' Mildred picked up a small brown paper parcel beside her. 'This came for you.'

'Oh, a parcel? From Spencer?' She recognised his handwriting.

'Perhaps a little something for Bailey?'

Olivia untied the string and opened the paper, out fell a letter and a small iron bird. A shiver went down her spine as she stared at it.

'That's so sweet.' Mildred admired the bird.

'A swallow. My brother Stu had a swallow just like this, Father made it for him when he was a baby. He made me a ladybird, and he made Lachie a frog. I lost my ladybird as a girl. I took it into the garden and lost it. Lachie put his frog in the hamlet's pond, thinking it would float and when it sank, he was so upset. He was only about three or four years old.'

'Your father must have been so talented to make such things out of iron.'

Olivia opened the letter and read it out loud for Mildred to hear.

My dearest love,

I am at present writing in a school room in a village. Outside the rain is pouring down and halting our advance. We have been in the thick of battle for over a week and although we managed to claim a good advantage against the enemy, the Germans have rallied to counter-attack and pushed us back. The weather has also turned against us. Winter is biting hard with deep frosts when it's not raining, that of which we receive a great deal.

You must be wondering at the bird. Do you recognise it?

Olivia's rapid heartbeat thumped against her ribs. She swallowed and kept reading.

I met a Canadian cavalryman during the battle. He and his horse were hit by a shell when we were under intense shelling. I went to his aid. I thought it odd how he had such pale blond hair and piercing blue eyes the same as my wife.

I was knelt beside your brother, my darling.

Stu joined the war in Canada where he'd been living. My heart aches for you as I write this. Regrettably, Stu died from his wounds. I am so sorry, my love.

Mildred gasped. 'Oh, Liv.'

Olivia strove to keep her voice under control as emotion tightened her throat. She blinked to clear her vision as the words blurred slightly in front of her.

I was with him until the end. He was not alone. He remembered me. I told him that we were married. I told him about Bailey. He was impressed that you had married me, a toff. They were his words.

Olivia could easily imagine Stu's cheeky words and she smiled. She swallowed with difficulty. 'Stu would say something like that,' she said to Mildred. 'He never took anything seriously. Life was one big adventure.'

'If he travelled to Canada, then he was courageous and spirited. It seems to be a family trait,' Mildred said with admiration.

'Or we're just stubborn and want our own way,' she acknowledged and continued to read.

The bird was in his pocket and being made of iron I thought it might be a link to your father's forge or that Stu had made it himself using the skills your father taught him. I thought you would want it.

Stu told me that he missed you, your father and Lachie. I could not bring myself to tell him what had happened after he left the forge. Nor could I mention Lachie's fate.

My darling, I must end this letter now as the mail cart is leaving in a few minutes and I am not sure when we will see the next one as we are on the move again soon. I wish I was there to comfort you as you read this terrible news. I'm sorry I cannot be there to support you. I love you.

Give my fondest regards to Mildred and the neighbours. I hope Tess is coping better with her loss.

I miss you most desperately. I long to be with you and hold you in my arms.

Give Bailey a kiss from his father and to you my heart, I send all my love and devotion.

Spencer. xx

'Oh, Liv. I'm so sorry.' Mildred hugged her tightly.

She felt numb, in denial. Her family was gone.

Leaning out of Mildred's embrace, she stared down at the swallow. 'I haven't seen Stu for three years. Not a word. What are the odds of Spencer being there when he died?'

'It's a miracle.' Mildred nodded with conviction.

'If Spencer hadn't been there, I'd never have known Stu was

dead. He was a Canadian cavalryman. He was in Canada not America as we thought.'

'He died a hero, fighting for the freedom of us all.'

Olivia gripped the swallow, a spurt of anger flaring. 'I've lost two brothers now. That is enough. They can't take Spencer from me as well.' She grabbed her apron and tied it on, ready to resume painting. 'All I have left of my family is my mother's tea service, Lachie's few things in a box upstairs and now this swallow. It doesn't seem much evidence of a whole family, does it?'

Mildred gripped her arm. 'You carry the memories, their love in your heart. You were brought up in a home full of warmth and kindness, by parents who cared for you and adored you. Consider that the very best evidence left of your family, Liv. Many do not have half of that.'

Chastened by the truth of the statement, she nodded. 'Forgive me. I sounded selfish.'

'Shall we go to church and offer a prayer, light a candle for your brother?'

'No. Not today.' She'd shield herself from words of sympathy for a little while longer. She preferred to imagine Stu in Canada, riding horses across the plains or trekking up mountains. 'I want to finish the painting.'

'Let yourself grieve, dearest.'

She straightened her shoulders. 'No, now's not the time.'

'There is no correct time,' Mildred murmured. 'If you don't grieve for them, it'll eat away at you. I've seen it before.'

'I'll grieve when the war is over.' Olivia couldn't afford to break the wall of sorrow, for it would consume her and she needed to be strong for Bailey, for Spencer. When Spencer was home safe and well, then she could grieve, but not yet. The ache in her heart would stay lodged, untouched, until she felt ready to let it go.

Mildred folded away Ralph's letter.

To distract herself from memories of Stu, Olivia tucked the

swallow back into the paper and returned to the previous conversation. 'What has Ralph confirmed?'

Mildred left her husband's letter on the sofa and tied on her apron before picking up the paintbrush. 'He tells me he has been spending time with some of the New Zealand regiments. He writes that the ones he's conversed with are lovely fellows. They have told him all about New Zealand. So, after the war, Ralph wants us to emigrate to New Zealand. He will apply for a parish there, if there is isn't a missionary placement.'

'New Zealand?' Olivia raised her eyebrows in surprise.

'It's incredulous, isn't it?' Mildred painted the walls with angry strokes. 'I have no intention of going to New Zealand. I'm not sure I could find it on a map.'

'It's near Australia,' Olivia supplied, taking up her paintbrush. 'At Hawthorn Manor the Broadbents had a globe. I used to polish its brass base. Often, I'd carefully spin it to learn about countries around the world. There's so many of them. I was fascinated by those countries at the bottom of the globe. I'd joke with Flora, the chambermaid, that surely those countries would just fall off? Flora was frightened they would. I used to laugh at her.' She smiled at the memory. 'Australia is many times larger than New Zealand and there are vast oceans around them. To me, they seemed lonely, forgotten, down at the bottom of the globe.'

'Typical. I'm the forgotten wife and now I'll be living in a forgotten country at the bottom of the globe,' Mildred fumed.

Olivia's mouth lifted slightly. 'New Zealand might fall off before you get there.'

Mildred fought a smile, wanting to stay angry. 'Seriously though, how am I supposed to feel? I barely see Ralph when we are living in a small village, imagine how it would be in a strange country where I don't know anyone, and nothing is familiar?'

'But imagine the experiences you'll have.' Olivia tried to put a positive spin on the idea.

'I'm not like you, Liv. None of that excites me. I'm in awe that you were willing to travel to America and only didn't because of Lachie's refusal to leave Wakefield. Now you're considering Australia.'

'With Spencer beside me,' she said wistfully. 'I will go wherever he wishes to go.'

'That's because you are secure in his love for you.' Mildred sighed. 'Ralph rarely told me he loved me before he left and never does in his letters. Even when he proposed to me, he spoke in such a way it might have been a business arrangement, and I was so desperate to be married... I did love him as well. I still do, but it's becoming harder...' Mildred blushed. 'I've said too much.'

'Who else are you going to talk to about such things if not me?' Olivia looked at her from across the room. 'You're a sister to me, Mil. I share everything with you, and I'd like to hope you do the same with me.'

'Of course, I do, which is why all this is so difficult. If we go to New Zealand, I'll never see any of you again. I'll miss watching Bailey grow up and any other children you and Spencer have.'

'Then write to Ralph and say you won't go.'

Staring at her, Mildred's expression revealed her anxiety. 'Become estranged from Ralph?'

'As I see it you have two options. You go with him to the other side of the world, or you stay here in England.'

'And do what with my life if I stay here? Become a governess, a teacher, and be alone for the rest of my life neither a wife nor a spinster?' Mildred rubbed her forehead. 'I want a family, Liv. I want a baby like Bailey. I want a beautiful family and a warm loving home. I'm not asking for the moon, or for the intense passion you and Spencer share...' Unhappy, Mildred continued to paint.

Olivia's mind whirled with thoughts as she painted. 'What if you told Ralph that you are willing to emigrate but only to a country where me, Spencer and Bailey are located?'

Mildred spun around so fast she nearly fell off her chair. 'What do you mean?'

'Well, Spencer is joining his father's business and as you know Stanford wants to open offices in different parts of the world, either Paris, which we've ruled out, New York, London and possibly Australia.'

'Is New Zealand on that list?' Mildred joked, continuing painting.

Olivia gave her a wry smile. 'No. I was leaning towards going to New York, because I thought Stu was in America, which was silly and naïve of me.' She smiled sadly. 'He's not there and never has been.'

'You don't want to go to New York?'

Dipping her paintbrush into the tin she gave an honest answer. 'Not really, no. If I was meant to be in America, then I would have gone before the war started.'

'So, where are you thinking?'

'Spencer told me in one of his letters that he doesn't want to stay in London because that's his father's domain. Spencer wants to strike out on his own. He mentioned starting an office in India, but Stanford wasn't keen because of the unrest there against British rule.'

Mildred nodded. 'Yes, I've read about the unrest in the newspapers many times.'

'Me, too, but I also read in the newspaper that it can take only forty days to sail between England and Australia now.'

'Instead of months as it used to.'

'Exactly.'

Mildred's eyes widened. 'What are you saying?'

'Well, my idea is...' she grinned, 'let's see if those countries at the bottom of the globe will fall off. Let's go on an adventure. Me, Spencer and Bailey with you and Ralph.'

'Australia?' Mildred dripped paint onto the floor. 'What if Ralph won't agree?'

'Then you can come with us anyway, if you wish.'

'You'll let me come with you?'

'Absolutely. I couldn't leave you behind. You're my family, and I have precious little left of it.'

'Oh, Liv. I don't know what to say.' Mildred started crying.

'Mil, put the paintbrush down or the floor will resemble a dalmatian dog.' Olivia went to her and helped her down from the chair. 'Spencer mentions in his letters about the Australian soldiers, of their bravery, their laid-back attitude to life, their willingness to give anything a go. They sound interesting, and Australia is part of the British Empire, they speak English, have English ways, which will help us settle. And, lastly, Lachie wanted to go there. I want to do it for him.'

'Will Spencer be happy to have me go along with you, and hopefully Ralph?'

'Of course. What did I just say? We're family.' Olivia rubbed Mildred's arm in reassurance. 'I'll write to Spencer and say I definitely choose Australia and that you are coming with us, one way or another. You can write to Ralph and say the same. I'm sure Australia needs vicars just as much as New Zealand does.'

Mildred didn't look convinced. But now the idea had grown root in her mind, Olivia felt a surge of excitement for the first time in years.

CHAPTER 20

June 1918

After a rain shower the day before, which washed away the dust, the summer weather returned warm and bright as the square made ready for a wedding. Jonnie and Margy were getting married, and the square was hosting the party afterwards.

Not long after dawn broke, the neighbours brought out tables and chairs, setting them up in a horseshoe shape. White tablecloths were ironed and spread over the tables and bows tied to backs of the chairs. Above, strings of bunting stretched from house roof to house roof, even the pub on the corner had wheeled around their piano for them to use.

Despite the food rationing, the neighbours and Margy's family had cooked and baked to mark the special day the best they could.

In the kitchen, Olivia brought out of the oven a tray of scones while Mildred places small egg custard tarts on a stand. Bailey was in the front room playing with a wooden train set that Stanford brought for him on his last visit a month ago.

The back door opened, and Tess came in looking splendid in a dove-grey dress with a matching hat sporting white feathers. 'Are the feathers too much?' Tess asked worriedly. 'Larry say no, but he's a man what does he know?' Tess tilted her head from side to side. 'What do you think?'

'I think you look magnificent,' Mildred said admiringly.

'Really?' Tess's shoulders lowered in relief. 'It's our first wedding of one of our boys and I want it to be prefect. I don't want Margy's family looking down on us.'

'Why would they?' Olivia placed the scones on the cooling rack. 'They live on Duke of York Street not in Buckingham Palace.'

'Aye, but we're a mining family.'

'And her father is on the railways, not a lawyer in a courthouse.' Olivia patted her shoulder as she went past her to the sink. 'Relax. It'll all be fine.'

'Aye, it will. The square looks wonderful.' Tess bent to tussle Bailey's fair hair as he walked into the kitchen holding a teddy by the paw. 'Look at his smart suit.'

Olivia beamed with pride. Bailey wore a white and navy sailor suit bought by Stanford from Selfridges in London. At twenty months, he was turning from a baby into a little boy and was adored by everyone. Olivia thought him to be the most beautiful and cleverest of any child ever born.

'I'll go up and get ready.' Mildred covered the food with a clean cloth.

Olivia wore a blue dress printed with small white flowers and edged with white lace at the cuffs and collar. She untied her apron. 'That's the last tray from the oven. We'll make the sandwiches when we get back from the church. How is Jonnie doing? Nervous?'

'Aye, a little bit. Larry has taken him over to the pub for a small whisky to bolster his courage. I said no ale until after church.' Tess glanced at the clock above the fireplace. 'We need to leave in ten minutes, I'd best go and fetch them.'

Olivia picked Bailey up as he tried to climb a chair to get to the food on the table. 'It's going to be a fabulous day, Tess.'

Tess sighed. 'Aye, lass, it is, but we're missing a few from the table, aren't we?'

'They'd want us to carry on and live for them. We have to make the most of every day.'

Tess nodded. 'Jonnie asked me and his father this morning if he and Margy can live with us when they get back from their honeymoon.'

'I thought they were going to her parents' house until they saved enough to rent their own place?'

'So did we, but Margy's had a bit of a falling out with her father.' Tess lowered her voice but couldn't stop the grin from appearing. 'I'm not supposed to say anything yet, but I'm about to burst if I don't say something soon. It seems I'm to be a grandmother, lass!'

'Oh! Oh, that's wonderful!' Olivia clapped in happiness and Bailey did the same, grinning.

'Aye, it is, *we* think it's great news, but her father's found out and he's fit to explode, apparently. He's disgusted they didn't wait until their wedding night and the daughter he's walking down the aisle in white isn't as pure as he thought she was. Jonnie told us there's no way in hell he's living with Margy's old man now.'

'That would be awkward.'

Tess grinned. 'It's their loss. I'll have them here and soon we'll have a little grandbaby to spoil.' She tickled Bailey's tummy. 'And you'll have a little friend to play with, my lad.'

'And maybe soon a brother or sister,' Spencer said from the doorway.

Olivia spun so fast Bailey nearly fell from her arms. The baby laughed, thinking he was being twirled. 'Spencer!'

He held out his arms, and she hurriedly stepped into them still in shock at seeing him. Her kissed her several times before he acknowledged Bailey, who wiggled between them. 'Look at our son. My, he's handsome and strong-limbed.' Spencer gazed lovingly at his boy.

'He's his father's son.' Olivia beamed.

'Give the boy to me, lass.' Tess took Bailey. 'I'll take him to the pub with me to fetch Larry and Jonnie.' Tess gave Spencer a look of tenderness. 'Welcome home, Major.'

'It's good to see you, Tess,' he said sincerely.

'Right, my lad, let's go and get the groom, will we?' Tess said to Bailey, as she walked him out of the house.

Olivia raised her lips for Spencer's kiss, holding him tightly now she had both arms to do so. It'd been a year and a half since she had touched him, and she couldn't get enough of him. They kissed deeply, achingly. 'I've missed you so much,' she whispered against his lips.

'I've dreamed of you being in my arms for months. It's been too long since I've seen your precious face.' He kissed her again, his hands cupping her cheeks. 'Needing to return to you and Bailey has been the only thing keeping me going.'

Laughter in the square broke them apart a little. She raked her gaze over him. He was thinner, a little more grey at the temples, but seemed unhurt. 'I read in the newspapers the German spring offensive was brutal. Are you well?'

'I am unharmed. Exhausted as always. The battle of the Lys was fierce, we lost a great number of men.' He exhaled heavily. 'So many in fact that our division has been pulled out of action. We've suffered such heavy casualties our numbers are vastly reduced. But the consensus is that the Germans were giving it their last big push before the American troops land in France shortly. The Germans hoped to secure victory before fresh soldiers join us. So far, the enemy has failed to claim that victory. Reports are that the German people have had enough, they are starving, and revolution is in the air back in their homeland.'

'It might soon be over?'

Spencer pulled her closer and kissed her. 'I hope so, my darling. The German prisoners we capture are often pleased to come with us. They've had enough of war and are in poor spirits and hungry.'

'How long are you home for?'

'With you, a fortnight, then I must return to my barracks in Cambridge to train new recruits for a couple of months.'

'You'll be in England for months?' Relief flooded through her.

'Until the autumn I hope.' He smiled tiredly. 'A day's train's ride away from you and Bailey. I'll find time to visit when I can, but let's not talk of that now. We have two weeks together and I want to forget the war entirely.'

She kissed him, utterly joyful to have him in her arms. 'There's a wedding on today, but I'm sure Tess will understand if we don't attend.'

'No, my darling. I want to do normal things, celebrate their happiness, be with you and Bailey, not sit inside and sleep away my time.' He turned hearing a noise behind him.

Mildred came slowly down the stairs, blushing at disturbing them. 'I'm sorry.'

'Don't be!' Spencer went to her and embraced her.

'I'm so happy you are home safe, Spencer.'

'Me too,' he said gratefully. 'You're looking so well, Mildred. Delightful in fact.' He admired her dress of deep rose and the soft arrangement of her hair under a small hat. 'Am I not a lucky man to be escorting two such beautiful women?'

Mildred blushed further at the compliment.

Spencer whispered to her. 'My brother is a lucky man as well, even if he does not recognise it.'

'Has he written to you about not going to Australia?'

'He has. I told him he was a fool.'

Mildred nodded unhappily. 'I have tried to convince him, but he insists on New Zealand.'

Olivia pinned on her hat with blue roses on the brim. 'We must go, or we'll be late.'

'We'll talk more of Australia and my brother later,' Spencer promised. 'But try not to worry. Father and I are working on changing his mind and even if we don't succeed, New Zealand is only four days sail from Sydney. You will not be entirely isolated.'

In the golden sunshine of the afternoon, the square rang with good cheer and laughter. After the church ceremony, the happy couple were celebrated in the square with food, and drink and songs played on the piano which turned jauntier as the evening went on and dancing began.

Olivia sat by a table as dusk threw long shadows across the square. Spencer sat beside her with Bailey asleep in his arms. Throughout the day she had to pinch herself that she wasn't dreaming. Her husband was here safe with her. They had two weeks ahead of them where they could love each other in private at night and during the day Spencer could learn about his son.

Dancing with one of Margy's uncles, Mildred laughed at something he said.

'The transformation of Mildred is wonderful to witness,' Spencer said quietly. 'She is a different person to the mouse-like creature Ralph married. When I first met her, she barely spoke to anyone. Gran thought she was a simpleton.' He chuckled at the memory.

'Mildred is anything but that,' Olivia defended.

'No, she has serene intelligence about her. When you've written to me telling me how unhappy Mildred was with Ralph I didn't quite understand, but after meeting up with Ralph a few times and further from what Father has told me, I can see that Ralph is more devoted to his beliefs than to his wife.'

'And Ralph is adamant he won't come with us to Australia?

You've written to him to tell him that it would help us all to settle better if we are together?'

'I have mentioned it several times in my letters. Ralph is set on New Zealand, so Father tells me. Father met me in London when I got off the train, we spent an hour together before I caught the overnight train here.'

'Stanford will visit us while you're in England?'

'Yes, he said he will. There is much to discuss. He is considering travelling to Sydney to begin the setup of the business, but I told him to wait. That I would like to do it myself.'

Olivia smiled. 'Your father has trouble letting go of control.'

'True, but he must if I am to take over the whole business, eventually.'

'Are you sure that is what you want to do?'

Spencer nodded. 'I know imports and exports isn't very exciting and I have a lot to learn but I want to build something for us, Liv, build something for Bailey and any future children we might have. I can't be a career solider anymore once this war is over. I have served my time.'

She reached for his hand and held it. 'Is Australia the right thing for us to do?'

He stared at her. 'Are you having doubts?'

'No, not really. But it will be just the three of us in a strange country, are we making the right decision? You'll be far away from your father, your gran and sister in Paris.'

'I have always lived far from them while I've been in the army. I'm used to it.'

'And I have no family left to miss, except Tess. Mildred will be in New Zealand, not too far away at least.'

'I will do my best to change Ralph's mind. He can be stubborn but he's not entirely stupid.' Spencer grinned and jerked his head towards Mildred dancing. 'And he's not seen the transformation of his wife yet, either, that might change everything.'

'I hope so for I fear she will not stay with him otherwise. They aren't as lucky as we are.' She lifted his hand to her mouth and kissed his palm, relishing in the feel of its strength as his fingers curled around hers.

Desire flared in his eyes. 'I think, my beautiful wife, that we should take this little man up to bed and turn in ourselves.'

She chuckled. 'I was just thinking the same thing, husband.'

CHAPTER 21

Bohain, France
November 11th, 1918.

IN THE ONCE GERMAN occupied village, as the sun rose over the horizon on a cool dry morning, Spencer spoke French to one of the village women who was collecting water from a well, assuring her the news spreading across the country was true. The war was nearly over. The armistice was being signed that morning between the Allies and the Germans.

Her weathered face showed confusion and then wariness. She shrugged her shoulders and carted the bucket of water away, not trusting him. He couldn't blame her after living through four years of war, surrounded by a devastated village and confronted by fear and death every day, the woman was allowed to not consider it was all coming to an end.

Strolling back towards the mess cart that had brought up food from HQ, Spencer rolled the stiffness from his neck. Unable to sleep last night, knowing today would be the beginning of the end, hadn't been conducive to his rest. So much had swirled around his mind, mainly getting home to Olivia and Bailey.

His men were waking and coming out of their billets to wash and shave. An exhausted weariness had taken hold of the company after their last big battle in September.

He had told all of his officers the previous day about the signing of the armistice and that they were to keep the news to themselves until it was official, but word had already spread across the country, through the army units, of the peace deal being arranged. The French and British newspapers were full of it. Not many believed it yet.

'Sir.' Bishop brought him a cup of black coffee, a drink Spencer had grown fond of. 'Your breakfast will be ready in ten minutes. I have your shaving kit out ready and warm water.'

Entering the cottage where he slept, Spencer stripped down to his bare chest and began to lather the soap against his face. 'Today is a momentous day, Bishop.'

'Aye, sir, so *they* say.'

'You do trust *me*, don't you?'

'Aye, sir. You've told me that today the war ends, and I trust your word,' Bishop said, tidying up Spencer's belongings.

'Your enthusiasm is incredible to behold,' Spencer joked, shaving. The little mirror he used fell off the stack of boxes Bishop had propped it on.

Bishop picked it up and held it for Spencer to see as he shaved.

Spencer glanced at him, pulling the razor up over his jaw. 'What do you plan to do when you get home?'

'We *are* going home, sir?' Bishop's stare was direct.

Lowering the razor, Spencer nodded. 'We are, I promise you.'

Bishop's face transformed into pure joy. 'You wouldn't lie to me, sir.'

'No, I wouldn't.'

'In that case, I plan to get me a little stall on Brick Lane market like me granny used to have.'

'And what will you sell?' Spencer continued shaving.

'All the stuff I've been sending home for the last four years.' Bishop grinned cheekily.

'Stuff?' Spencer dreaded to think what the man had been purloining on their travels across France.

'Aye, sir, I've been sending things I've… found to my cousin in Hoxton. He's kept them all in his front room.'

Chuckling, Spencer washed his face. 'Well, I've written you a reference, in case you need it. The envelope is on top of that pile on the desk there.'

'Thank you, sir. That's kind of you, but don't be offended when I tell you that I don't intend on serving another man in my life. Not that I haven't enjoyed serving you, sir, but I'll not be doing it no more.'

'I totally understand, Bishop.' Spencer washed and dressed in his full officer's uniform. 'Oh, and, Bishop?'

'Yes, sir?'

'Try not to strip the place clean before you go. Leave something for the French,' Spencer said with a wry lift of an eyebrow.

Bishop laughed. 'I'll try not to, sir.'

He finished his writing correspondence while he ate breakfast and then held a meeting with his officers, telling them that no activity will be undertaken today. He ordered for his company to gather for roll call.

Once roll call had been completed, a runner on horseback dismounted and handed him a telegram. Spencer read it and keeping his emotions in check, he stood in front of the rows of his men. *His men.* Faces he'd become familiar with, voices he knew, their courage he'd witnessed.

He checked his watch. 10:58 a.m.

He lifted his head and spoke to the men of his company.

'I have a telegram from HQ. I will read it to you now. At five hundred hours this morning, the armistice was signed between the Allies and Germany. All hostilities will cease at eleven hundred hours today, 11th November.' Spencer checked his watch and a shiver rippled over his skin. 11:00 a.m. 'Gentlemen, the war is officially over.'

Stunned silence greeted him.

'Your bravery, your devotion to your fellow soldier, to your company and to your regiment has been commendable. I will add that, personally, it has been an honour to serve with you all and may you all find happiness in the future.' He straightened to attention and saluted them.

As one they stood to attention and saluted him back.

His throat tight, Spencer let his hand drop and then grinned at them.

'Three cheers for the Major!' Matlock called.

The cheers rang loud across the village.

Spencer held up his hand in thanks, too emotional to stay he stepped backwards and turned away.

A loud whoop was shouted from the back row and was soon joined by others. The men erupted into shouts and hollering, throwing their hats up into the air, which brought out the village folk who cheered with them.

Sergeant Matlock shook Spencer's hand. 'Thank you for everything, sir. It was a pleasure to serve with you.'

'And you, Sergeant.' Spencer slapped him on his shoulder. 'You're a fine good soldier.'

He shook many other hands and was kissed by the village women, even the sceptical one he spoke to by the well that morning.

Finally, he turned for his cottage and the tasks awaiting him. He'd give the soldiers the afternoon and night to celebrate before the army required more from them. Demobilisation was going to be a long and slow process, but he didn't want them to find that out just yet.

Sir.' Lieutenant Dawes saluted him outside of the cottage.

'Yes, Lieutenant?' Spencer answered the salute, wondering what grievance Dawes wanted to discuss now.

'I believe you have resigned, sir?'

'That is true. I leave tomorrow. Captain Bowman will take over the company. He will need your assistance. There is a lot to be done. Any German units in our vicinity will surrender all weapons to us, but patrols will still need to be maintained as I mentioned in the meeting earlier.'

'Yes, sir.' Dawes lifted his chin. 'I personally want to thank you, sir. Your leadership has been exemplary.'

Shocked, Spencer stared at him.

Dawes reddened. 'I have learned a great deal through serving as your lieutenant, sir.'

'You have?' He couldn't keep the surprise from his voice.

'Yes, sir. I have decided to stay in the army and hopefully, one day, I will end my career with the respect and thanks that you have gained.' Dawes held out his hand. 'Thank you, sir.'

Utterly bewildered, Spencer shook his hand. 'Thank you, Dawes. I wish you well.'

'Thank you, sir.' Dawes saluted him. 'Goodbye, sir.'

Watching him march away, Spencer questioned if today was all a dream.

* * *

STANDING IN THE SQUARE, on a cold but dry day, Olivia held Mildred's arm on one side and Tess's arm on the other side. Church bells rang and factory sirens wailed around all of Wakefield and the villages beyond, indeed throughout the country, signalling the end of the war.

It was over.

As the neighbours rejoiced and embraced each other, Olivia stood, head bowed and finally let the tears fall. Great sobs wracked her body, shaking her shoulders. The well of grief broke its walls and flooded her, buckling her knees until she sank to the freezing cobblestones utterly distraught.

Tess knelt beside her, holding her tight, crying, sharing the same sorrow.

Bailey, distressed at his mother's mournful sobs, tried to climb onto her lap, but Mildred carried him away.

Larry picked Olivia up off the cold ground and cradled her in his arms and took her inside the front room. He placed her on the sofa before the fire, where they let her cry in solitude.

The tears fell in an unrelenting torrent. When she thought she'd cried enough and raised her head, something, a memory, would flash through her mind and grief would overtake her once more.

She cried for her mother, aching to hear her soft voice again.

She cried for her father, desperate to see his wry smile on his sooty face.

She cried for Stu, as she clutched his swallow in her coat pocket.

And she cried for Lachie, the pain unbearable in her heart. Never again would she see his cheeky face, or hear his jaunty whistle.

It was impossible to think of living beyond the war without them. Of course it made no sense, she lived without her parents and Stu before the war, but the war had taken over all aspects of her life, burying her mourning for her parents. There was no time to mourn them when she had to care for Lachie. Then Lachie left her as well, and in his place, she devoted herself to Bailey, pouring all her love and attention on him to ease the ache of grief.

Without the war to concentrate on, and the fear of it taking Spencer from her as well, she no longer had a buffer to hide behind. She had to face the fact that her family was dead.

Her tears flowed once more as she hugged herself, giving into the relief of Spencer making it through the war. She felt the baby kick in the stomach and suddenly stopped sobbing. She'd fallen pregnant from Spencer's last leave in June. Was this overwhelming despair harming the baby?

She wiped her eyes with her coat sleeve and sucked in a deep breath. She rubbed her stomach. 'I'm sorry, little one.'

Shuddering with one last sob, she took calmer breaths. The fire crackled, the sound barely heard over the continuous ringing of the town's church bells.

Closing her eyes, she sank back against the sofa. Spencer was safe. His last letter arrived only that morning and he was safely billeted far behind the lines.

Spencer would be coming home to her.

They had a future.

Bailey's excited voice heralded him before she saw him as he ran into the room and climbed up onto her lap.

'He got away from me!' Mildred apologised.

'Come by the fire, you must be cold,' Olivia invited.

'We are a bit, aren't we, Bailey?' Mildred held her hands out to the fire. 'Shall I put the kettle on?'

Olivia nodded and cuddled her son, resting him against her small bump. 'Your papa will be home soon.'

This time when the tears fell, they were healing, joyful ones and she let them fall. She had a future to look forward to, and a family she was growing.

CHAPTER 22

Northern France,
October 1919.

As the final notes of the 'Last Post' died away, the bugler lowered his instrument.

Olivia bent and placed a bouquet of white flowers against the simple wooden cross marking Lachie's grave. Beside her, Tess did the same for Colin.

Olivia kissed her fingers and touched the cross. 'Rest in peace, dearest Lachie. You will never be forgotten.'

She took a step back as Spencer and Mr Parkinson saluted the graves and the action moved her deeply. A tear lingered on her lashes before trickling down her cheek.

The group surrounding the graves stood in silence, even Bailey who didn't understand the occasion and wanted to run around as three-year-old boys liked to do remained quiet in his grandfather's arms.

Next to Stanford, Mildred held the handle of the pram, looking after her baby nephew, William, while Ralph stood behind her.

All the Hobson family had gathered, including Margy and the twin girls she gave birth to last year. They slept contentedly in their pram.

Lined in rows, hundreds of wooden crosses stood like sentries guarding the bodies of the brave young men beneath.

A few hundred yards away the small village was in the process of slowly being rebuilt. Mr Parkinson had learned that Colin and Lachie's bodies had been moved from their original burial place beside a dusty road a mile away and brought to this newly erected cemetery along with hundreds of other fallen soldiers.

It gave Olivia comfort to know that Lachie was not only with Colin, but with other brave men.

The villagers had spoken to Olivia and Spencer that morning, telling them of the honour of caring for the graves of the young men who fought so hard for their freedom. Some remembered Lachie, the young man with the pale hair who cared for the horses. Many of the village women said they'd make sure the graves would be cared for and Olivia had thanked them.

'Darling, the others are leaving,' Spencer said, slipping his hand into hers. 'But we can stay.'

She nodded. 'Just a few minutes more?'

'As long as you want.'

She glanced over at Tess, a mother standing head bowed over her son's grave. She stepped closer to her and read Colin's name on the wooden cross. 'I remember the day I first met him. He could barely say a word to me.'

Tess sniffed and wiped her nose with a handkerchief. 'I think, at first, he fancied you, then soon realised that you were way too old for him.'

'The cheek!' Olivia tutted, smiling.

Tess wiped her eyes. 'You became a sister to him.'

'That's nice to know. He was a credit to you and Larry.'

'Aye, he was.' Tess raised her gaze to the horizon. 'Tomorrow, we go and stand by Lance's grave. Mr Parkinson has been such a gentleman to organise this visit for us all.'

'He has done an amazing thing,' Olivia agreed. She looked over to where Mr Parkinson and Spencer chatted with the others. Mr Parkinson had returned from Egypt at the end of the war and caught the Spanish flu, but he'd overcome it, thankfully, and fallen in love with the nurse who'd cared for him in hospital. The nurse in question now held onto his arm, her face full of concern as they walked back to the village in the cold air.

'And you will go to visit Stu's grave tomorrow,' Tess stated.

'Yes. Mildred and Ralph will look after the boys for us and Mr Parkinson will drive us there. It's an hour's drive away.' Olivia would never forget Parky's kindness. He had been so good to organise this visit to the graves in France, something he'd arrange while convalescing himself. Stanford had paid for it all, including the travelling costs of the Hobson family.

When Spencer resigned from the army and returned to England a week after armistice, the plan had been for Olivia and Bailey to join him in London as he learned about his father's business. However, with the Spanish Flu epidemic spreading rapidly he didn't want Olivia and Bailey in the capital. Instead, each week he made the trip to the square to spend time with Olivia and his son. Olivia decided she'd stay at the square until after the new baby's arrival.

Two weeks after William's birth, in March, Spencer's grandmother died. Olivia couldn't make the funeral in Paris and with the Spanish flu epidemic still lingering, Spencer had agreed with Olivia that it was better for her and the boys that she stay at the square until she was fully recovered from the birth and the epidemic had lessened.

However, by the middle of April, Olivia had declared that the flu was not going to stop her from being with Spencer. She had waited long enough. She packed up her and the boys' belongings and closed the door on number seven for good. They were going to London.

Leaving the square for the last time, Olivia had given all her neighbours a hamper basket of goods as a goodbye gift. Tears were shed and embraces were given as she waved to them all a final goodbye. They had all welcomed home the men of Woodcock's Square. Ezra, Mr Muldoon, Mr Berry and Sadie's Gerry. None of them saw Winnie and Martha anymore, but heard she was happy living with her mum. Her vicious husband had long disappeared, and house number one had been taken over by a young couple with a small child.

Olivia would see the Hobson family again soon, but it was still one of the hardest days she'd had. The square, a place she once thought she'd never like, had given her a different kind of family, and she loved them all. Happily, her home had been taken over by Jonnie and Margy and the babies, which pleased Tess greatly.

Now as a cool breeze lifted the ends of their coats, and the sun dropped low, Olivia knew the time was coming when she'd have to say goodbye to her dear friend.

Tess tucked her handkerchief into her coat sleeve. 'When does Mr Middleton take our dear Mildred to New Zealand?'

'They leave next week.' The sadness of Mildred emigrating to New Zealand was still deep, but she put a brave face on it for Mildred's sake. Ralph had refused to consider going to Australia when he returned from France. He'd collected Mildred and they'd gone to live in London with Stanford, but Mildred had come back to the square to help Olivia through William's birth. Olivia had missed Mildred terribly in the months she was gone.

'Mildred isn't going with you to Australia then?'

'No. Ralph had forbidden it.'

'Did he now?' Tess asked, darting a quick look at Olivia. 'I didn't think our Mildred would stand for that.'

'She wants a baby, Tess. She can't have one if she leaves him.' Olivia shrugged. The situation was hopelessly gloomy.

'The poor lass. What a dilemma. And you're all set to go?'

'Yes, in two days. Our luggage has been sent to the ship in Nice and we're going by train from Paris to Nice once we've seen Stu's grave. Stanford is coming with us to help get us settled in Sydney. Then he'll return to London next year.'

Tears flowed down Tess's cheeks. 'How will I be without you, lass? You're like a daughter to me.' She hunted for her handkerchief again.

Olivia hugged her tightly, her voice raw with emotion. 'We'll come back and visit. No doubt you'll be swarmed with grandchildren when we do.'

'They give me such joy.' Tess wiped her eyes that didn't stop leaking tears. 'Never stop writing to me, lass. You know I'm not good with words, but I'll do my best. Margy is a better writer than me, so she'll help me. I want to hear all about Australia and how the boys are doing.'

'I'll tell you everything,' Olivia promised. 'You know how I love writing letters!'

Tess chuckled and hugged her once more before staring down at the graves. 'It was one of the best days of my life when you moved to the square. You gave me the chance to have a daughter, and I want to thank you for staying when I know you wanted to flee and thank you for becoming a member of my family.'

Olivia linked their arms and rested her head against Tess's shoulder. 'I'm so grateful to have you in my life. I wouldn't have survived without you.'

They stood together by the graves for a little while longer until Spencer and Larry came over to them.

Olivia glanced down once last time at Lachie's grave and said a silent goodbye to him.

'Ready?' Spencer smiled down at her.

'Ready.' She nodded, receiving his kiss.

'Let's go and find some sun with our boys.' Spencer shivered in the cold as they walked away.

'Oi you, Major, don't rub it in,' Tess rebuked him, pulling up her scarf.

'I'm not a major anymore, Tess.' Spencer told her for the hundredth time since leaving the army.

'You'll always be *Major* to me,' Tess said stubbornly.

'Can we go and have a drink?' Larry whined. 'It's cold enough to snap the balls off a brass monkey.'

'Larry Hobson!'

'I'm only saying.' Larry shrugged.

'Keep that up and I'll send you to Australia with our Liv,' Tess told him.

Olivia grinned as they walked into the village inn to join the others. She would miss Tess so dearly.

Mildred came over to her. 'The boys are warmly wrapped in blankets in the motor car waiting. Bailey has had a drink of hot chocolate, and I took him to the inn's lavatory out the back. William is stirring for a feed. Stanford is holding him in the car.'

'Thank you, I'll feed him on the way back to the apartment. Are the drivers waiting for us?'

'Yes, they are ready to go.'

Olivia heard William crying from outside. 'I have to go say goodbye.' She went to the bar to say goodbye to the Hobson family who were leaving to travel in the other direction to visit Lance's grave.

Finally, Olivia embraced Tess for the last time in what would be a long while. 'Goodbye, my dear friend.'

'Take care of yourself, lass, and those lovely lads of yours.' Tess held her tightly. 'We'll see each other again one day.'

'We will, I promise.' Olivia kissed her wet cheek and then swiftly walked out of the inn and to the motor car, taking William from Stanford and cuddling him to her.

Spencer joined her and they set off for Paris. While she fed William, Spencer sat Bailey on his knee, and they pointed at things out of the window as the car drove through the countryside.

'I'm glad I'm not in Father's car,' Spencer said, giving Bailey a sandwich from the hamper and passing one to Olivia. 'You could cut the tension between Ralph and Mildred with a knife.'

'Can you blame her? You've seen how Ralph is with her. He treats her like a cousin, or a good friend. His letters to her during the war were something like friends would write to each other, polite, courteous. I couldn't stand it if you weren't passionate towards me.'

Spencer took her hand. 'My passion for you will never diminish. It's quite the opposite. I fall more in love with you every day.'

Her heart melted at his beautiful words. 'How did I get so lucky to have you?'

He kissed her hand. 'Darling, not everyone can have what we have. We can't interfere in Ralph and Mildred's marriage.'

'But I hate to see her so unhappy.'

'They have to work it out for themselves.' He shrugged as Bailey bounced on his lap saying he saw a cow.

At Stanford's opulent apartment in Paris, Olivia changed her clothes to an evening gown while a sweet young Frenchwoman, employed as the boys' new nanny, gave them a bath.

'I still can't get used to not bathing my own children,' Olivia said to Spencer as she donned the silver diamond earrings he'd given to her on the birth of William.

'Your whole life is going to change now, sweetheart.' He smiled. 'You'll soon get used to it.'

Running her hand along the shining wood of the dressing table, she thought back to the days when she was a housemaid at his grandparents' manor. Then, she had been the one to polish the fine furniture she now touched. 'I think I will adjust better once in Australia.'

'How so?' Spencer fastened his cravat in the long mirror.

'Because no one will know of my humble background in

Sydney.' She waved her hand airily and tilted her head up as she'd seen ladies do at the manor. 'I will tell any new friends we meet that my father was *"in iron"* and let them guess the rest.'

Spencer walked to her and placed his hands on her shoulders. 'Darling, look at you'. He spun her to the mirror. 'You look like you were born to this life.'

She admired the fine green silk dress she wore. 'But I wasn't, Spence, and I don't want to embarrass you or the boys in our new life.'

'You could never embarrass us.' He kissed her. 'I really don't want you to fret about it. We'll find our way in Australia and be happy.'

'I hope so.'

'You met Anthea and her family yesterday, and you both got on so well.'

'Your sister is kind and looks past my background of being her grandparents' housemaid.'

'Anthea sees you, the person, not what you did for work.'

'That's a rare gift, most people don't have that ability to see beneath a station.'

'My sister likes you because you make me happy. That's all a sibling wants for their family. Would you agree?'

'Yes.'

'You'll be fine. You already have my father, sister and Parky on side. You need no one else!' Spencer joked.

She stared around the plush bedroom. 'It'll just take me some time to get used to this kind of life after living in the square.'

'But you're adventurous, so I know you'll meet this challenge and conquer it.' He tilted her chin up with a finger. 'And I really want to take that dress of you and make love to you…'

'We'll be late for dinner, and you'll mess up my hair.'

'See?' He grinned. 'You're already acting like a high-born lady.'

She slapped him playfully.

'Seriously, no matter where we live or who we associate with, you'll always be my Olivia, the beautiful girl who stole my heart standing outside of her father's forge. I never want you to change into someone you think we want you to be. Promise me you won't?'

She reached up and kissed him. 'I'm Olivia Brodie Middleton, and I promise to never change.'

They walked through to the main reception room where Stanford and Ralph were talking by the fireplace and Mildred sat alone on the elegant sofa.

Olivia sat beside her.

Suddenly, Mildred clutched Olivia's arm. 'I can't say goodbye to them, to the boys, or to you. It's breaking my heart.'

'Don't think of it as goodbye.' Olivia felt so sorry for her. 'You'll only be four days sail away from us. We'll visit, often.'

Mildred dabbed at her eyes. 'I can't do it. I can't go.'

'But you want to have a family, Mil,' Olivia whispered. 'You must think of that.'

'And be trapped in a lonely marriage.' Mildred's expression showed her fear of the prospect. 'Children might not even happen. Then what will I do?'

'Mildred?' Ralph came alongside them. 'What is wrong?'

Lifting her chin, Mildred stared at her husband. 'I want to go with Olivia and the boys to Australia, and not to New Zealand where I'll be lonely with just *you*,' she declared through clenched teeth.

He jerked back as though slapped. 'We've talked about this.'

'No, you've talked and not listened.'

'You feel so strongly about New Zealand?'

'I feel that *strongly* about you and your stubbornness to only please yourself!' Mildred whispered harshly. 'You do not consider my needs, my wishes! You talk only of what you want to do, where you want to live, how this will benefit your career! I can't be left alone again, Ralph, not after living with Olivia and the boys and being surrounded by people who *care*.' Mildred's face crumbled.

Ralph frowned, agitated. 'Everything is arranged, Mildred.'

'Then you go without me!' She ran from the room.

Ralph stared after her and then glared at Olivia. 'What did you say to her?'

'Me? I have said nothing.'

'Oh, I think you've said plenty since Mildred went to live with you. Why she did so, I'll never understand.'

Annoyed, Olivia stared up at him. 'She came to me because *you'd* left her, and her home was taken over by *others*.'

'She could have gone to my father. Why would she choose a Wakefield slum when she could have been in a more suitable house in Mayfair or York?'

'Possibly because she felt more at home with me?' Olivia defended, striving not to become more angrier.

'Enough, Ralph,' Spencer stepped in. 'Olivia is not at fault here, you are.'

'Stay out of this, Spencer,' Ralph snapped.

'I'd gladly do so but not when you accuse my wife of wrongdoing.'

Ralph's nostrils flared. 'Mildred was totally herself when I left for France, then suddenly she has fled to Wakefield to live with someone she barely knows. She changes her hair, her clothes, her views on life. Tell me none of that involves your wife.'

Olivia shot to her feet, fed up with his attitude, his blindness. 'Everything Mildred has done is of her own accord. And I'll tell you something else, Mildred was not herself when she came to me. She was heartbroken by your actions and grieving a lost baby!'

Coming back into the room, Mildred faced her husband. 'Olivia is correct. Living with her showed me how I had allowed my life to simply pass me by without truly living it. You, Ralph, swept me aside to foster your own interests. At the vicarage I was alone, lonely and terribly unhappy. You were the reason, but I was also to blame for not standing up for my needs, my desires. You went to France and left me alone to deal with the grief of losing another baby. That was unforgivable.'

'I was grieving too!' He threw up his hands. 'You make me out to be some kind of monster.'

'I don't mean to...' Mildred lifted one shoulder in despair. 'I love you, Ralph, but I don't want what you want. I cannot be the biddable wife you left behind.'

Ralph's face lost all colour. 'What are you saying? Do you want to divorce me?'

'That's up to you.' Mildred raised her chin defiantly and stood as tall as her short stature allowed. 'But I shan't go with you to New Zealand. I will go to Sydney with the others.'

'Mildred, please...'

'No, Ralph. I want to be loved.'

'I do love you.'

'Do you? Really?'

He tutted and glanced away. 'Do you want me to be obsessed as Father was with my mother? How Spencer is with Olivia? I refuse to be. I've seen the effects of that tortured kind of love, and I refuse to feel it and be controlled by it. Father has grieved for my mother for all of his life, so much so, he wasn't a good Father to us children until only a few years ago. And Spencer, he searched for Olivia like someone possessed. I won't give in to such powerful emotions.'

Stanford lowered his head, despondent. 'I am sorry. I am *trying* to make it up to you all.'

Spencer patted his father's back. 'We know.'

Mildred took a step further into the room, her anger gone and replaced with desolation. 'I deserve some happiness, love, affection. If I can't have it with you, then I'll have it in other ways with Olivia and the boys, and Spencer. I'll be a sister and an aunt and share my life with them,' Mildred said firmly. She turned on her heel and walked back into the bedroom.

A maid waited by the dining-room door, ready to announce dinner. Stanford indicated they weren't ready, and she slipped away.

Spencer strode to the drinks cabinet and poured everyone a drink. 'You're the biggest fool, Brother.'

'So, it seems.' Slightly shaken, Ralph sat down on the edge of the sofa. 'I'm sorry, Olivia. I shouldn't have accused you as I did.'

'I only want the best for you both,' she told him sincerely. 'Mildred has become a sister to me. I know her very well now.'

'Yes, probably better than I know her.' Ralph accepted the drink of whisky from Spencer. 'I don't know what to do.'

'Do you love her?' Olivia asked gently. 'A deep love? A love where the idea of living without her seems impossible?'

'Like the kind you and Spencer share?' He took a gulp of the drink. 'I honestly don't know. She's changed while I've been away.'

'Then do you wish to get to know her all over again?' she prompted.

'I believe I do. This new Mildred is actually rather interesting.' He flushed, embarrassed.

'Tell her that. Embrace this new Mildred for who she is and forget the mousy woman you married. She wants to be your partner in all things, let her.'

Ralph took a deep breath and gulped back the rest of the drink. 'There could be hope for us if I agree to Australia?'

She smiled a little. 'Isn't it worth the chance?'

'I think we should go out to eat,' Spencer announced, 'and leave Ralph and Mildred to talk.'

'Perfect idea.' Stanford hurried to the entry cupboard to retrieve their coats and hats.

Ralph stood. He took Olivia's hand. 'Thank you.'

She nodded and watched him walk towards the bedroom.

Spencer came to her and wrapped his arms around her waist. 'I'm proud of you. None of that was easy.'

She tilted her head at him. 'You Middleton men should remember that you have strong wives. You shan't get it all your own way.'

Spencer rolled his eyes. 'I'm learning that fast.'

She reached up and kissed him. 'Oh, don't worry, we have the rest of our lives for me to teach you.'

He laughed and crushed her to him.

AUTHOR NOTE

Thank you to all my lovely readers who sent me such warm comments about book 1, *A Sister's Sacrifice*. I really hope you enjoyed the sequel, *Where the Poppies Dance*. I loved writing it. The characters swept me up in their lives as they always do. I upset myself when writing Lachie and Colin's end scene. It's very difficult to type when your eyes are misty with tears!

As I mentioned at the end of book 1, Woodcock's Square in Wakefield no longer exists, but it was a real place and where my great-great grandparents lived. Like a lot of the poor areas of Wakefield, many 'yards' and slums areas were demolished in the 1930s.

In both books 1 & 2, I took the liberty to use author's licence in regards Spencer's army unit. I loosely based his war movements on the 2nd Battalion, York and Lancaster Regiment and the role they played in WWI. I researched that battalion's war timeline, but as Spencer is fictional, I could use some leeway, but by using a real battalion's movements, I could create a realistic timeframe for Spencer and place him at villages where battles took place. I did learn that some officers were able to come home more often than an ordinary private could, etc.

For Simon's small storyline I was inspired by an episode of Who Do You Think You Are. A celebrity's ancestor's boat was torpedoed, and they were rescued and taken to a port in North Africa, and I thought that was an interesting aspect to include (you never know where story ideas come from!).

Stu's storyline of enlisting in Canada is something I learned while researching WWI. A lot of British-born men who were living in Canada, and other overseas countries, would enlist in that country's army. My own great-grandfather Patrick (and his brother) had gone to America to work in coal mines in Kentucky in 1910 and they enlisted in September 1918 – two months before the end of the war so they didn't have the time to train and be deployed before the armistice. My great-grandfather was 39 years old at the time. The family returned to Wakefield three years later.

Emigration features heavily in my books, simply because I draw on the fact that so many of my family members left England to start new lives in other countries, mainly Australia, but also Canada, America and New Zealand. As working-class folk, they took whatever opportunities they could to better their lives. My great-grandfather, Patrick Kittrick, left Ireland in 1900 to try his luck in England, then travelled to America before returning to England. However, his two oldest children remained in America. My own parents left England in the 1960s, as ten-pound poms, and came to Australia. I have left Australia to live in England for some years before returning home to Australia (my brother and sisters have done the same). We are a family of adventurers, I think, and so are my characters.

As always, I thank my family for their support, especially my husband, Mark, and I'd like to thank my editor, Jane Eastgate, for her help in finding my errors. We try our very best to eradicate all mistakes, but some do slip through, sometimes, and I apologise in advance if there are any (we are not A.I. robots, although I think, at times, my husband wishes I was so he could unplug me. Ha!).

Until next time, lovely readers, stay safe and thank you once again for coming on this journey with me.

Best Wishes,
AnneMarie Brear.

AUTHOR BIO

Author of over forty novels, AnneMarie Brear has crafted sweeping historical fiction with atmosphere, emotion, and drama aplenty that will surely satisfy any fan of the genre. AnneMarie was born in a small town in N.S.W. Australia, to English parents from Yorkshire, and is the youngest of five children. From an early age she loved reading, working her way through the Enid Blyton stories, before moving onto Catherine Cookson's novels as a teenager.

Living in England during the 1980s and more recently, AnneMarie developed a love of history from visiting grand old English houses and this grew into a fascination with what may have happened behind their walls over their long existence. Her enjoyment of visiting old country estates and castles when travelling and, her interest in genealogy and researching her family tree, has been put to good use, providing backgrounds and names for her historical novels which are mainly set in Yorkshire or Australia between Victorian times and WWII.

A long and winding road to publication led to her first novel being published in 2006.

She has now published over forty historical family saga

novels, becoming an Amazon UK best seller and with her novel, The Slum Angel, winning a gold medal at the USA Reader's Favourite International Awards. Two of her books have been nominated for the Romance Writer's Australia Ruby Award and the USA In'dtale Magazine Rone award and recently she has been nominated twice as a finalist for the UK RNA RONA Awards.

AnneMarie lives in the Southern Highlands of N.S.W. Australia.

Please visit her website to learn more about AnneMarie, her books and to subscribe to her quarterly newsletter.

http://www.annemariebrear.com

Printed in Dunstable, United Kingdom

80720628R00160